MILES OF FILES

MILES OF FILES

MICHAEL J. SAHNO

WELCOME

I'm truly grateful to you for taking the time to read this novel. It is among the great accomplishments of my life.

If you'd like to check out my other novels, please visit my website at http://www.msahno.com/books. If you join my free email newsletter, you'll get news on upcoming events, along with my free e-book, Marketing for Authors.

For today's independent authors, book reviews are like currency. If you enjoy this novel, please post a review of it on Goodreads or Amazon. If you email me to let me know that you've reviewed it, I'll send you a special bonus PDF of exclusive material.

Of course, if you like the novel, I hope you'll recommend it to others and follow me on social media. You can follow me on Twitter at https://twitter.com/MikeSahno or like my Facebook page at https://www.facebook.com/sahnocomm.

Thank you all.
- Mike

Published by
SAHNO PUBLISHING
P. O. Box 46506
Tampa, FL 33646

Second Edition
Printed in the United States of America

ISBN 978-1-944173-04-3

Library of Congress Control Number: 2015916580

Publisher's Cataloging-In-Publication Data
(Prepared by The Donohue Group, Inc.)

Names: Sahno, Michael J.
Title: Miles of files / Michael J. Sahno.
Description: Second edition. | Tampa, FL : Sahno Publishing, [2017]
Identifiers: LCCN 2015916580 | ISBN 978-1-944173-04-3
Subjects: LCSH: Insurance companies--Employees--
    Fiction. | Embezzlement--Fiction. | Whistle blowing--Fiction. |
    Employees--Dismissal of--Fiction. | LCGFT: Thrillers (Fiction)
Classification: LCC PS3619.A46 M55 2015 | DDC 813/.6--dc23

Cover Design by
Mario Lampic

CHAPTER 1

AT 5:38 ON the morning of his forty-first birthday, Graham Woodcock awakened to the sound of a cat retching. He heard three distinct thumps as the cat's larynx contracted, then a sound with a different quality, liquid, gurgling: no doubt the discharge of some vomitous hairball. Or, worse, an entire meal. He saw it in his mind's eye as he glared through the dark at the red numbers of the alarm clock.

When he finally decided to rise—after another hour's sleep—he was roused not by the urgency of cat puke, but by the urgency of the breakfast hour. Not his—the cats'. One of them leapt on the bed and nuzzled his outstretched hand with phony affection, a clear message: get up, get up. Giddyup.

Graham crept into the kitchen, trailing the cats in darkness. He scanned the floor to avoid any cat vomit that might be there, but there was none. He flipped on lights and fed the cats, then wandered from room to room in search of vomit. Nothing.

He sat down to eat his breakfast, and everything was fine until one of the cats began to move its bowels while Graham was finishing his cereal. It was Truman, no doubt, whose bathroom routine was maddeningly predictable.

He decided to ignore it and finish the cereal in spite of the odor. Then Truman strutted into the kitchen, waving his tail like a dog. Somehow he'd managed to snake his tail across the gloppy pile of excrement in the litter pan, and a streak of it glistened in his fur like a grotesque flag.

"Bloody hell."

The cat approached the breakfast nook, still switching his tail back and forth, and each motion left a faint brown brushstroke against the cream-colored paint. He created his own masterpiece right beneath the kitchen counter.

"NO, no, no. Shit," Graham said, then realized the irony. He picked the cat up by the scruff of the neck—the only way he could hold him without getting himself painted—and carried him into the bathroom. "You little bastard." He swallowed the urge to slam the cat against the wall.

"I hope this isn't an indication of the kind of day it's going to be."

But it was. On the side of the bathtub stood a cockroach the size of Graham's thumb. He froze, dropping the cat as the roach scampered down into the clean white tub. "Christ!"

He cranked the hot water all the way on to drown the brown beast, which swam around with frantic leg movements. At last it succumbed to the boiling hot water and floated toward the drain, which was too small for it.

"Why the hell did I ever come to this godforsaken swamp?" he muttered. "All I ever wanted was a nice house in the hills and a bit of crumpet on the side. Now I'm stuck in Florida with the cast of *Deliverance*, killing roaches that look like Harley fucking Davidson motorcycles. If it weren't for the 401(k) program, I'd bloody well sod off."

The Harley Davidson was dead now, and Graham grabbed it with a wad of toilet paper before flushing it. Unfortunately, he'd scalded himself in the process, and small pink welts like fever blisters rose on his arms.

He remembered the cat, and knew it was too late. Sure enough, as he walked from the bathroom he saw light brown feather-strokes at odd points on the burgundy carpet. Some were barely visible, like the first one he stepped on—with his bare foot, of course.

"Happy fucking birthday," he said between his teeth.

CHAPTER 2

PAUL PANEPINTO SAT at his desk, the phone pressed to his ear. On hold as usual.

Dave Johnson from Underwriting walked up to Paul's desk, paused, and cocked his head. In a phony British accent, he said, "Sir Graham not in today, old boy?"

Paul shook his head. "No."

"Wot a pity." He laughed and walked away.

Paul's mouth twitched. Well, he thought. Happy Friday.

Although no one in the office was close enough to Graham to know it, Friday, May eighteenth, was his birthday, and in the twenty-one years he'd been working, he'd never once worked on his birthday. Paul found out only that morning that Graham Woodcock would be out that day, not that it was his birthday, though the information wouldn't have mattered. Like any other day, Paul would still have to pick his way through a minefield of lapsed policies and customer service inquiries so banal and idiotic as to be almost incredible. And since Maggie Brown, the claims supervisor, would also be aware of Graham's absence, she would take the opportunity to harass Paul with requests for favors, always via e-mail.

He slumped back in his chair. The hot chocolate in the Federal Funding mug was now cold chocolate, and his hands were brittle from the overzealous air conditioning system. He listened to the muzak while on hold with Mortgage Depot and drummed his fingers on the desk's surface. Without consciously looking at his monitor, he glimpsed the small envelope in the bottom right hand corner indicating a new email message. He blinked and glanced over at it.

Ay, caramba. Now what?

Just a short time ago, he'd had a position of some responsibility, an actual management job. Now, stuck here at Flambet Insurance, he had moments of irritation and boredom so profound and impenetrable that they were almost mythic. The whole weary world receded, and what was left remained meaningless as falling stars. He watched the ripples on the pond outside the window, small undulations and an occasional spray of mist from the fountain, and the trees would nod and bow their mute adoration of nothing while the sun went slowly down....

He had good moments, too—uproarious laughter at a dirty joke from a fellow employee, slow periods when the whole room felt the release of tension like air from a tire and people took time to straighten up desks, wash coffee mugs, water plants. And, more noticeable than the rest, days when the big bosses were gone and people stood outside during breaks and traded war stories, basked in the literal warm sun of the present and allowed themselves to forget the jammed fax machines and computer crashes and all the other ulcer-inducers of a typical day.

Sometimes in the slow season, when claims only trickled in, he sat at his desk without a word for hours at a time. He played CDs on the computer: Howling Wolf and Prefab Sprout, Miles Davis, the Velvet Underground. If things got especially slow, he opened up a psychedelic screensaver and stared into swirling paisley patterns, listening to horns and electric guitars. Several others did the same thing, and they'd nicknamed the practice "Desktop Spacing."

Paul glared again at the envelope in the corner of the screen. Had it really been a year and a half in this menial position? He marveled at it, the astonishing truth of it, and at his own intestinal fortitude. How had he done it? But he knew how. Had it not been for his painting, the time he'd devoted to it evenings and weekends, he would surely have put a noose around his neck.

No, he thought dryly, a gun would be more reliable.

But he also knew he wouldn't have been able to sustain this torturous period if not for Inocente Madrigal Fuentes. Inocente, with her bright eyes and studied touch, her brave attempts at *inglés*, her crazy jokes and imperturbable smiles. Sure, she was nuts, but she'd made the past year and a half bearable…and just because she was presently incommunicado didn't mean she wasn't a factor.

He remembered the assault well: "Hablas inglés, puta," the man hissed, his teeth clenched. "You're in the United States of Fuckin' America now."

Before Paul had even been able to react, Inocente, eyes big with disbelief, reared back like a puff adder while the man smiled his strange sneering smile, not understanding. And when her fist came up into his mouth, he looked so surprised—like someone about to die an undignified death—that she could barely refrain from laughter even as she pulled back her teeth-slashed knuckles. The blood from his mouth came up so fast she saw it still purplish, turning red as it hit the air. Though some of it covered her aching hand, the majority trickled down his chin, dotting the front of his shirt as he doubled over, tears in his eyes and both hands over his mouth.

"You spic bitch," he muttered. "I'll get you for that. You dirty bitch."

"Bite me. Asshole." She stooped down herself, clutching her hand, so that they glared at each other like gladiators. "You're nothing but a bigoted asshole. Ow, my fucking hand."

Well, okay. Sure she was in the past, a past that receded faster by the minute. She was an *ex*-girlfriend. But the past brought him to the present. To *here*.

And here in the present, he sat in this office, this windowless bin, still somewhat bleak, though the floor-to-ceiling windows helped immeasurably…what he could see of them, anyway. He'd never seen such a huge, open office space fill up so quickly, and he'd liked the view better when the room was still empty. Now, all he could see were the tops of trees and a high arc of spray from the fountain in the middle of the pond.

Another e-mail from Maggie Brown, he said to himself. Let's check this out.

PAUL, it said, all capital letters, like some moronic banner of boredom, CAN YOU CALL RELIABLE MORTGAGE AT 201-555-1797 AND ASK THEM TO FAX THE DEC PAGE FOR ACCT. #601-HO-79? THANKS. M. B.

You lazy wench, he thought. Why don't you ask one of your own peons to do your little chores? He clicked delete with a sense of futile glee, and Maggie Brown's message disappeared into the cyberspace void.

He began to daydream, and only the thought of Suzanne Beidertyme kept him from dropping from the precipice of consciousness. Five seven to his five ten—the perfect height—she worked down the hall in Claims, something to do with worker's comp. Her hair was dark and long, and her eyes were dark and sexy, and he would have overcome his nervousness and asked her out if she hadn't been a fellow employee. The "office romance" situation held no appeal.

But sexual fantasy wasn't out of the question, and he decided to indulge himself while the air conditioning froze his fingers and the muzak segued into yet another song. Good God, a muzak version of *Reelin' In The Years*…there's got to be some kind of law against this. Pulling the phone away from his ear slightly and closing his eyes, he imagined office sex with Suzanne. Of course, such a thing could only happen in a world where he could snap his fingers and everyone on the planet froze in place except him and the object of his desire. And when he commanded it—later, much later—they'd all continue on as if time hadn't stood still, unaware that anything had happened.

In that world, he and Suzanne made love now, right there on the carpet in front of the copier. He created a surprisingly tame fantasy, really, with a lot of kissing, and nothing aberrant at all about the foreplay or even the consummation. Just uninterrupted sex, glorious and free and—

"Thank-you-for-holding-how-may-I-direct-your-call?"

Paul's head snapped forward, and a little of the cold chocolate in the Federal Funding mug sloshed out onto the papers beside his keyboard. Jane Garrett, one desk over, looked at him strangely.

"Yes, this is Paul Panepinto from Flambet Insurance. I'm trying to locate someone regarding some lapsed policies—"

"One moment."

Back the muzak came, a version of *Sweet Jane*, and Paul slumped forward onto the desk as if someone had just gently and quietly knifed him.

CHAPTER 3

DOWN THE HALL, Suzanne Beidertyme nibbled a bagel while Cora Gable talked about men.

"You know," Cora said in a low voice, as people wandered in and out of the break room, "I don't think a lot of people would admit it, but *I* think some of the hottest guys around are the Flambet brothers."

Suzanne choked on her tea, felt her face redden. "Jesus," she said, "are you kidding? The Flambets? Which one, James the Dork or Mac the Slime?"

"He's not slimy, come on. Admit it, there's something about him that spells danger. And he likes you, you know."

"I think there's something about him that spells venereal disease. He gives me the creeps. You realize this guy is thirty-six and he's been married *four times*? Those beady little eyes…."

Cora leaned back in her chair, her perfume like a wall of verbena, and when she spoke again, her voice went up an octave. "Mac doesn't have beady little eyes."

"He does too. He scares me. I mean, seriously."

"Oh, stop. He's just real intense. And besides, those guys like Mac and James…they're seriously alpha males, you know? They've got money *and* power. They're not like these mama's boys who act like they're eighteen when they're twenty-five…."

"What do *you* know about them, other than what you see here? Is Lakeisha giving you dirt on them?"

She leaned forward, conspiratorial. "Lakeisha's been cleaning for that family for almost two years. She knows all the dirt…she sees it, literally!"

Suzanne laughed. "*All* the dirt."

Cora reached up and patted the stiff helmet of blonde hair that moved slightly against the pressure. "And you know," she said, "even without getting serious with any of them, some of these guys can really show you a good time, if you know what I mean."

Suzanne laughed again, pretending not to be disgusted, and swatted her on the arm. "Cora! I didn't know you were such an animal."

"Well, I'm not necessarily." She leaned back in the chair again. "I mean, I was just talking about some fine dining and dancing, or a Broadway show —"

"Yeah, right."

Cora laughed shrilly. "I don't think you're taking this conversation seriously."

"How could I?" Suzanne thought for a moment about how untrustworthy Cora was.

"Trust me," Cora said. "Mac Flambet is the man. *And he likes you.*" A singsong, the schoolyard *I-know-something-you-don't-know.*

Suzanne glanced down, as if to appraise her slight chest with disdain. "Oh, please." This actually meant, "Oh, please spare me Mac Flambet," but Cora wouldn't have guessed it. Was Cora actually trying to set her up with Mac?

"No, no," continued Cora. "He does like you. I'm sure of it. You didn't really mean that about him being a slimeball, did you?"

"Well —" She glanced away. "I just don't think he's my type."

"Think it over, girl." Cora got up, suddenly and decisively. "It could be the time of your life. Have you seen that Jaguar?"

Their eyes met. "Yeah, actually," Suzanne smiled.

"There ya go." And she flounced out of the room.

Alone in the room, Suzanne took a deep breath and shook her head. "I don't think so," she said.

CHAPTER 4

FLAMBET INSURANCE CORPORATION, owned and operated by James Irving Flambet (Chief Executive Officer and "chief cook and bottle washer," in his own words), grew out of the need for the family law firm to diversify its holdings and provide more stability for its wildly fluctuating portfolios. The family law firm started out as Flambet, Cohn, Weisenstein and Montrachet—frogs and hebes, old man Flambet always said, frogs and hebes—and it grew through a series of outlandish permutations until at last it reached its present incarnation of Flambet, Flambet and Weisenstein. Jean Bertram Flambet was the old man, known to all as "J.B.," like an old-time Hollywood director. He got a lot of mileage out of Weisenstein's name, pretending he'd picked the name out of the phonebook. He had an elaborate pantomime routine: "Let's see, Weisenborn…Weisenheimer…Weisenhoofer… *Weisenstein!*" He'd formed the first version of Flambet Insurance Corporation in his thirties, and when he decided to spin off a group of limited partnerships in addition to it, it only made sense that his elder son James should take the helm at the insurance firm. By that time, his younger son Mac had already established a prominent place for himself in the family law firm. James, something of a black sheep since he'd never achieved the MBA, was two years older than Mac and in need of a job better than the one he had at Tampa's Westchase Country Club, so it wasn't reasonable, really, to make Mac try to run an insurance company. Besides, Mac was a good attorney with a sharp eye and an instinct for the kill, and no one doubted he'd become a senior partner within a year or two at most. In fact, he did just that.

On the Friday that Graham Woodcock took off, James Flambet stayed home also, though not for the same reason. He'd planned to work, but his daughter Eugenie announced she had a fever that morning, and with James' wife Celia out of town on business, he had to stay home. Eugenie, a striking seven-year-old, would normally have been comforted and nursed all day by her nanny, a Northampton girl named Pamela Mae Swenson, but Pamela was sick, too. So James Irving Flambet, Chief Executive Officer of Flambet Insurance Corporation, a man of some sophistication and an agreeable degree of material comfort, spent the morning eating buttered scones and oranges and watching *SpongeBob SquarePants* videos with his daughter.

Of course, he broke out the paperwork at length, and gave a perfunctory moment or two to the numbers at hand, especially the figures regarding a morass of legal problems he'd nicknamed The McDillon Nightmare. But the numbers didn't add up, he found weird, inexplicable omissions in the spreadsheets, and it all fatigued him. So many problems in the firm these days, it felt like he was bailing water out of a leaky sailboat. Every time he discovered a new scheme to raise capital, down came another disaster, and the juggling act of creditors and debtors became more and more convoluted and futile. Where would it all end?

He put aside The McDillon Nightmare and went idly through printouts of payroll records. He didn't have a compelling reason to look at them, but it diverted him from anything else. Since the company had grown so large and impersonal, three hundred employees in the home office alone, he felt somehow comforted flipping through these records of past and present employees.

Part nostalgia trip and part "new hire" update, mostly it was just a diversion.

Lucy Hedges, he thought, thumbing through the pages. There's a name I haven't heard in a while. John Alsup. Hmm, thirty-five thousand a year. Must be a new processor. Philip Banks. Don't remember him. Must have retired. Says here he was born in…that would make him about sixty-seven now. Can't place the name or the face. He was here a while, too, look at this—stock options, the 401(k)…I've got to keep up more with this stuff, he thought. Shake a few hands.

Philip Banks, he mused. Nope, don't remember him at all.

CHAPTER 5

ACROSS TOWN, PAUL stood on the threshold of discovering Philip Banks for himself. He'd swallowed his pride and done a few things for the ubiquitous Maggie Brown, and then it turned out he had to do a few things for Graham in the big boss' absence. Maggie, acting on orders phoned in from James Flambet, gave Paul one of Graham's sign-ins, a password into areas of limited access in one of the company databases. Paul opened the Teleclaim program and, while searching for a file called *claimtemp3*, he must have accidentally hit the wrong key. Blood throbbed in his temples as he realized he didn't know how to undo what he'd done. Hitting *Escape* didn't work. He hit *Enter*. Nothing. He clicked on *Help*. Nothing. Just the slow inexorable blinking of the cursor.

He was afraid to try a function key, since that was probably what he'd inadvertently pushed in the first place. For all he knew, it might damage the whole database. So he sat and tried to figure a safe way to escape, his left forefinger idly tapping the surface of the *Tab* key.

Suddenly, he realized he must have actually pressed the *Tab* key. The screen changed dramatically, fading to a duller shade of blue and prompting him to enter a password. Another password. Shit. He punched *Escape* again, hoping for luck. Nothing but a beep. Reluctantly, he reentered Graham's sign-in. And voila, he was in. He didn't know where he was, but he was in.

He was looking at an employee profile of a kind he'd never seen. It had a résumé, a screen that showed a whole history of company-related transactions enacted by the employee, and a financial statement of some sort related to the company's 401(k) retirement plan. Apparently the guy made pretty good money before retiring from Flambet Insurance.

His name was Philip Banks.

Later he would be hard pressed to say why he'd suspected something was wrong. He'd just say it was luck, a hunch. Maybe the name did it: a pun, Philip Banks, like Fill Up Banks. Somehow it just didn't sound real. Possibly it was just the oddity of Graham having this strange-looking file, isolated from the rest of the company's records.

He found another, of course. An employee named Dolores Buenas. Maybe because of his Latino background, or maybe just the prompting of Fill Up Banks, he transliterated Dolores Buenas into Dólares Buenas, "Good Dollars," so quickly and intuitively, it felt like an epiphany.

He scrawled the social security numbers and phone numbers of both Philip and Dolores on a piece of paper. He knew he was onto something. He knew that these two names, names he'd never heard—and there was nothing in the whole file besides their records—would lead to something secret and unsavory and probably illegal.

In fact, he decided to do more than write down numbers. He went through every page of the file, hitting the *Print Screen* button on the keyboard at each page, terrified lest he should be too late getting down the hall to the printer before someone else saw part of it. He slipped the piece of paper with the phone numbers and social security numbers into his pocket in case something went wrong, just so he'd have something. When he went down the hall, he was relieved to find no one near the printer, a lucky break. He pulled the last few sheets from the printer and put them face down on the rest of the stack, his forehead and back damp with perspiration.

He had it all, whatever it was. And he walked back to the computer, knowing he didn't know how to back out of the limited access file, knowing the computer guys would bitch at him for turning off the hard drive manually while he was in the middle of a file, knowing he would lie and say the thing had just crashed and not caring that he'd have to lie. He had it all. Whatever it was, it was his now, too.

CHAPTER 6

THE NEXT DAY, in the public library, Paul found nothing to allay his suspicions, just as he'd expected. More impressive still, when he logged onto the Internet, he quickly found that the social security numbers were bogus, since it was easy enough to get modest-sized information files on virtually anyone in the country just by jumping through a few hoops. But no one had those socials, and none of the people he found named Philip Banks or Dolores Buenas matched the profiles.

He tried the phone numbers. One out of service, and the other a Chinese restaurant named Hao Wah.

Once again, Paul scanned the materials. All very thorough and apparently legit. Except for one thing: they didn't exist.

Without even using any imagination, he'd deciphered the mystery. Philip Banks and Dolores Buenas were fictitious characters—Graham Woodcock's brainchildren and heirs to a small fortune that he would undoubtedly amass within a few years, assuming their portfolios did well. Simple enough.

The only real mystery was how Graham had been so careless as to let the phony records be accessible. But then Paul thought back to how he'd gotten them: sheer accident. He'd hit the *Tab* key, of all things, which was never used as a command to open an application. It wasn't even really a function key. Somehow, Graham made it one and, naturally, figured that was safeguard enough.

And why not? The personnel files and résumés he'd taken great pains to create would have been sufficient "proof" for any snooper. Who would go further? Nobody ever checked up on these things, least of all an easygoing CEO like James Flambet.

Just for fun, Paul contacted the universities Philip Banks and Dolores Buenas had supposedly attended. No such students on file.

So in theory, he had Graham Woodcock by the short hairs, and no one would deny it. But did he? He had no legitimate way to retrieve the files for anyone else. He'd found the files through a series of keystrokes too bizarre and mysterious to reproduce; not just the *Tab* key, but the one prior to that, the accidental keystroke. Paul was pretty sure it must have been a function key, but the keyboard had twelve of those, and anyway, he'd need one of Graham's sign-ins to get back in…probably the exact same one.

Of course, he had hard copies, but what were they worth? Graham would obviously deny it all and destroy the records, and besides, who would believe it? The risk was too great. Graham was completely responsible for the 401(k), and with his other responsibilities, he was like an executive vice-president. Who else was higher up? Only James Flambet himself.

Paul picked up the phone and dialed.

"Hello?"

"Hey, Suzanne, it's me, Paul."

"*Hi*, what's up? I was just —"

"Listen, I have to talk to you."

"What's wrong?"

He cleared his throat. "Can we get together later? I don't think I should talk about this on the phone."

"Uh-oh. You haven't been reading one of those conspiracy-theory books again, have you?"

He laughed. "No. But if I do have a conspiracy here, it's a conspiracy of one."

"What are you talking about?"

"Meet me at the Café Con Leche at eight o'clock?"

"All right. Do I have to wear black, like a spy?"

"No, smartass, you don't have to wear black. Although I like black…."

"Well, I told you I was the artistic type. Didn't I ever tell you my greatest goal in life was to work as a dance instructor?"

He pictured her in a dance studio, an enticing visual. "You still taking night classes to get your dance degree?"

"Oh yeah. Wednesdays and Thursdays."

"All right, well, I'll see you at eight o'clock, then, right?"

"Okay. See ya then."

He hung up the phone, sat back, and started to count the hours until eight.

CHAPTER 7

MAC FLAMBET, thirty-six years old, tall and lank and hungry-looking, rose at five each morning and looked in the mirror before doing anything else. It was a mark of character for him that he stood before the great Victorian nightstand with its burnished chest of drawers and, as religiously as if he were performing some mysterious sacrament, always looked searchingly at his face and smoothed down his hair, paused to glance out the window at the Jaguar—this as much a ritual as the mirror—then back at the mirror for a last complacent look before retreating to the vanity in the bathroom or to the kitchen for breakfast.

Of course, the hair he smoothed down was not too thick, receding back farther and farther from the high colubrine forehead and the small cold eyes like the eyes a taxidermist would use, slick and dead-looking. But the smile was complacent nonetheless, and behind the expressionless eyes and the sharp incisors lay a mind sharper still that knew what it wanted and how to get it, and knew that he was not entirely wrong to fancy himself something of a lady-killer.

Someone had recently asked how old his kids were and, without thinking, he'd replied, "About three and a half marriages." And that was true, though since he hadn't found number five yet, he still hadn't gotten completely over ex-wife number four. He'd told the psychiatrist as much the previous Friday.

"I still think about fucking her sometimes," he'd said thoughtfully, his eyes fixed on some distant unseeable point beyond the St. Petersburg skyline. "Anybody would think about fucking her."

But in getting over his last wife, he'd had to have numerous affairs. There'd been a hooker somewhere in there—the thought of HIV never frightened him—and a young college student or two. *No need to worry about them*, he'd told himself, *their immune systems are strong*. The most exciting and, to his mind, fulfilling candidate was Andrea Heatherstone, a married woman of twenty-seven with the body of a swimsuit model and a face like a young Audrey Hepburn. She was absolutely magnificent, and in his frenzy for her, he'd done something he'd never done with a woman: gotten down on his knees, kissing her hand. He'd kissed her fingers, his heart pounding with lust and mad joy, kissed her wedding ring itself, knowing it was taboo—one of the most excessive taboos he could imagine—and yet it was dreadfully exciting, a shiver of excitement and revulsion passed through him and he breathed a little harder as she began to moan. He'd made violent love to her then, and he remembered the climactic moment when the orgasm hit him in the knees, a savage blow, and his legs twitched like the legs of a dreaming dog.

He stood before the mirror and smoothed his hair, and he chuckled. What a trip. Well, that was in April, and it was almost June now. She was something, though. Maybe it was worth pursuing yet, trying to pick up the loose thread.

He went into the kitchen and poked through the cabinet, looking for oatmeal. Damned if that cleaning woman hadn't rearranged everything again. He'd have to have a talk with her.

To add gasoline to the fire, he stood and ran a bony finger across the top of the refrigerator. Sure enough. The lazy negroid whore. He rinsed the finger carefully, then thought better of it and went ahead with the anti-bacterial soap, washing both hands completely.

When he left for the law offices of Flambet, Flambet and Weisenstein that morning, his watch already read six, later than he liked to be leaving. When he wasn't in court, he usually worked from 6:30 to noon, ate lunch, then dove back in from lunch until about nine or ten, always working, stopping only for a brief dinner at the country club on nights when the firm's caseload was light.

More often than not, though, he waited until he got home at eleven or twelve and had some fruit or cheese and crackers in lieu of dinner before bed. Mostly, he just liked to make sure he was in his office before seven, since that gave him one more thing to lord over the slackers who didn't have the kind of vested interest in the firm he did. And since he had nearly an hour-long commute, he liked to leave between five-thirty and quarter to six.

But the building was still dark when he eased the Jaguar into parking space number one at 6:55. He got out and pressed the car alarm button, and as the alarm chirped in response he stepped toward the door lightly and with good cheer in his step. He was first again.

Stacks of documents awaited his signature. The ones in his in-basket typically held little importance, and could have been signed off by any of the partners. Others, mostly those set with care in the big leather chair behind his desk, required his signature alone: documents from his father, documents relevant to the office lease, documents from one of his ex-wives. He sighed and scrawled signatures across the bottoms of the pages, not even troubling to read them.

Ida Stephan, one of the firm's oldest legal secretaries, did most of the work around the office, and Mac had known her since he was a boy. She'd come down to Florida from Canada in the fifties and gotten a job with the firm not long after it opened. She was like family, and of the few people Mac trusted, he trusted her most. For that reason, he forbade anyone in the office other than Ida to leave signature-required documents on his chair. If Ida put it there, he didn't have to read it; he could just sign it.

CHAPTER 8

ON THE BOOKSHELVES in Suzanne Beidertyme's cozy apartment, side by side with Anaïs Nin and Jamaica Kincaid, she had the *Rubaiyat* of Omar Khayyam, plays by Beckett and Mamet, books on ballet. On the southeast wall hung a print of Dali's "Resurrection," while a painting of early New England farmland opposed it in sunny tranquility, like some poor imitation of the Hudson River School painters. The furniture was perversely heterogeneous: an antique lamp, a paint-spattered wooden chair, a nondescript sofa. Even the bathroom's magazine rack, an aberration picked up from British friends, held a copy of *The Practical Cogitator* in its wooden embrace.

She regretted telling Graham Woodcock she'd had friends from the U.K. He had launched into his usual list of the praises of Mother England, waxing eloquent about bangers and the silly sods of some "football" team. In the process, he'd roped Mac Flambet into the conversation, and Mac watched her from beneath his beetle-like eyebrows, his cold eyes taking her in as he ran a hand across his thinning brown hair and wiped his oily forehead. She averted her gaze. Only a moment before, he'd looked across the room at her like a bee contemplating an orchid.

She pictured him as she scrubbed the shiny porcelain base of the toilet, pausing to dip the washcloth back into the bucket of soapy water beside her. How could she avoid him? She did not so much mind being polite to him—as the boss' brother, that was inevitable—but she resented his eyes on her, leering at her small breasts, her hips, probably even—but no, she shook her head and shuddered.

How could she avoid him? Impossible. She could leave her cubicle any time under the pretense of going to the ladies' room, and she'd even done it once. But it wouldn't solve anything. He'd surely still be there when she returned, waiting, *because he knew where she was.*

It was disgusting, the humiliation of it all. Naturally, he knew she wasn't interested, but she knew he didn't care. He wanted to watch her squirm, the sadist in him was undoubtedly turned on by it. The bastard. Thank God he didn't actually work there.

Suzanne remembered overhearing Graham and Mac talking about women, a disgusting conversation: *Of course,* Graham had said, *in Americar, one meets so many women…but I've found almost all of them—the good-looking ones, anyway—are frightfully ordinary. And they're almost always paired off with some bloody swaggering Cro-Magnon man who's got all the tact and delicacy of a Mongolian idiot. Undoubtedly, it makes these women feel marvelously sophisticated and intelligent—*he smirked—*which, of course, comparatively speaking, they are, aren't they?*

Well, said Mac, *pussy is pussy. It's all the same to me. Frankly, I think women should be flattered men spend so much time and energy fantasizing about having sex with them. I mean, trust me, once she's fifty or sixty years old, not a whole lotta people are gonna be fantasizing about her anymore, you know what I mean? Maybe a few other fifty- or sixty-year-olds.…*

Suzanne wrung out the washcloth again and paused, gazing unseeing down into the barely rippling water in the bowl. God, this is ridiculous. We've only gone out on two dates, and here I am making my toilet clean enough to eat out of, and all because Paul might come back later.

Okay, three dates. But come on, it's *Paul.* Like he's really going to notice if my place isn't spotless. It's practically clean as Mom's place right now, for Pete's sake.

She tossed the washcloth in the bowl and stood. Screw this, I'm not cleaning anything else. It's almost seven-thirty. We may not even come back here later.

But she was kidding herself. She'd been out with Paul three times, and each time, he'd somehow managed to get her to invite him in. She still wasn't sure how he did it. Nothing had happened, but the thought made her pause.

Was he as interested in her as she was in him? It didn't seem likely, unless he just played it cool for effect, but he'd certainly managed to get comfortable with her place quickly. He'd sat back in one of the big easy chairs, hands behind his head, and looked for all the world like a little boy imitating a man lazing behind a desk. She would not have been surprised if he'd put his feet up on the coffee table and grinned at her.

The phone rang and she leapt across the room for it. "Hello?"

"Hey." A woman's voice.

"*Hey?*" She leaned into the phone.

"Suzanne?"

"Who's calling, please?"

"It's me, Cora."

Her heart thudded. Shit. "Hey Cora."

"Guess who I just got off the phone with? Lakeisha Bennefield."

"Lakeisha Bennefield," she repeated, wondering how Cora got her phone number.

"You know, Lakeisha."

"Ah, sorry, I—I was just on my way out. The name didn't register. Can I call you back?"

"Yeah, sure. But you remember Lakeisha, right? From the Flambets."

"Yeah. Oh yeah. All right, I'll talk to you."

"See ya."

She hung up. God, Cora Gable was calling now. Life had become a cartoon.

CHAPTER 9

GRAHAM WOODCOCK PICKED up his cell phone and punched in the toll-free number for the Philip Banks and Dolores Buenas accounts.

"Thank you for calling —"

"Yeah, yeah. Fuck off." He punched in more numbers, interrupting the recorded greeting.

"Please enter your —"

"Yeah, yeah." He punched in the PIN.

"Your total portfolio value is eleven…thousand…seven hundred…dollars and…two cents…."

"Jesus, that's it? Fucking hell." He disconnected the call, hit redial, punched more numbers. He sat silently at the traffic light, working his phone and glancing at the black Lexus beside him, a carbon copy of his own car.

"Your total portfolio value is thirty-seven…thousand…nine hundred…."

Graham hung up and sighed deeply. He tapped the cell phone impatiently several times, then stopped when the light changed and gunned the car through the intersection and across several more.

"Thirty bleeding grand…less than four months' pay. I should have created ten of the little bastards instead of two." He sighed and began tapping again. Outside the car window, buildings went by like glimpses of shadows, quick and meaningless. A ragged man stood on the corner of an intersection. Ten days' growth. *Will work for food.*

The clock on the dashboard read 6:05, although the real time was 7:05, thanks to daylight savings. He hadn't figured out how to reset the new car's clock, and since he usually spent eleven to twelve hours each day at work, he hadn't had time to read the manual either. Still, knowing it needed updating created a sense of urgency, and he cursed the device all the way back to the beach.

The one saving grace in the whole nightmare was that beach. Facing the Gulf of Mexico, the condo complex stood silent, a vast rectangle of glass and steel and concrete like a giant hotel squatting at the outermost tip of Redington Beach, two miles north of John's Pass. On Sundays, he sat on the balcony in an ergonomically designed chaise lounge, drinking Manhattans and staring out into the vast blue abyss of the Gulf, looking through it somehow, and—when the universe was merciful—not even thinking.

Today was Friday, though, and he knew he would be working at least another twelve hours every day the following week. It had been one of those sixty-hour weeks, each day from seven to seven, and since he was salaried, it felt like a loss: always the same pay, regardless of the number of hours. Of course, he knew he made more than three times the average salary in the area, but that was no consolation.

He looked down at the laptop on the seat beside him and scowled. You little bugger, he thought, I ought to throw you into the fucking Gulf. Call up Flambet and tell him somebody stole it out of the car. "Sorry, old boy, couldn't get anything done *this* weekend." Serve him right, too, the yuppie bastard. Fifteen years as CEO and all he's got to show is that snobby bitch of a wife and a daughter with a French name. Fucking wanker.

He entered the condo to the tune of the two cats meowing for food. "All right, all right." He took food from the cabinet, poured food and water into the bowls. "Right, now piss off." He turned to go to the bathroom, then noticed the voice mail light blinking.

"Graham, it's James. Listen, we've got a real problem here with this McDillon nightmare. Some missing fields of data, or at least it looks that way. I tried you at the office and they told me you were gone, so I tried your cell, but apparently it's not working. Anyway, call me on my cell, thanks."

"Fuck off, you stupid bastard." He sighed bitterly. "The end of the world could come and nothing would matter except bloody McDillon. Bastards."

He picked up the phone and threw it across the room. The cats bolted like children from a drunken parent. The dial tone hummed plaintively, and tangled phone cords stretched taut across the floor.

"Ah, Christ," he said to himself. He put the receiver back on the hook, then carried it back over to the nightstand. He glared down at the laptop.

How many more years of this have I got to take? I can't possibly work another twenty or twenty-five with these miserable sons of bitches. I want out now, for God's sake. Even if I could transfer all the mutual funds to something with a higher yield, I'd still be looking at fifteen years *minimum* before I'm home free.

He sighed. I've got to marry some little rich bitch or knock somebody in the head. If I could find some way to make those little buggers multiply without creating more of them…but how do I increase the contribution to a 401(k) plan of someone who's supposed to be retired without using my own money? I've got to develop a whole new source of damn income.

He dialed James Flambet. "What's up?"

"Hey Graham. Yeah, do me a favor Monday and see if we can pull one of your people to take a look at that McDillon thing. It's mostly just a matter of doing the auditing, maybe re-running some reports to see if the data is corrupted or what. I can't waste any more time on it, and I sure as hell don't want you wasting yours. You've got enough on your plate." He chuckled without humor.

"Yeah, well, I may not be in on Monday. I've got a bloody great sinus infection, and my head feels like it's in a vise. I'm about to take two aspirin and call no one in the morning."

"Sorry to hear it."

No, you're not, Graham thought.

"Well, let me know if there's someone who can do some overtime on it. Maybe Paul or somebody."

"Paul Panepinto?"

"Yeah, or whoever. Okay?"

"Right-o."

"All right, take care of that sinus headache, buddy."

"Right, bye."

James hung up, and Graham glared at the phone before putting it down. "Sinus *infection*, I said, not headache. And I am not your fucking buddy. Phony bastard."

Suddenly, as if the word *phony* had opened a great door in the wall of reality, it came to him. That's it: a phony blackout. I'll tell the whole lot of them the fund's getting a new administrator. And there'll be a blackout period during the transition where no one will be able to monitor how their funds are doing. The thing's bound to be up and down during that month, or two months, or whatever the hell I decide to make it, so no one will really track their losses or gains with any kind of accuracy. They'll just assume that things aren't terrible, as long as the market has its normal ups and downs. No way in hell they'll see all funds going up or down every day if they look them up online.

All I've got to do is figure out the best way to skim the cream off the top. That's the only hard part. But Christ! What a bold damn idea. Skim the top off the whole lot. Three hundred people in the Tampa office alone. If I helped myself to five dollars from each of them, it would be fifteen hundred; if I made it fifty, fifteen grand. Five hundred…God, it's beautiful!

He sat down with the laptop and began to work.

CHAPTER 10

PAUL RAN OUT of things to do early Monday morning when Graham was again out of the office. He'd told Suzanne all about Graham's scheme when they'd met that night at the Café Con Leche, and she'd blanched, then laughed and called it "the Graham scam." He dreaded seeing Graham, so his absence was like a gift.

Paul called James's secretary twice, but James was on the phone each time, and he was on the phone again when Paul went down to his office.

"Yeah," James was saying, "because of the loss history we can't rewrite it in our preferred market. Exactly. Okay. Right." He hung up the phone without saying goodbye.

Paul tiptoed into the office, and James smiled his best presidential smile. "Hey, Paul."

"Morning."

"What's up?"

Paul's glance flickered on one side of the room and the other. He grinned feebly when he made eye contact again. "Well, Graham's still out, and I've pretty much hit the wall on what he left for me to finish. What should I do next?"

James stood and took a step away from Paul and from his desk. He crossed his hands behind him. "Well…what would you *like* to do?" He grinned again, laughed shortly through his nose.

I'd like to go home, thought Paul. I'd like to get the fuck out of here and never see that thieving bastard Woodcock again, or have to think about him or what he's doing to your company. What he's doing to you.

Instead, he smiled and played along. Softly, softly. "Ah—coffee break?"

They both laughed, then James returned to his desk and sat on the edge of it. "Yeah," he said, "why *don't* you take a break. If you'd like, you can come back in about fifteen minutes and help me wade through this McDillon mess. In fact, I suggested to Graham that I ought to have one of you guys work on it, but he never got back to me this weekend. Sinus problems. It's mostly a no-brainer, just numbers, but once the basics are sorted out, I still need the final analysis. I just don't have time to screw around with all the math."

"Great. I'll just grab some coffee and come right back."

"No, no, take fifteen." He scowled the scowl of someone who is being magnanimous and knows it.

"Okay. Thanks."

James gave him a big thumbs-up. "All right."

Paul walked to the break room, then picked up the comics section and sat down on a large stuffed chair. Only two other people sat nearby: Cora Gable and a young woman from another department named Jill Martin.

"So how bad are things under Mr. Wood Cock?" asked Jill.

"Not too bad," said Cora, "not too bad. He's out again today, so that's cool. How's Maggie's World?"

"Maggie's on the rampage this week. John got his review, and she gave him three unsatisfactories and a couple of averages."

"That fucking bitch. On *John?* The guy puts in almost seventy hours a week." Cora glanced at Paul. "Sorry, Paul."

"Doesn't bother me," he said, turning back to the comics. "John must be bummed, though." Anything goes in this place, he said to himself as the two women walked out.

In some ways a typical modern company—cubicles with computers and phones, dull walls brightened somewhat by generic office art—the place was much looser in other ways than what people thought of as corporate America. For one, every day was casual day to an extreme: jeans, shorts, tennis shoes and sweatshirts were just as de rigeur as polo shirts and penny loafers. Even more important, the unofficial "Flambet Attitude" was more a byproduct of working for Flambet Insurance than an actual personality trait. People became careless about language, saying the work *fuck* loudly over something minor, like a jammed photocopier. Character assassinations ran rampant.

Paul remembered that, on one occasion, a male employee jokingly offered to go down on a female employee if she'd only find a certain file for him, and everyone in the room laughed. No one was even slightly offended. All it would take was one relatively conservative person walking in on a joke like that, and there'd be a sexual harassment case the size of Alaska. If the wrong client overheard Cora Gable referring to Maggie Brown as *that fucking bitch*, a big account could vanish into the ozone.

Truth be told, the company was an insane asylum, a place where even the most well-adjusted among them ate antacids like candies and ran from task to task taking desperate sips of coffee from Styrofoam cups. And although it was no longer a small company, it was still one of those offices appareled for every holiday season, as if consciousness of its insignificance created a manic need to stand out: jack-o'-lanterns in October, turkeys for November, poinsettias at Christmas. Still, Paul thought, there was something poignant about it all. They ate politically correct junk food at the office parties, peanut brittle from the rainforests of Brazil, sugarless candy packaged by Somalian farmers.

Paul's mind suddenly returned to a night with Inocente, just after a Christmas party, standing outside beneath dim streetlights. He remembered the cool, damp air, the smell of woodsmoke and orange blossoms in the air contrasting with the palm trees and live oaks beside them, the kudzu-covered trees…how all the night had felt unreal somehow, the party, the people, and then the strange walk to the car. They hurried down the dim road, their breath coming out in a slowly-dissipating stream, the two of them shivering in their long coats like peasants in some Russian novel instead of the unreality of a Florida winter, which made him think wryly of St. Petersburg.

The options narrowed before him clearly, the honing borne of the need for certainty and direction. He saw both Suzanne and Inocente in his mind's eye, their separate worlds, and how he was drawn to each in different ways. Inocente, the Latino girl, from his own culture, and Suzanne, the white girl, so much more like what he thought he was himself. His parents were professionals. He'd been born here, had no accent. And their personalities: where Suzanne offered a kind of comfort and security, a predictable warmth and peace, Inocente provided an almost equal measure of uncertainty, but more excitement, unpredictability. More risk.

And straight down the middle, like a line separating the two worlds, he saw the path he would travel if he chose neither. He wondered if that choice was any choice at all or really just drifting, letting his life be a series of disconnected incidents. Or maybe he'd make a choice if he held his hand close to his vest and didn't let anyone see his cards. Since neither relationship was a romance in the conventional sense, maybe he should see who else came along.

He decided to give it another thirty days.

The sun broke through heavy cloud cover behind James Flambet when Paul returned to the CEO's office. James stood behind his desk with one hand in the air, motioning to Paul to come in. Behind him, sunlight through tinted glass gave him the appearance of a halo.

"So where does it look like you'll be next month?" said the man he had on speakerphone.

James winced. "Right now, it looks like we're about the same place as last year at this time—I'll be right with you, Paul—" he made eye contact a moment "—sorry, Rob, I've got someone else here in my office…anyway, we're not out of the woods yet. It's a little like bailing water out of a leaky sailboat, but we're doing a pretty good job of sealing up the existing leaks, anyway." He looked up and winked at Paul.

"Well, do you want to call me next week?" the voice asked.

"Tell you what, call me Monday, and I'll see what we can do."

"Okay, James. Thanks."

"Thanks, Rob. Take care." He pressed the button and sat back down behind the desk, frowning.

"Did you need me to come back later?" Paul asked.

"No, no. Just thinking." He looked up again. "Talking to one of our many creditors."

"Aha."

"As I'm sure you know from working with Graham, we've incurred substantial debt this year, primarily from taking out loans in order to pay off creditors. And though we're making money, our outstanding expenses, combined with our debt, actually put us in the red. So we're doing a little juggling act. It's not *your* problem, and I don't want you to worry about what's going on with the company, because we're all right. But part of the situation now is this McDillon nightmare I need you to work on, so just bear with me and I'll explain it."

"All right."

"I just thought you should know where we stand and what this is all about before you get started."

Paul nodded.

"These spreadsheets are the first thing I want you to review. There are some weird omissions I can't account for, so anywhere you see a blank field, we need to try to find out what the deal is."

"Right."

It took ten minutes to explain it all, and by the time Paul carried the file folders back to his desk, he wondered if he was in over his head. His job had become so simple it almost felt dangerous to take on a task of such importance. But then he thought about the work he'd done at National, and realized how similar this was. This might signal an opportunity for advancement down the road. He was so preoccupied, he didn't realize until after he'd passed Suzanne Beidertyme in the hall that he'd only smiled blankly in response to her hello.

CHAPTER 11

THE FIRST JOB Eula Yi ever got in a Chinese restaurant was at a place called Diang Chi Nan in Clearwater, right on the beach. The place had a reputation for great food, but an even bigger, and unfortunate, reputation for serving dishes with quirky names and spices that did not quite meet customers' expectations. The one that Eula Yi remembered, and would in fact remember always, was Chairman Mao's Chicken.

She knew it shocked customers no end when she took their orders. She'd glide over to their table and say, in her sweet southern drawl, "Are yew ready to order?"

Men with ruddy faces and short sun-bleached hair had been known to slap the table and say, "God dang, girl, you ain't no Chink! You're from the south, ain't you?"

And with the greatest effort, she said, "I was born in Georgia, sir. My parents are Cantonese." Then she smiled, as diplomatic as if the word *chink* were a congressional medal of honor and the moment was no different than someone pointing out that her hair was so black it was almost blue.

She'd been twenty then; hard to believe ten years had gone by. Ten years had left a little mark on her—two marks, in fact—neat little curved lines on either side of her mouth that remained visible even after she stopped smiling. But otherwise, she was as beautiful as she'd been at twenty. She looked like an Asian model, one of those women on posters advertising soft drinks or movies in Hong Kong, her face long and slender. She worked hard, had no apparent vices. She was dependable as a clock.

Jorge Arce walked into her apartment with a little red beret cocked to one side on his head. "Hey," he said.

"Hey." She smiled, brief and formal.

"What's up, home kitty? You look kinda down."

"Home kitty? *Home kitty?*"

He shrugged. "Just an expression. A little joke, kinda like my paycheck."

She smiled in spite of herself.

"Seriously, you okay? Look like you seen a ghost."

"I'm all right, Jorge." She pronounced his name unlike the Latinos, drawing out each syllable, so that it sounded like *whore-hey*. "Can we talk about something?"

"Sure," he said, suddenly all tender solicitude. "Didn't I just ask you what's wrong? So, what's wrong?" He took one of her hands between his own, pressing it lightly.

"That girl called for you again."

"Girl? What girl?" He let go of her hand.

"Pamela Mae Swenson," she said, with the voice and manner of a snooty Northeastern girl.

"Oh." He relaxed. "She just the nanny, hon. She like a co-worker. Probably just wants to know something about a dish I left in the fridge. Like food allergies or something."

"I don't like her. She never talks *to me*. Just at me. Like she takes for granted that I'll be here to take messages for her. She doesn't know me."

"I know," he said. "I know."

"I don't like her," she repeated, as if he might not have understood.

"Forget about her," he said. "Let's go get some Chinese."

On the drive to the restaurant, the subject of the Flambets came up. "I'm getting tired of working for those people," said Jorge. "They're crazy, I'll tell you. That Mac, he's a real beauty. I don't see him much, 'cause he don't come over to visit old J.B. and Alexis that often."

She smiled. "How is old Alexis these days?"

"Alexis?" He glanced over at her for a moment, then back at the road. "Ah, she'll be a bleached blonde when she's a hundred."

Eula giggled. "You're mean."

"I'm serious. She a typical rich old lady. Always workin' on some painting or goin' off to some volunteer club. Everything's all *dahling* this and *dahling* that."

"I remember."

"Sure, I told you about her. That Mac, though, he a trip."

"The lawyer?"

"Mm-hm. He got some problem at work with some woman who works for him. Gave him something to sign that he shouldn't have signed. He didn't even look at it, I guess. I overheard him talking about it."

"What was it?"

"Something from one of his ex-wives."

"*One* of?"

"Yeah, he got like three or four of 'em."

She shook her head. "Damn, no wonder you never seem to want to think about marriage. Working for people like that."

Jorge's eyes darted back and forth on the road ahead, and he hunched his shoulders up a little. "Ah," he said, "I can't think about that kind of thing on an empty stomach."

She lifted her left foot as if to press it down on his accelerator foot. But he only said, "Hey," and she pulled it back again and was silent.

CHAPTER 12

THE MEMORIAL DAY weekend provided Graham with time to work out his scheme to the last detail. It wasn't actually feasible to black out the company plan for more than a month. People would get suspicious. But two weeks was only one pay period, too short a time to skim very much. So he settled on a month: two weeks to help himself to money from half the employees, and then two weeks spent on the other half.

He started with an arbitrary figure of fifty dollars per employee, but some employees didn't contribute enough to the plan for fifty to be feasible, and for others, he had to admit, fifty was surely not enough. He worked it out so elaborately that he knew in advance how much he would skim from each employee, contingent, of course, upon how much the various mutual funds were up or down in a given pay period. A hundred dollars or so from this one, seventy to eighty from that one.

As long as he timed it well, and the funds had the normal ups and downs, no one would miss a bit of it. If the funds all went up and only up, he was sunk: end of game. If they went down and down, it would be a bonanza. He mapped it all out on a spreadsheet, studying the allocation of mutual funds each employee had chosen, as well as the contributions to each fund. He felt like a child planning for Christmas, anxiously anticipating what he would get.

Then he had to implement phase two. The only way to do the thing was to divert money so that nothing appeared amiss, either to the employees or the fund managers. Consequently, it had to look like an ordinary month on paper. This required a whole new strategy, and would entail a software purchase.

He went out to the computer store at six, and since he hadn't eaten all day, he stopped off at a Chinese restaurant for dinner. He stood outside, perusing the takeout menu and thinking maybe something with shrimp. In front of him in line, a young Latino man and a young Asian woman were talking about an attorney. The young man's hair was styled in an ugly, flat-topped buzz cut, so that from a distance, he looked rather like a bald man wearing a fez.

"No," the young woman said, "I bet he started that insurance company just to make money to pay for his legal problems."

"No, no," the young man said. "I told you before, a long time ago, his *father* started it."

"Well, whatever. He's gonna need some extra money if he's got legal problems."

"But that's the thing: his brother ain't no great businessman, the way they talk about him around the house. Lakeisha told me that. She said, *James may be a nice guy, but he ain't no great businessman.*"

"Well, what makes you think Mac's such a great lawyer?"

Graham's ears perked up.

"He's a son of a bitch," the young man said. "Anyone's a son of a bitch, he probably a great lawyer. You can find good lawyers who ain't sons of bitches, but you find a lawyer who's a son of a bitch, you can just about guarantee he great."

She gave him a playful shove. "I think you're silly."

"I think I'm right." He looked around for confirmation and nodded at Graham, who nodded sagely back.

"Well, so anyway, what was this thing he signed? You don't remember?"

"I told you, it was from one of his ex-wives. Wait 'til we get a table, and I'll give you as much of it as I can remember."

Graham decided not to get takeout after all. "Beg your pardon," he said to a passing waitress when the two were seated. "May I have a booth beside that young couple?"

"I'll check, sir." She looked confused, but when he smiled and bowed slightly to her, she flushed, then hurried away. A moment later, she returned. "Right this way, sir."

"Thank you," he said.

"So that's it?" the woman said when Graham reached the table beside them.

"As far as I know," said the young man. "I know it was something from one of his ex-wives. And I know that, whatever it was, it's some serious shit. He said he signed it without looking, he *shouldn't* have signed it, and that when *his* lawyer called him up to ask him what was going on he just freaked."

"Who's this woman who put it in his in-basket?"

"On his chair. She's the main secretary, been with the company forever, Ada or Ida something-or-other, I forget. He said he trusted her like she was his own mother."

"Damn...."

"Yeah. He was rantin' and ravin' like it was the end of the world. Talkin' about how could he salvage it."

"You think it's like something about child support? Or maybe his will?"

"Child support, maybe. I don't think his ex-wives could mess with his will."

"No, maybe not."

The conversation turned to other things, and Graham drifted off, scrutinizing the menu. So, Mac was getting a screwing. How absolutely charming, and how well-deserved. And this young domestic seemed to see the pure poetry of it too.

A waitress came over and he smiled.

She smiled back.

"I'll have the Pork Lo Mein," he said.

CHAPTER 13

MAC FLAMBET SAT in disbelief, looking down at the document he'd somehow inexplicably signed. He looked across the desk, an infinite sea of mahogany, into the sad brown eyes of his own attorney. "Do you mean to tell me that my ex-wife is actually my landlord?"

"I don't know what to tell you, Mac. You signed the thing."

"Goddamn it, Steve, I know that. Ida...."

"Ida put it in your in-basket —"

"On my chair. My chair!"

"— Right, and for whatever reason, you didn't look at it."

"I never look at that stuff. That's what I'm telling you. She knows that. The bitch paid her off. Or she just hates me. All those years of eating shit from us: 'Ida, hold my calls,' 'Ida, take a memo.' Christ, I don't know. Isn't there some way out?"

"What can we say? That you were held at gunpoint?"

"Why not? There'd be no witnesses for my side, obviously. How about it's a forgery?"

He looked down. "You'd have to perjure yourself, Mac."

"I know, but…shit. Come on, Steve, we're good attorneys. There's got to be an out. I've lived in that condo almost ten fucking years!"

"I know. I know. Look, this comes as a shock to all of us. Let me think about it overnight. Let's talk tomorrow. Give me a call in the morning and we'll chat. Okay?" He rubbed his temple with his fingers, not looking at him.

"All right." Mac sighed, sitting back in the chair. "I'll call you at nine."

"Okay, Mac. Thanks."

"All right," he said again. It better be okay, he thought. At four hundred dollars an hour it better be fucking okay.

He walked down the hall toward the elevator. His brain was boiling and his guts churned, like he'd had something he was allergic to for breakfast. *This comes as a shock to all of us.* Jesus, how lawyerly. It sounded like something he would have said himself, the kind of thing he'd say to someone whose divorce was certain to turn out badly, someone whose father has just been killed. Someone who's just gone broke. *All of us.* Jesus Christ.

He staggered into the blazing heat, his lungs filling with moist air. It smelled like burnt plastic, and the shock of walking outside from cool, dark air conditioning made him feel as if he'd been wrapped in wet flannel. My ex-wife is my landlord, he said to himself. My ex-wife is my fucking landlord.

His stomach lurched and rolled. Sweat beaded up on his forehead and ran in rivulets down his back. He was sick. He knew he was sick, and he couldn't blame it on breakfast.

As he headed toward the gleaming sanctuary of the Jaguar, he had to veer off and vomit bitterly beneath a tall palm surrounded by wood chips. He crawled on the wood chips on the little island with its border of curb and pavement. And as he stopped to vomit again, still on his hands and knees, he felt the hand of doom press down like a great weight upon his back.

Finally finished, he wiped his mouth with the back of his trembling hand and unlocked the car door. The Jaguar was a sauna, and he had to open the windows to prevent his sunglasses from fogging up. The stench of vomit stayed in the back of his throat, acrid, hovering in his sinus cavity. He cranked up the radio to drown the clash of thoughts in his head, but he found nothing but commercials. No doubt about it, it was a shitty day.

Traffic on I-4 four crawled like insects, and he seethed behind the wheel, glaring balefully and with resentment at the occasional person who slowed down beside him to check out the car. She would throw him out. She had clear title now.

Of course she'll throw me out. I'll have to rent. Rent! Jesus H. Christ, I can't imagine hearing some fat fucker's footsteps over my head. My God.

He approached his exit, slowing, and when at last he reached it, he found himself in a long traffic jam of cars waiting to get off the interstate. He sat in the right-hand lane while car after car passed on the left, and watched them, since they weren't going all that fast either. At length, he saw a familiar sight: Steve Dawson, his attorney, in his baby blue Porsche.

Steve held his cell in his left hand, his right on the steering wheel. Just as he passed by, he threw back his head, laughing into the receiver. He looked like someone at the top of his game. Someone having a good day.

Mac closed his eyes.

"Goddamn you," he said under his breath. "Goddamn you to hell and back."

CHAPTER 14

THE PHONE RANG three times and was beginning to ring a fourth when she picked up the receiver, just before it went to voicemail.

"Hello."

"Suzanne, it's Paul."

"Where have you been? It's almost eight." She had started to get comfortable on the sofa, waiting for him.

"Sorry. I know I said I'd be there before seven. Were you asleep?"

Embarrassed, she wavered, opting for the fib. "No, I just…it's been a long week, and I was – I needed to sit and space for a while, I guess. It's probably just as well you didn't make it here early…."

"Yeah, I got involved with something at the library."

"Graham again?"

"Yeah."

"Why are you still agonizing over that, Paul? You know there's no way to prove it."

"You're probably right. I was just reading up on corporate crime, and I found a good book on *preventing* it. I kept digging deeper and deeper, looking for something about detection, a way to proceed without a lot of evidence, you know? Naturally, the damn thing didn't have an index…."

"Naturally."

"I figured there had to be something in some of the case histories about how some of these guys get caught. But it was like reading one of those psychiatric evaluation books, where you keep plunging ahead, trying to find some magical answer. Some big insight into the workings of the mind."

"Which you've done, of course."

"What can I say? Mental health is one of my hobbies." He chuckled.

"You're almost a nerd, you know. Not quite, but very close."

"Thanks a lot."

"You're welcome," she said, smiling.

"But a dashing, debonair sort of nerd, right?"

"Aah, you're all right."

He laughed. "Screw you. You'd never go out with me, otherwise."

"What do you mean? Yes, I would."

"Ms. Personality. Women as good-looking as you never go out with someone they don't find attractive."

"That's not true. What do you mean 'Ms. Personality?'"

He laughed again. "Well, you were always so reserved before we started going out. Distant, I would say."

"I was not. Besides, I never said we were *going out.*"

"Trust me, we are. You wouldn't have answered the phone like that otherwise. 'Where have you been?'"

His falsetto made her laugh dryly. "Oh my God, you're so rude. All right," she said. "Maybe in your world we are. So are you coming over, or what?"

"What time is it?"

"Does it matter?"

"Not to me," he said.

"Well, okay, then."

"I'll be right over."

"Wait a minute," she said. "Did you check that book out of the library?"

"Yeah, as a matter of fact."

"Bring it with you. I want to take a look at it."

"To see if you can find something I missed."

She laughed. "Maybe."

CHAPTER 15

MERCEDES EDEN PAINTED a long black stroke down the middle of a perfect bright red fingernail and thought about the problem of Paul Panepinto, a much bigger problem than anything she'd ever had to face in the wonderful world of investment banking. The problem was how to get him interested in her friend Cora Gable, a problem as weighty as the pursuit of Frank Brenkus. Cora Gable wasn't on Paul's mind very much, or so it would appear. Just like I'm not on Frank's mind very much, Mercedes sighed. But at least the Panepinto problem felt workable, like there might be some hope of resolution one way or the other. The Frank Brenkus issue was a thousand times worse: personal, subjective, staggering beneath the load of unrequited love. Cora held no such illusions.

Mercedes was twenty-eight and Frank, ten years her senior, beckoned to her from the great height of television news like the northern star in the heavens. Meteorology, she thought with a chuckle. How did I ever fall for the weatherman? Nobody falls for the weatherman.

True enough. Frank was pale and boyishly appealing, in a way that appealed to aunts and great-aunts and great-grandmothers, but not much to look at from the neck down. Not exactly obese, she thought, but he was quite round in the lower portion of his frame, and none too muscular in the upper. She'd met him at a sports bar called El Toro, where they showed real Spanish bullfights beamed in by satellite, and when she first saw the white cherubic face with its rosy cheeks she thought him familiar for some reason. Kind of cute. Too bad he was so out of shape. She decided he must eat like a horse.

And sure enough, as if the thought was a stage direction, a waitress entered Mercedes' line of vision with a tray and headed straight for Frank. Double cheeseburger with all the toppings, a mound of fries almost big enough for a meal itself, and a tall lager. Frank beamed.

"Here you go, Frank," the waitress said, and her smile was maddeningly warm.

At that instant, Mercedes Eden experienced the defining event of her life. Almost at the same time, she felt an absurd pang of jealousy and a flash of recognition that he was a TV personality: Frank Brenkus, staff meteorologist for local station WRYY. Five ten, about two hundred and forty pounds, and suddenly, inexplicably, he was God.

She got up from the table as if in a dream and walked toward his side of the room, swallowing a rising wave of panic. "Excuse me, but aren't you Frank Brenkus?" Then, as if for clarity, "The weatherman from channel six?" she said. And immediately regretted it.

But he smiled again and all was well. "Yes," he said. "Would you care to join me, Miss…?"

"Eden. Mercedes Eden."

"Oh, excuse me." He wiped his hands on the paper napkin so he could shake the proffered right hand. "I've got to catch dinner on the fly sometimes in this business. I hate to eat in front of you, but —"

"Oh, no, no, no," she said. "Don't mind me." She laughed, a false nervous laugh that matched the look in her eyes. It was as if no one lived behind those eyes, and that moment decided it. No, he thought, she's not for me. Too bad. Good-looking girl. Damned good-looking. I wish she were my type, I'd do her in a New York minute. Nope. I wonder what's wrong with her?

Mercedes sat and pondered this amazing new being, the real Frank Brenkus, chattering away while he ate his dinner. She couldn't say what drew her to him or what held her there, except that he had charm. The more she looked at him, the less attractive he seemed. In fact, not one single feature of his face was attractive, but when you put the whole face together it had a certain seductive quality.

Maybe his personality overrode everything else? Who could tell? The nose was a bit too long and one eye tended to drift off slightly, giving the effect of him looking in two places at once. His teeth were a little crooked and his chin was rapidly becoming plural. No, it had to be something radiating out from beneath the external features, some indefinable version of charisma. Mercedes felt herself smiling, a warm glow filling her entire being.

And the glow continued on, days later, weeks later. She drew another bold black line down the center of another blood-red fingernail. It was nine o'clock, and in an hour, she had to meet Cora Gable and two other women at a bar in Ybor City, The Red Zone. There, she would dance until two or three in the morning, occasionally with one of the countless men who asked her, but usually just with the rest of the group of women, the four of them occupying one corner of the dance floor: remote and unattainable creatures, beings of a higher order.

She'd keep the men at arm's length, curtly refusing overtures toward any actual physical contact. To them, she appeared cold, since they had no way of knowing that they didn't exist in her mind. In her mind, only the ever-new image of Frank Brenkus turned and turned.

Except for now. She thought again about Paul and Cora. Paul didn't seem to know she existed, and now, according to Cora, the rumor mill had started to grind out something about Paul and Suzanne Beidertyme. Nothing confirmed, but Suzanne Beidertyme!

Mercedes knew nothing of Suzanne except what Cora reported—that she was a conceited little wench who'd resisted even the overtures of Mac Flambet, an attorney with a Jaguar, no less. Cora was still working on getting Suzanne to see the light, Mercedes knew, and now this rumor about Suzanne and Paul threatened to make the whole show go up in flames.

Mercedes painted the last nail and thought of calling Frank, who had given her his unlisted number after she'd gone out with him the one and only time. She decided it had better wait.

CHAPTER 16

SUZANNE AND PAUL sat side by side, drinks in their hands and feet up on her sofa, so that their knees lined up like four fence posts. She'd taken the book from him and it rested on her thighs, almost vertical: *Corporate Crime* in loud red letters, a comic-book tone masking the enormity of the words within. The library book's clear plastic cover caught the slight glare from the track lighting and reflected it whitely across the space between them, the only dissonant note in a room where their speech had grown languid, as if they'd just made love.

"What did you really think about all that McDillon stuff?"

"Who knows?" said Paul. "Maybe those missing data fields were really Graham's handiwork. Nothing would surprise me at this point."

"What good would messing up the McDillon thing do him? How would he benefit from that?"

"I don't have a clue, hon. He's the evil genius."

She laughed. "You know," she said, "we could probably use a little evil in our lives. All work and no play, right?"

He held her gaze and though the moment didn't feel as perfect as some other one would have, he thought it as good as any. He reached across her with his free arm and, with a smile that betrayed none of his nervousness, he kissed her. He could not help wondering if she felt his heart pounding, but it didn't matter, It would probably be endearing if she did.

He kissed her with a growing sense of urgency, holding back a little, though her response was sufficiently enthusiastic. Finally, yielding to practicality if not libido, he broke off, kissing her neck, an ear, the hair behind her temple. Without thinking, he kissed the top of her head once, then her forehead, each cheek, her nose: a peck, hardly enough to register.

He pulled back, searching her eyes, and her smile was mischievous, it crinkled up the corners of her eyes. For an instant, he saw how she would look when she was older, and he was not displeased. But the fact of the smile, its mischief, baffled him.

"You're funny," she whispered.

"What's funny? My kissing is funny?"

"No," she said. "You're kissing is great. It's just…kissing me on the nose."

He smiled, sitting back a bit from her. "I'd never kissed your nose before."

"You'd never kissed my anything before."

"Well, I didn't want to overlook it. Let's see, now, what else have you got that needs kissing?"

"Kiss my ass," she laughed.

"I hadn't planned on that next, but if you insist…unless you're just being sarcastic, in which case that's just a *little* rude."

"I couldn't resist the temptation," she said. "And no, I didn't mean it literally."

He tilted his head to one side. "Hm. Well, I think you did."

He made a lunge for it, and she squirmed, laughing. Before long, they were off the cushions and rolling around on the floor. At last, he relinquished control a little, but not until she'd rolled on top of him and was laughing down as if from a great height. He pulled her down to kiss him and for a moment her back arched like a cat's, but then she relaxed down onto him so that they were touching as much of each other as they could without being undressed. Through both layers of clothing he felt the heat of sex between them like some other being, a primal energy all its own, and he strained up against her.

She paused, but not before meeting him there. "I think we'd better stop."

He kissed her again. "Mm-hm."

"I'm serious," she said.

He kissed her again. "Okay." Then he continued.

"Hey." She laughed and sat up. "Let's go back to the sofa."

He sat up and looked at her.

"Oh no," she said. "Don't even think it."

"What?" He smiled, baffled again.

"You were looking at me like you're about to tear my clothes off. Like you were imitating Mac Flambet looking at me."

He snorted and shook his head. "Screw Mac Flambet."

"No thanks." They both laughed. "Come sit by me." She patted the cushions and sat back down on the sofa.

"Mm, I think maybe you were right. I really should get going."

"Who said anything about going? I just don't think we should be having sex on my living room floor. At least…not yet." She smiled coyly. "I'm not ready for that."

He smiled, hiding the irritation. Did she really think he wanted to make out for two hours, an aching erection beneath his jeans, sitting on the sofa fully clothed like a sixteen-year-old? He didn't know whether to be embarrassed for her or just shocked at the naïveté. He folded his arms.

"You're right," he said. "It's too soon. So, not to change the subject, but what did you think of that book—from what you saw?"

"You're angry."

"Why would I be angry? You said you don't want to be having sex on your living room carpet. Fair enough. I just don't want to be sitting here *aimlessly* kissing for two hours. Doesn't mean I'm angry."

"Aimlessly kissing?"

"Well—yeah, I mean…." He let it trail off. She was clearly as close to the brink of saying, *You men are all alike* as he was to saying, *You women….* And in the pause, the impenetrable sizing up, he decided to let it go. "I don't mean everything has to be goal- oriented. Let's just…talk. May I?" He gestured toward the sofa.

"Please." But the message was already clear: be my guest, Mr. Aimlessly Kissing. She gave him a dry look and pushed herself back as he sat down, her chin on her knees.

He wouldn't allow it, and slid close to her, putting his arm around her. "C'mere." For a moment, he struggled with the temptation to kiss her again, but he managed to reach the arm around her and lie back with closed eyes, so that they were still close together.

She sighed. "This is nice, too."

He murmured in assent.

"And," she said, "to answer your question, I think it looks like a good book. I hope you can find what you're looking for in it."

"If I'm honest about it, I'm not sure I know what I'm looking for," he said. "Part of me wants to nail Graham to the wall, but part of me says it's none of my business."

"You don't believe that, though. You can't just put your head in the sand. I don't believe that for a minute."

He sighed. "You're probably right. If I could just let it go, I would have. I wouldn't have checked the book out."

"Exactly my point."

"You seem to know me pretty well for someone who's only been out with me a couple times." He glanced over, smiling.

"We have worked for the same company for over a year and a half…."

"God," he said. "Has it really been that long?"

She smacked his thigh. "It's not that bad."

"It could be worse. I mean, I met you there, right?"

"Oh brother…."

"No, I mean it. If nothing else good comes of it, I did at least meet you."

"Now, don't get too sensitive on me."

"I'm not. I'm just…well, anyway."

"Just what?"

"Nothing." He wished he'd said even less. "Give me a kiss." She did, but then stopped, searching his eyes. "What?" he said.

She shook her head. "Nothing."

But a trace of a smile still lingered, and he suddenly felt himself at a loss, completely unsure about her, of what he was to her or even who she was at heart. Kissing her, closing his eyes, he felt all sense of self-possession slip away. He hovered above some great abyss, terrified lest he should make a wrong move and plummet into it like a suicide.

He kissed her with greater fervor, clinging to her as if in passion, but in fact, he'd never felt a more frightening sensation, an ego-dissolution he would have only ascribed to a drug experience or madness. The unselfconscious free-fall of the insane, the damned. He kissed her, dizzy, paralyzed with fear, and when he pulled back from her embrace he was breathing shallowly. He took a long deep breath, let it out, his hands on his temples.

"Are you okay?"

"I just got a headrush," he said. Even in his ears, the words sounded false, almost a lie.

"You're all right, though? Look at me." He opened his eyes, stared at her. "You're tired," she said.

He smiled wryly. "I'm all right."

"Well, you look tired."

"Thanks a lot." Already they were distant again, all irony and faint sarcasm.

"I don't mean it that way. Maybe we should call it a night, though."

He continued grinning. "Wasn't I just saying that a moment ago…?"

"Yeah, but not—smartass." She tapped his leg again and looked away sourly. But the eyes still twinkled.

"I guess I am a little tired." He pulled her close and they kissed again. "It was a pretty lousy day. But it was worth it to get here."

She folded her hands on her chest and looked melodramatic. "Our first kiss."

He gave her leg a little smack like she'd given his. "Okay, smart-ass. I'll see ya," he said and got to his feet. One brief final kiss on the lips and he was out the door.

CHAPTER 17

GRAHAM WOODCOCK WAS driving himself to the beach.

He'd grown tired of Indian Rocks and Redington and Madeira, he loathed the wall-to-wall feeling of the throngs of teenagers at Clearwater, and at last decided to take a drive up to Caladesi State Park, just over the Dunedin Causeway, where Honeymoon Island had a reputation for unspoiled beaches. The rainy season had come, and he knew severe thunderstorms inevitably arrived in the late afternoons, so he left early. As he drove along the causeway, looking at the palm trees beneath him along the shore and feeling the satisfaction of the lunch he'd just eaten, the tension from the city dissolved behind him.

On the horizon, clouds squatted like great bullfrogs, bluish white and grey. He was driving west toward the Gulf, and a light breeze was pushing all the clouds eastward, so that, through the windshield, their motion looked unnaturally fast, like a film of time-lapsed photography. Graham had never seen anything like it in nature.

He made a mental note of everything he'd brought—sunscreen, beach towel, a thermos of pre-mixed Manhattans, a crime novel. Change for tolls, a lounge chair suitable for the beach.

When he pulled up to the booth at the entry to the park, a park ranger greeted him and asked for eight dollars' entry fee. Tall and blonde, she wore long slacks and a short sleeve shirt, uniformly green and official-looking, almost military. She was friendly enough, but he felt relieved when she let him through. He pulled into the lot by the water's edge and went into the beach-house men's room.

When he came out again, the first droplets of rain were just beginning to spatter the sand. He had an idea it would be a brief shower, one of those classic Florida sunshowers that splash rain down with such intensity it's hard to believe the ground is dry again ten minutes later. He retreated to the car, slid inside, and had a Manhattan, watching in amusement as people fled the beach, started up their cars, and left the park.

An hour later, he still sat, brooding out on the gulf like some grim British Buddha. Rain hammered the roof of the car, lightning flashed in the distance. Thunder boomed, vibrating through his body and the body of the car. The water danced and rolled, crashing on the shore, the puddles in front of the car came alive with raindrops, and still the grey, flat-bottomed clouds kept coming.

Two pelicans flew across the sky, flapping their wings slowly, then gliding, hanging an instant in midair before one dropped for a fish into the water below, falling as if it had been shot. Graham looked at the clock. It was 1:30.

That bloody Paul Panepinto, he thought. Fucking wanker. *Sure, Mr. Flambet, I can run the reports. Sure, I can lick your black boots.* Fucking sod. *Oh, Mr. Flambet, there are some inexplicable omissions in the data. Shall I run the reports again?*

Go ahead, you little bastard, run them 'til your fucking heart stops. You'll never find what's really happened. Run them 'til doomsday. My 401(k) is still going to do what it's supposed to: it's a bloody locomotive running over your little reports.

He sipped the Manhattan and hunkered down over the steering wheel. The rainclouds were still coming at him, like bats.

Let them look for their bloody data fields, he thought. Let them drive themselves to despair with it. Mucking about in confusion.

Stupid wankers couldn't find their own asses with both hands. Fucking data fields.

He scowled, noticing that the Manhattans were taking effect with unusual speed: not even two o'clock yet, and he was slightly drunk. He breathed shallowly, leering out over the Gulf. Outside, several young women were walking toward the shoreline in spite of the rain. One group came from one car, and the other—a pair, one white and one black woman—had apparently come from another car. They were not all together.

Graham watched the black and white woman, ransacking his memory. They looked vaguely familiar, as if he'd seen them in a dream, or passed them in a shopping mall. Even from a distance, the white woman looked like a model, but as they got farther from the car, their features grew indistinct in the rain. He forgot them.

The women—Lakeisha Bennefield and Pamela Mae Swenson—worked for the Flambet family, Lakeisha being a regular part of the household staff in the capacity of cleaning lady, and Pamela, the nanny for little Eugenie, the seven-year-old. Lakeisha's hair was pulled back in dreadlock-style braids, while Pamela's hair whipped around in the wind and rain. She brushed the long strands back from her face, looking as though she wished she'd brought an umbrella, or at least a hat.

"What about that man?" Lakeisha said. "He still after you?"

"Who?"

"That TV man. The weatherman."

"Oh, God. Frank Brenkus. He's such a cheeseball douchebag." Pamela rolled her eyes and brushed back another strand of hair. "Yes, he still calls. I don't return his calls, but they keep coming just the same."

"He a little old for you, huh?"

She laughed. "Yeah. It's not just that, though. I don't even want to think about him."

"Yeah, he'd even be a little old for me. How old is he: thirty-nine, forty?"

"Something like that."

"Hell, and I'm only twenty-seven. You're what, twenty-four?"

"I will be in October."

"Yeah, you just a youngun. And that man chasin' you? He a dirty old man. Mm-hm." She shook her head.

"Why don't *you* go out with him?"

They both laughed.

"Me? I don't want no dirty old man. TV news or no TV news. You know who he need to go out with is that girl Mercedes."

"Who's that?"

"You know her. From that little sports bar. El Toro, El Whore-o, whatever it's called."

Pamela Mae laughed at the El Whore-o. "No, doesn't ring a bell."

"She pretty. Almost pretty as you. Not quite. Somethin' about her look a little strange. Anyway, she in love with Frank. Follow him around like a lost puppy."

"Somethin' about her a little strange, then. You said it."

They laughed again.

"Yeah, he ain't interested in no Mercedes. He only got eyes for you. You must be a Rolls Royce!" She laughed and laughed.

Pamela shook her head. "Spare me," she said.

"That's right, Pamela Mae," she said, enjoying the joke. "You must be a Rolls Royce." She laughed again, then wiped a tear. "Too funny," she said. "Too too funny."

"Ha ha."

"I'm sorry, Pamela Mae," she said. "That Frank, he just crack me up. Big old bug eyes and that fat little body. He'd be kinda cute if it weren't for that fat little body."

Pamela pursed her lips. "Mmm."

"I'm sorry," she said again.

"Well," Pamela said, "not as sorry as I am." But she smiled to show no grudge.

They walked on, talking, but Pamela's mind wandered off, thinking of home, back in Massachusetts, how much she missed the music scene there, how she loathed the music scene in Florida. She'd seen the best-loved acoustic artists of her time in Northampton in her teens, Patty Larkin and Shawn Colvin, Greg Brown, singer-songwriters in the traditions of Joni Mitchell and Bob Dylan. She'd loved it all, and had taken the ticket stubs from those shows and arranged them in a scrapbook she'd had for years. And on dark summer days at the height of the rainy season, when big clouds like oil tankers loomed in the afternoon sky and a stream of rain poured down on the roof above, she sometimes flipped through the scrapbook, reading the names—Cheryl Wheeler, Lui Collins, Suzanne Vega—dreaming on the names and dates, feeling again the old feelings of the shows, friendly old ghosts in the pit of her belly.

That was all forever ago, she thought. Far away. She missed the cold winter nights as much as she despised the humidity of Florida, and she thought of the time that had come and gone.

She and Lakeisha reached the far end of the beach, where the sand trailed off into scrub grass, and retraced their steps back toward the lot where the cars were parked like sentinels. She looked across the sand and saw a man, drinking alone in his car, but he was a stranger, and she looked away again.

CHAPTER 18

THAT MONDAY, PAUL saw Graham for the first time in ten days, a full week after James Flambet asked him to do the work on the McDillon Nightmare. He'd found nothing, just confirmed what James already knew: the omissions in the spreadsheets were inexplicable, due only to either a computer problem or some major tampering by an employee higher up in the firm than himself. He'd had to give the reports back to James with a shake of the head and an apology. No explanation to be found.

He wasn't thinking of anything related to the issue now; he was relaxed and calm. But when Graham walked into the office, for an instant it seemed as if Graham somehow bored down into the earth and drilled through layers of sedimentary rock. Paul felt the ground collapsing under his feet.

"You did some extra work for me last week, eh? Some of the McDillon report?" He smiled, his teeth like a row of razors.

Paul laughed feebly. "Well…I tried."

"Find anything?" He sipped his coffee.

"Not really. There were some omissions in the spreadsheets all right, but I couldn't find anything out about them. Dead ends everywhere I checked."

Graham nodded, then leaned back on his heels and dug one hand casually in his sportcoat pocket. "Hmm. Well, easy come, easy go, eh? As you say here in Americar."

Paul smiled again, trying to avoid his eyes. "I guess."

"Anyway, thanks for looking into it. I'll take it from here."

"Yeah, James has all the stuff."

"Right-o." He nodded, and a light went out in him: back to business. He paused an instant longer, like he wanted to stress the sincerity of his thanks, then turned and walked back to his office.

Paul realized he'd been holding his breath, and he exhaled, slowly and completely. Omissions in the spreadsheets, he thought. Was that really all there was to it? Of course he'd hit the wall on it, but what if that was the whole point? He couldn't think of any reason for his blood to run cold at the sight of Graham other than intuition. What if somehow the McDillon thing had a connection with Graham's phony 401(k) scam? Dolores Buenas and Philip Banks. But what connection?

He walked back down the corridor toward his desk. Here I am investigating my own supervisor, I don't see him at all for over a week, and now I've got seventeen piles of lapsed insurance policies to deal with, not to mention a massive stack of customer inquiries. Then the son of a bitch walks in, and I feel like someone's just shot me up with truth serum. What the hell's going on? What does all this McDillon stuff have to do with our old pals Dolores Buenas and Philip Bank, if anything? On the way down the hall he passed Cora Gable.

"Hey, Paul. How's Suzanne?"

He paused. Had they become gossip already? "Suzanne? Fine, I guess. How do you mean?"

She sashayed over and stood in front of him, one hip slung far to one side. "Oh, a little bird told me you two are an item. Did I hear wrong?"

He blushed and cursed himself for it. "Ah, we're just friends, Cora. Not good to bring the love life to work, you know what I mean?"

"I don't know. She blushed almost as much as you did at the same question."

"Well, maybe we'll elope," he said, and laughed. "That would settle it, wouldn't it?"

"I would think so, Mr. Studley." She gave him a little poke in the chest and sauntered away. He pondered the strange gesture and thought of a line from some old movie: *You're a big man now, aren't you?* So much said and unsaid in such a short space. So much ambiguity.

The hell with her, he thought. Now I know why the office romance idea never appealed to me. That's the price. With a sigh, he walked back to face the piles of lapsed policies and customer questions.

CHAPTER 19

DOWN THE HALL, Suzanne battled the same issue among four co-workers. She had been working on a new case when they interrupted her, generating forms headed *Florida Department of Labor & Employment Security Division of Worker's Compensation: Notice of Injury.* She had to fill in each field with pertinent information: the patient's name, social security number, and so on. It was all terribly tedious, of course, except that occasionally the "Employee's Description of Accident" was inadvertently comic – "Hit left eye with box flap." "Felt strain in neck while lifting large bag of dog food." "Slipped off gondola when getting box off top shelf." And her personal favorite: "Bent over at time clock to punch in and back muscle popped."

Jane Brighton from Accounting pulled Suzanne out of her work-induced reverie: "So what's the scoop, Suzanne? Are you and Paul doing the nasty, or what?"

Suzanne blanched, immediately distracted. "No, we're doing nothing of the kind, smartass." She forced an angry smile into a rueful one. "We're just hanging out," she said. "It doesn't have to be anything more than that."

"Methinks the lady doth protest too much," said another.

"Ah, go back to your Shakespeare, girl," Jane said. "Come on, level with us, Suze. You guys aren't even interested in each other?

You know you make a cute couple. Don't even tell me you haven't noticed the way he looks at you."

"The way he looks at *me?*" But she did know, and they all saw it. Worse, she suddenly couldn't keep a straight face, and when she started to laugh, they did too.

"All right, come on now. No more bullshit. Out with it."

"Okay, okay," she said, still laughing. "Three dates. No big thing, okay? Just dates. We're just hanging out together. No sex."

"After three dates?"

"No."

"No foreplay?"

"Jane! No, okay? No foreplay. Jesus. Now, come on, no further questions, your honor. I don't want this all over the damned email by three o'clock. He's very sensitive about the whole office romance thing."

Cora walked in at the tail-end of it, saying, "Who's sensitive about the office romance thing? Paul?"

Everyone laughed again except Suzanne. "Yes, Paul, if you must know." She smiled, grimly polite. "I just told these guys, we're not exactly an item."

Cora sneered. "Paul just denied the whole thing too."

"I'm not denying anything! I just said we aren't on the floor… much."

The other women laughed, but Cora shook her head, unsmiling. "Could've been Mac," she said. "Oh well." She turned and walked away. "See you all later," she said over her shoulder.

Jane turned back to Suzanne. "Mac? Flambet?"

Suzanne rolled her eyes. "Cora seems to think I'd be the luckiest girl on earth if I'd just see the light and finally get interested in Mac Flambet. Like I could do it without holding my nose."

"Not exactly your type, eh?"

"Not my type? Honey, the only things that nasty bastard chases more than women are ambulances. He's a pig. I don't know why he thinks he's such a great catch. He finds these little bimbos somewhere who go for the Porsche or Jaguar or whatever."

"Jeez, Suze, why don't you tell us how you really feel?"

They all laughed. "Sorry. I don't mean to go on about it. He's just so *gross*."

"I think Cora just wants you to go out with Mac because she likes Paul," said Jane.

Suzanne cocked her head to one side. "Really? Cora and Paul? I can't picture that one."

"Neither can Paul," Jane said.

Again they all laughed, even Suzanne, in spite of herself. "You're bad."

"Well, hey, he's interested in *you*, right?"

Suzanne smiled. "Well, let's keep this whole thing in perspective. We're just hanging out, that's all. Let's not make it some big thing."

"Ah, Suzanne's in love."

"Come on, I'm serious here."

"You notice she doesn't deny it," one of them said.

"You guys." She shook her head. "Please don't say anything to Paul, though, okay? God only knows what Cora said already."

"Okay, we won't."

Suzanne searched their eyes, looking for clues. She read nothing definite there. "I hope I'm not gonna regret this."

CHAPTER 20

PAUL TRIED NOT to think too much about Dolores Buenas and Philip Banks. Rage became anger, anger became sullenness, and soon, the only feeling left was apathy. The days turned to weeks, and before long, two months went by.

He had the daily round—work, some cherished time with his palette and brushes, plans with Suzanne—and, when time allowed, a night out with some of the guys. He didn't so much abandon the search as forget it. Life eclipsed it, at least until he overheard a conversation in the break room that set him thinking about Graham, the 401(k), and the "blackout period" when the plan was supposedly switching administrators. That Monday morning marked the receipt of quarterly statements for the second quarter. In the break room, Don Taylor and Jeanette Page were talking about theirs when Paul walked in.

"I don't see how I could have made so little last quarter," Don said. "I mean, I sort of follow the progress of my funds in the paper, and it doesn't seem like I got as much as I should have. Seems to me they were more up than down during those three months."

Jeanette yawned. "I don't even look at mine. You gotta think long term anyway, you know? Besides, the contributions are probably like a month behind."

"Yeah, I'm just saying it doesn't seem like I got as much as I should have."

"Well, greed's always a great motivator for me."

He laughed. "That's not what I meant, but I see your point. Oh well."

They continued talking as they walked out, and Paul heard nothing more. But the phrase *it doesn't seem like I got as much as I should have* resounded in his head like a lyric from a song he'd heard long ago. It stuck with him. And suddenly, without planning it, he was back on the same track.

He ran into Suzanne during lunch. "I got my 401(k) statement today," he said.

"And…?"

"Did you get yours?"

"Yeah. I didn't really look at it." They sat down.

"This morning, I overheard Don telling Jeanette Page he doesn't think he got as much as he should have."

She paused, searching his eyes. "Graham?"

"Could be." He chewed a bite of his sandwich.

"I thought you'd given up on all that."

"Not on purpose."

She smiled and leaned back in the chair. "What does that mean?"

"Just that I never actually abandoned the whole issue. I mean, I haven't been pursuing it, I know, but I'm starting to wonder if maybe I should."

"How?"

"I don't know."

"Can you track how the funds did for that whole quarter?"

He pondered it. "I suppose. I could probably get some solid numbers by calling up the company. You know, some percentages."

"And if you're right?"

"If I'm right, he may have ripped us *all* off."

"But the question is how to prove it."

"Yeah. The question is how to prove it." He paused, thinking.

"Do you think you've got a shot at it?" she asked.

"I don't know."

"What about that program he had? With Philip Banks and Dolores What's-her-name?"

"Dolores Buenas, yeah. I was just thinking about that. I don't know, hon. I don't have a clue how to get in there again. I'm not even sure what I'd say to the computer guys if I asked them to help me."

She sipped her iced tea. "You think they'd rat on you?"

"I doubt it, but who knows?"

"Do any of them really despise Graham?"

He smiled, drumming his fingers on the top of the table. Then the smile vanished. "Not as much as I do."

CHAPTER 21

FRANK BRENKUS, local weatherman on WRYY television , a station with slogans like "R-Y-Y: Why not?" and "We've got *our* 'Y' on you," accompanied by a large picture of an eye with a "Y" in it, stared into the silent flickering screen of the computer monitor, almost weeping with rage. This day was the disaster to top all disasters.

He peered down into the cavern of the monitor, down past the electromagnetic field, past the blue maw of the screen that only moments ago had been filled with the text of the weather report, past wavering pixels that danced like some strange electronic meadow of bluebonnets. He could almost see the words in his mind, standing before him in long neat rows, in the midst of which the cursor blinked its slow and inexorable blink, when at last he realized he had stopped breathing. His head grew lighter and lighter, and with considerable effort, he breathed again, labored and heavy. With a great exhalation of anguish and terror, he sank down into the chair and covered his face with his hands.

How long, O Lord? How long? Outside the window, above the faded green of live oaks with their Spanish moss hanging down like limp bodies, the sky hung murky and grey, and let a feeble light down into the room. He tried to think of something to calm him, but the only thing he could think of was sex. He imagined Mercedes, pictured her with her dress hiked up, her legs open, then pictured her pushing herself against his body, kissing him hungrily, then sliding down while he ran his hands through her black hair until she was on her knees before him, putting her great wet lips over—but no, it was too much, it was obscene to fantasize her in this situation. Like thinking about incest, bestiality, some dreadful taboo.

Pamela Swenson was a different story: he was actually interested in her. But Mercedes? No, it would be criminal, more than just a callous seduction; almost a rape, really. He'd be using her like a tissue and discarding her. Well shit, he thought, it's only a fantasy. Not even.

Mercedes Eden. He thought about her name, staring down into the blinking cursor. Who the fuck would name their kid Mercedes Eden? It was like Dow Pasture. Or Marlboro Meadows. He almost laughed aloud at that one. Marlboro Meadows, that's good.

Mercedes Eden. She was the best friend of Cora Gable, another real piece of work. In fact, he realized, one of the things that made Mercedes singularly unattractive was her friendship with a character as unsavory as Cora Gable. Unsavory, he thought with another small thrill of self-congratulation; that was the word for her, all right. It wasn't like Mercedes was ugly, or an idiot. She just had unattractive characteristics. Bad taste. And she likes *me*, he thought. That's just not right.

He blinked twice and realized he was still looking down into the blue abyss of the computer monitor. The vision of Mercedes vanished as suddenly as it had appeared. There wasn't any way to get out of it: he would have to go on camera and read whatever they rolled out across the teleprompter, probably something from another station. No rehearsal.

In his mind, he heard the strained robot-voice he would inevitably have, saw how idiotic he'd look to viewers as his eyes followed the unfamiliar lines of whatever report they had on the teleprompter, and with apocalyptic despair, he realized that Pamela

Swenson might be free that night, might even see the broadcast. His heart bounded across the cage in his chest with a thud, and he belched. The only thing that could make things worse would be a fit of incurable hiccupping.

Eighty minutes until showtime, and he stood before the mirror in the studio, grimacing at his hair. He rubbed the makeup in quickly, patted his hair. Unthinking, he grabbed the spritzer. Unthinking, he sprayed. Then he ran a hand over his hair. Good enough. Hell with it.

It was summer in Tampa, and he knew what the weather would be: mid 90s, low 80s. Late afternoon thunderstorm you could almost set your watch by, great thunderheads rolling in off the bay like grey monsters. At least a hundred lightning strikes per summer, some of which would, in all likelihood, hit something. Nothing human, one must hope.

"Frank," said a voice from the next room. "Are you ready?"

He sighed. "About as ready as I'll ever be." He squared his shoulders and walked toward the door.

CHAPTER 22

PAUL STOOD LOOKING at the night sky, a fourteen-year-old with a head full of romance and rage and fear and wonder and a lungful of marijuana smoke. He exhaled deeply, watching the stars shimmer in the sky like electric white birds, and in his mind rang the same phrase over and over, a name: Melissa. Sweet Melissa.

A song, a sound, a dream of grace, and the pleasures of love just out of his reach, sacrosanct and protected by the values and strictures and morals, the code stamped on him by his culture and parents and the clergy and even, truth be told, his teachers, for sex education did not exist in that town in that time. But he said to himself he must have her, he must, no matter the cost, he thought of the poem he'd written her…*tiny gestures like the way she holds my hand*…and he said again to himself that he must have her, he would have her, and to hell with rules and guidelines and the code. It could not wait another hour.

And in some ways, it became the defining moment in his life, although he did not know it then, would never know it would forget it in a year or two or three and look back in later years as an old man with only the haze of nostalgia and the tender recollection of romance, forgetting the rage and frustration the determination hot as flame that drove him down that road that long night, a sad-eyed wise-eyed fourteen-year-old with his cynical mannerisms and his tightly rolled joints in his cigarette pack and his black leather jacket, Hendrix cranked up on the little portable tape player blaring tinnily through the headphones and dreaming of a car and a girl and a moonlit beach thinking *if I just had a car* and *if we were just a little older* and saying *I've got to have her*, and then the long road ahead street after street and the ache in his legs and then the pebble tossed into the air toward the shuttered window and the clatter when it dropped back to his feet futile and hit the asphalt and the same fearful underhand toss again and again until at last it made the long-awaited contact and then the moon-like face at the window floating looking down in wonder, and was it fear or anger or love that made her come down and the ache in his heart and brain and loins while he waited for her to come down the stairs and out the front door and his heart hammering in his chest as if to escape him, and he wondered doubted himself again should he have worn the cologne should he not have smoked the joint should he have brought the bottle of peach brandy stolen from his brother's bottom drawer, he stood quite still trying to look sullen and aloof and then the feeling that hit him when she came across the lawn in the long white shirt flowing down so far below the terry cloth shorts it looked as though she might be naked below the waist her hair flowing out behind her, and even as her whisper of reproach reached him he knew it all meant all it all meant everything all she was all she all yes

What are you doing here

I came for you

You shouldn't have done this

I know

If my parents see

I know I'm sorry

Paul

Yes

Paul

Yes

Do you

Yes

You don't know what I

Yes

And then the kiss the long slow suspiration of breath and the warmth of the enveloping warmth of the yes and yes and then the sounds of cricket and cicada and all fading and the scent of lilac and all she was all, and the cool grass of backyard and the long shirt and all and wet heat straining and longing and the rising and falling and she and he and all and yes no more longing and no more night and no more and yes and no and yes and yes, and he had known she was going to ask him if he loved her and he had said yes and she had known he knew and he knew she knew he knew and all it was she was and he was and all and yes

And the long walk down to the trail to the lakeside and the whispers and the do you love me and the yes and will you always love me and yes and all to be forgotten by both in a year or two or three but not forgotten merely buried back in the abyss of the heart beneath the layers of all else, and he would come back to it again and again in later years and see the beauty and longing and the great wide world opening up to him like a symphony and forgetting the frustration and fear and rage, and still he would not see the moment shining in that moonlight on that road a moment standing out alone from other moments something not connected to the rest, still he would not see that it had been the defining moment all that all and all that rage and desperation and yes defiance and all yes and all yes shining out around him, and the moment had come and he had seized it and he had said I must live as I choose I must I cannot walk the path someone else chose for me and if that means I must break their rules then so be it and if I must then make my own rules then so be it and yes so be it yes amen amen amen amen

And a year or two later, walking down that long dirt road with Philip Marin passing the joint between them so casual as if it were a bottle or a book taking deep hits holding them as long as possible so that only a wisp of smoke came out when one of them exhaled (where did it really go, he thought, did it stay in the bottom of your lungs) and the harsh strong burnt hay taste of the smoke hung in the back of the mouth filling the nasal passages with its fragrance, the road appeared to stretch out far ahead of them as if it were so much more than just another road that would soon be another suburban development in another town, it looked longer and longer in the dark the end of it already in view as they headed downhill looking in the darkness like a bend in the road or maybe a cliff as if the dark forest ahead were actually sky and the boulders at the end that the bulldozers had been unable to move hunkered down like great Cadillacs and Fairmonts and Bel-Airs at the edge of some phantasmic Lovers Leap, and it seemed as if it would always be here he could not conceive that someday children might be playing video games behind bedroom windows on this spot where he was walking down the starbright road smoking and talking with his only friend, he could not conceive that there might someday be blacktop and asphalt over this pebbly road undulating beneath the dark night sky

They walked on and on, and at last they did reach that end of the road and found no cliff there no bend in the road just the giant boulders that squatted there almost as tall as they were, and beyond the dark and mysterious woods with its oaks and elms and pines wavering a little now in the night wind and almost obscuring the lights of the city below them, and then the night of freedom came to its end inevitable coming faster than it could have and the long slow incline of the road lay before them and they walked with hearts of lead and ashes back up the long road, the inescapable comedown of the grass and the burning in their lungs their legs beginning to ache as if at sixteen they had that summer already started to age and weaken and never a thought that the grass and the cigarettes might prove responsible detrimental never a thought for mortality, and even as they reached the opening out of the long slow incline out of the woods and into the silent subdivision, even as they tossed the peppermints into their mouths they were talking about smoking another joint saying they wished they could and how unfair it was to be so young so long and never to be carefree and they said how bad it felt to always hear these ancient people around them saying youth was wasted on the young and how it gave them that awful joke that time spent wasted is not wasted time and how cruel and vicious a thing it was to tell young men that these bright and painful days would be the best days of their lives, and in that dark naïveté and ignorance of youth and having nothing to refute it with they had to wonder if it would wind up being true if even in the fullness of time it would prove inescapable and before long they would be old and impotent men with arthritis and hemorrhoids and ulcers stretching their dark wrinkled bodies on lounge chairs in the nursing homes of their twilight years looking back fond and regretful at the wasted years gone by, recalling that time when their biggest problems had been getting beaten soundly by some savage tower of a football player at a keg party in the piney woods or riding the crest of the raging buzz of hormones passing by Debbie Antonini in the hallway in a paroxysm of priapic and anguished lust or standing at the top of the tower above Daytona talking about Judy Grant's suicide, how reasonable it had appeared in the end looking down at those crashing waves on the beach roaring like bombers thinking Because I could not stop for death he kindly stopped for me and To sleep perchance to die what was that line out of old Bill Shakespeare and then those thoughts of mortality would linger like buzzards around them not connected to the present to the grass and the cigarettes and suicides but to some far-off distant time when death might start to look inviting by contrast to that dark implacable second infancy when even the football beatings and the tortures of involuntary celibacy would be a source of some kind of nostalgia

And then thinking back to that time with sweet Melissa under the summer sky and the falling stars and how he knew she knew what he was going to say and how she knew he knew what she was going to ask and how they hadn't had to say anything and life had been just that, just the falling stars the wet grass the sweet lightness in his head the scent of lilac the backyard sounds of cricket and cicada the rising and falling and how she kissed him and how they knew what they knew and now she was gone and life had grown so much harder so much more complicated yet narrower darker it grew a little narrower and darker every year.

CHAPTER 23

GRAHAM WOODCOCK LOOKED down at his tanned, wrinkled body stretched out on the green and white chaise lounge and, because summer had settled down on Florida with its promise of highs in the nineties and sometimes no cooler than eighty at night, he thought of the winters of his youth those times of celebration past the long sad elegiac tone poem of autumn the cold air became almost bearable, and after a month or two he started to like it and would go sledding in the hills around Sussex, he remembered when he lay on the sled in the icy winter afternoon and looked down across the white hills of the English countryside it felt as if the days would last forever they were so long and bright and clean and he breathed like smoke into the afternoon breath so cold and heavy he was certain he could see actual molecules in the fog of breath when he watched it, and beside him the dogs Ranger and Travers two great Siberian huskies standing erect as horses and to his childish mind almost as big against the white snow and the grey and white clapboard houses and the woods and river beyond they stood and barked at each other sniffing and wagging their tails furiously before pulling him down the long incline on the wooden sled wind bringing the water to his eyes and freezing his ears but the ride itself bringing only the wild and unabashed joy of its own inevitability, he laughed and laughed the sled picking up speed and beginning to overtake the huskies dividing them like a schooner creating a wake and before long they were running on either side of the sled panting tongues lolling smiling at him and increasing their pace trying to lead the sled once more racing him down the long incline until they reached the first hill and began to pull ahead and to slow down as the weight of the sled and the boy brought the tension back into their haunches, they pulled him up the hill and over into the next wide outspread vista of valley and sunlight and bare tree branches and he knew in his heart that these days would never end he would always be a boy on a sled with the wind roaring in his ears and the dogs running with him through the valley and the lea and over the frozen brook while the sun sank pale and harmless in the grey horizon beyond them like a sun in some old faded storybook

And now more than thirty years later, he was not a boy and never would be again and never would think again about what it would be like to grow up and get married and have a son of his own who might also love to go sledding down through the valley with his own dogs on a beautiful winter afternoon, he remembered where he was and that he hated not just Florida but the whole country all of it the complacent self-seeking lot of them unwilling to even contemplate for a moment the notion that all might not be quite so well as it looked, and even though the thought of his own mortality made him sick with fear it did not feel quite so bad as the sadness he felt when he realized the waste of days gone by how close he had been to choosing a different path how it all converged on him now all points led up to this winter day where he lay on a chaise lounge in the sun as inevitable as a train racing down a track, and he knew there could be no escape he had to go on with it every last detail from the deception of the fund administrator at National Fidelity to the actual embezzlement of all that money from the ignorant sons of bitches at Flambet, and if it hadn't been him he told himself it would have been someone else and if not for this single act of desperation and courage and genius on his part he would have to languish another fifteen or twenty years in the unthinkable position of toting home the goddamned laptop every weekend taking the occasional vacation to relieve a modicum of stress in the whorehouses of Bangkok or Guadalajara, and soon he would have to leave for another position in another firm just to get away from these sorry bastards with their Yes Grahams and Okay Grahams their daily charade of competence in the face of disillusionment computer crashes cancelled policies and all the petty burdens that made up an average day, he would have to start anew somewhere else not just to give his life the semblance of an upward and logical progression but for the change of scenery for the break in the monotony and pain of the daily grind at Flambet and for the delusion that things would somehow be better somewhere else, but if he could secure a sufficient amount of money and take early retirement he could live off the interest until he had to start drawing on the 401(k) funds and then things truly would be better on the beaches of St. John and in the whorehouses of Bangkok and Guadalajara, and he knew the possibility still shone out of the darkness ahead of him and that he needed to make every last effort to make it happen and so the time had come again for work and he eased himself slowly off the chaise lounge and picked up the warm Manhattan beside him and went back into the cold air-conditioned condo to face the laptop and the dream again.

CHAPTER 24

THE DANCEHALL FELT claustrophobic to Paul, despite tables set up next to the walls to accommodate the faded wooden dance floor. The ceiling was a kind of A-frame, the lowest points in the corners of the room just seven feet high, which gave the entire room an eerie nineteen-fifties look. The spinning mirrorball and hanging lamps, though modern enough, did little to alleviate the effect.

The annual dance of the Benevolent Protective Order of Elks could just as easily have been a low budget wedding reception or a fortieth high school reunion. Sallow young men with dark moustaches and women with thick glasses and barrettes in their hair went from table to table, pausing to adjust a black bowtie or brush a speck of lint from a ruffled sleeve. They were the youngest people in the room, curiously foreign-looking as they served the elders.

Just before the music began to play, promptly at 9:20, a grey-haired woman with the coiffure of a 1920s flapper and a heavy sequined dress said, "They were supposed to play from nine to one. It's not fair for them to be this late: people are *waiting*." It was hard to imagine her even staying awake until one, but who could tell? Perhaps she'd been to see Art Blakey in Bleecker Street cafés, grooved to Little Richard at Madison Square Garden or the L.A. Forum, stomped her feet for Elvis or Fabian.

The quality of sound coming from the speaker system was truly abysmal, the high end cutting loudly like an aural knife through the murky low notes, so that the overall effect was one of massive distortion. Had it not been for the familiarity of the band's repertoire, and the exuberance of their playing, the audience surely would have found it intolerable.

At the bar, a man in a silk tie ducked his double chin around at the barmaid and asked for a Dewar's in a frosted glass. He was explaining something to her about the sprinkler system, only interrupting himself to place the order. He glanced at Paul, who had just walked up to the bar, before he continued: "Yeah, you'll be all wet if that sucker goes. But you won't have to do a thing. The fire department will be here in minutes. You'd have to get out of the way mighty fast, though, if you hit that switch."

"Oh, shit," she said. She looked sideways at Paul and flushed slightly. He stood waiting to order his drink, expressionless.

"Sure," the man in the silk tie said. "Just make sure you don't hit that switch, or it'll be all over." He grinned to show her he was teasing, enjoying his little joke.

"What else can I get you?" she asked. She looked anxious to change the subject.

"Ginger ale."

"Ann's not drinking tonight?"

"Every other drink," he said. "She's on a diet."

"Well, she looks terrific."

"Yeah, she's doing great with it. I'm on one, too, but I'm not too worried about it. If the weight goes, it goes...."

"Sure."

"And then I'll be excited to see the scale in the morning."

He paid and left. Paul stepped forward.

"A virgin sea breeze."

"Okay."

"Actually—make it two. That way I'll be gone twice as long."

She chuckled. "All right."

He paid and walked back to the table by the dance floor. He was planning to eavesdrop on J.B. Flambet, but this was proving to be like work: the Flambets were nowhere in sight.

Behind him, the band sang,

Edelweiss, edelweiss,

Every morning you greet me…

The song ended, and everyone but Paul applauded.

A white-haired man in a tuxedo stood up behind a microphone and called for attention. "Ladies and gentleman, each year at this time we have the opportunity and privilege to congratulate this year's Elk of the Year. Now, this is a very difficult proposition, because there are over seven hundred Elks in this lodge. And it's quite a dilemma to have to choose just one Elk out of all these Elks to be Elk of the Year."

He cleared his throat. "But I had to do it. Now, just so you're aware, there are exactly seven hundred and forty-one Elks in this lodge, and thirty-eight or thirty-nine of them have been Elk of the Year. Now, the only criteria here are that the new Elk of the Year must not be an officer for the lodge that year, or a past Elk of the Year. I believe that we have at least six or seven Past Exalted Rulers here tonight, and I'd like to introduce them to you before we honor this year's recipient."

He droned the men's names…Elmer Chance, Jean Bertram Flambet, Mel Cox. They formed two lines flanking the micro-phone, like people in a wedding reception. There turned out to be eight of them, and after they had all been introduced and had received their obligatory rounds of applause, the white-haired man continued.

"And now I'd like to introduce this year's Elk of the Year. He's been on the Major Emphasis Committee, the Major Emphasis Advisory Committee, the Antler Committee, the Armchair Racing Committee, the Memorial Services Committee, the Mother's Day

Committee, the Spring Fling Dance Committee, the Men's Clambake Committee, and the Memorial Barbecue Committee. His service to this lodge for over thirteen years has been absolutely without precedent, and his loyalty to all of us has been a tonic. He is truly an inspiration. Ladies and gentlemen, please welcome *Harry Ames*."

The room shook with thunderous applause. Harry Ames stood, looking slightly dazed and overcome. He seemed to teeter for an instant, and approached the bandstand on unsteady legs. Waves of applause buoyed him up. He became steadier as he neared the microphone, and by the time he arrived, he walked with the confidence and purpose of a man nearing a long sought-after goal.

Not until he reached the microphone could the crowd determine that the strange sobbing and retching noises they heard came from Mrs. Harry Ames. Overwhelmed with emotion, her great bosom heaved like the throat of a bullfrog. Her sobs rent the air, and the woman next to her patted her arm.

Harry Ames was asked to preside over the eleven o'clock retrospective, where all the souls of Elks past are honored with the strains of *Auld Lang Syne* and *God Bless America*. Before the crowd could be led in song, Harry first had to deliver a speech about the brotherhood, which he did with all splendor, surrounded by a respectfully weighty silence.

"...Yes, brothers and sisters," he concluded, "the elken heart swells and throbs, and a friendly message chimes on the night wind, pealing through the pines and welcoming, *welcoming* all travelers in need of charity, fidelity, justice and brotherly love who join us as we trudge down the path of elkdom."

Paul coughed phlegm discreetly into his handkerchief and headed back to the bar for more pistachio nuts.

CHAPTER 25

"SO, HOW WAS IT?"

Patches of sunlight lay across the table, and Paul looked at them bleakly, slumped back with his hands in his pockets. "Waste of time," he said. "Like a bad movie."

Suzanne's face tightened. "Was the band any good, at least?"

He looked up, grinning. "The band," he said, "was terrific." He got up and waltzed her around the room, singing: "*Edelweiss, edelweiss, every morning you greet me….*" He stopped abruptly and sat back down. "What a fucking nightmare."

She laughed. "Well, it *was* the Elks club, after all."

"I know. I know." He covered his face with his hands.

"What did you hope to get out of it, anyway?"

"Aside from hanging out with Jim while he endured playing drums at that horrible gig? I don't know. I was going to shadow J.B. Flambet for a while—you know, eavesdrop a little at the bar—see if I got anything about James or Graham or whoever. Didn't work out."

"Obviously not."

He looked up. "Got any aspirin?"

"Just ibuprofen."

"That'll work."

She went to the medicine cabinet and came back with the tablet and a glass of water. "What did you drink, anyway?" She sat down.

"Nothing. That's the rottenest part about it. Just a lot of cheap juice and some pistachio nuts. Maybe it was the pistachio nuts." He downed the tablets, wincing at the cold water's bite.

"Oh, I thought you were hung over. My brother had to go to the hospital once after eating some bad pistachios. Serious food poisoning."

Paul arched an eyebrow. "Thanks a lot."

"I mean it. If you're really sick, Paul...."

"I'm all right." He waved it away, then paused to think about it. "You know, it's funny. I always thought an Elks dance would be kind of cheesy. And I was wrong. I was really wrong."

"It wasn't?"

"No, it wasn't kind of cheesy. It was unbelievably cheesy."

She laughed and gave him a little shove. "You're bad."

"I'm serious." The ghost of a smile hovered there. "I mean, I'm sure they do a lot of good, but...Jesus. It was like being *in* the old Lawrence Welk Show."

She laughed. "Sure you're not exaggerating a little?"

"Not a bit." He stretched his arms out like an old-fashioned singer and recited, as if from memory:

If you're an Elk
Or of that ilk,
Ya gotta love Welk:
He's safe as milk.

Suzanne shook her head. "Well," she said, "tomorrow's another day, right?"

"I suppose. Hell, today's another day. I just don't feel up to doing anything about it."

She looked at him. "I realize this may not be the best time to bring this up, but I need to talk to you about something."

"What's that?"

She looked down, tracing circles on the tabletop. "It's about work…well, not about work, exactly, but about you and me…in the context of work, I mean."

"You lost me."

She looked up again. "I don't know how to ask you this. Do you ever get the feeling I treat you differently? Like I treat you one way at home, another way at work, another way when we're out with friends? Do I seem to do that?"

"No. Not that I've ever noticed. Do *I*?"

"That's what I wanted to talk to you about."

He bristled slightly. "Well, there's a time and a place —"

"I know, I didn't mean we should be having wild sex on the floor at work —"

"I had a fantasy about that once."

"I just mean—oh, you did, did you? Pervert. No, I'm just saying sometimes it seems like you don't want other people to see you care. I'm not criticizing you. It's just the way it seems…sometimes." She looked down and away again, tapping her foot.

"Do you remember a conversation we had a while back about us going out? And I said you wouldn't have answered the phone the way you did unless we were going out with each other?"

"Not really," she said. "No."

"Well, it went like this: I said you were always so reserved before we started going out. And you said, 'I never said we were *going out*.' Then I said, 'Trust me, you wouldn't have answered the phone like that if we weren't.' And you said, 'Okay. Maybe in your world we are.'"

"I remember it now."

"Well?"

"Well, what?"

"So, are we going out, or what?"

"Of course we are." She laughed and tapped him across the table. "Come on, Paul, that was months ago."

"Okay, maybe two months."

"More than that. Of course we're going out. I mean, we don't have to make some formal announcement."

"No. But I still figured we should cool it at work. You knew how I felt about the whole office romance thing, and I'm still not thrilled that you could be sitting there at lunch with somebody from Claims talking about the fact that we haven't had sex yet."

"I don't do that!"

He laughed. "I'm not saying you do. I'm just saying…."

"Well, okay. Do you really mind if I show a little affection while we're there? You know, wink at you while I'm walking past your desk? I mean it, seriously."

"No, of course I wouldn't mind that. But just one requirement."

"What's that?"

"If you're going to go switching by my desk and wink at me…."

"Yeah?"

"You have to wear those little white ankle socks."

She laughed and smacked him on the arm again. "You are so bad."

"Hey, what can I say? It turns me on."

"You want me to put my hair in pigtails, too?"

He pursed his lips, scowling. "Couldn't hurt."

She slapped him on the arm across the table, hard, and he roared—first with pain, then laughter.

"Hey," she said, "I've got an idea to cure your Elks club indigestion. Let's go talk to my girl Pamela. I usually meet her for a late morning brunch around this time anyway. She may have some dirt on the Flambets for you, or at least be able to help us out with this whole thing with James Flambet and Graham."

"Who the hell is Pamela?"

"Pamela Swenson. That's right, you never met her, huh? She's about three years younger than me."

"And who is she?"

Suzanne looked up at him and blinked twice. "She's the Flambets' nanny," she said.

"They have a nanny?"

She took on a mock-haughty tone. "Yes, for their daughter, *Eugenie.*"

"Oh brother. Well, I guess that's to be expected. Okay, far out. Let's meet up with her. How do you know her?"

"She's good friends with Lakeisha Bennefield."

"Who in the fuck is Lakeisha Bennefield?"

"She was in *your* graduating class in high school, Mister Sociable."

"Oh. Well, hey, I knew a lot of people, but I didn't know everybody."

"She knows who you are."

He scowled again. "Is that good or bad?"

"I don't know." She smiled mischievously.

"I don't even want to know what that means. So how do you know *her*?"

"Best friends with Cora Gable."

"Oh, brother, now I really am going to be sick."

She laughed. "Hey, now, come on. Cora likes you."

"Spare me, spare me."

She laughed again. "That's exactly what I said when Cora tried to sell me on the idea of going out with Mac Flambet."

"Mac? *Mac?* Holy crap," Paul spluttered. "Why would she want to do a thing like that to you?"

"Because she's my *friend.*" She smirked. "Also, then she could have you all to herself."

"God, that is twisted." He stood and finished the rest of the water in the glass, then smiled. "Let's get out of here, before you tell me something that's such a shock to my system that I can't stand up for the rest of the day."

CHAPTER 26

THE FLAMBET ESTATE was tucked into that part of South Tampa just north of the bay, where Himes Avenue ended and began again half a block later after a right on Neptune, a left on Frankland, and a left on San Miguel. Five or six of the new homes there belonged to the nouveau riche, couples from Wisconsin or Michigan who built huge two-story structures with pillars and porticoes, but most of the neighborhood consisted of old money like the Flambets, and it showed. None of their lawns were mapped out in the newer styles, landscaped by architects with master's degrees in xeriscaping and environmental biotechnology. Instead, they stood as neatly and trimly manicured as the plush lawns of homes in New York or Connecticut, miracles of carcinogen-heavy pesticides and the labors of on-site maintenance men.

Like several of the others, the Flambet estate featured servants' quarters in the back, a series of cottages like those on old-time Southern plantations. The entire staff—in fact, the entire family—fluttered about in a whirl of activity based largely upon the whims and wishes of the queen bee: seven-year-old Eugenie, who was James's only child and, if no one else issued forth from the Flambet loins, heiress to a small fortune; assuming, of course, that the family fortune remained a reality and not just a series of bits and bytes in some computer program subject to the winds of Wall Street and the International Monetary Fund. Which was, unfortunately for Eugenie, becoming increasingly possible.

Pamela Mae Swenson had just left the queen bee behind after a full week's worth of nannying, nursemaiding, and biting her lip in general, when she paused to take stock of herself in her car's rearview mirror. Twenty-three, petite, she had green eyes and the kind of long brown hair that turned heads on city streets, but Pamela Mae felt embarrassed by her looks and always thanked other women when told she was pretty, then promptly changed the subject. In a way, she was the last of a vanishing breed, undeniably attractive, yet warm and compassionate, and that was what landed her the job with the Flambets, though she was certainly qualified as well. She ran a finger carelessly across her lower lip, blinking again at the rearview, and drove off. She looked fine.

Pamela Mae retained living quarters with her employers, but she lived on weekends with a roommate in a South Tampa apartment complex two miles from the bay. Even on weekends, the Flambets frequently required her services, so that the apartment, though modest, still assumed the aspect of a getaway for her. The roommate, Sarah, thought the situation ideal, since she reaped the benefits of sharing the monthly rent while living virtually alone.

Even before Pamela Mae reached the top of the stairwell, she could hear Sarah's guttural cries through the wall, and she slowed to a trudge, then stopped.

Damn it.

Oh yeah oh yeah oh yeah, went the cries.

She stood for a moment near the top of the stairs, trying to clear her mind. Where could she go to kill an hour?

Oh yeah oh yeah oh yeah.

Well, the hell with it. Might as well hit the donut shop early, before she was supposed to meet Suzanne, maybe grab a coffee and read the morning paper. She stepped down the stairs again cautiously so as not to be overheard, not that it was at all likely, and pushed open the glass foyer door, almost walking directly into Suzanne and Paul.

"Hey, fancy meeting you here." She pulled up short.

"Hey stranger," Suzanne said. "Paul, this is Pamela. Pamela, Paul."

"Hi."

They smiled at each other politely.

"We can't go upstairs, or I'd invite you in. My roommate has a *guest.*" She rolled her eyes as she said the word.

"Yikes. Well, you wanna get coffee a little earlier than we'd planned? We were just dropping by to see if you wanted to go… and so you could meet Paul, of course."

"Sure. I figure I'd better kill an hour."

"Wow, I think you're really overestimating Ron there, girl."

The women cracked up, and Paul shook his head, grinning.

"Come on," Suzanne said. "We'll take my car."

On the way to the coffee shop, Pamela Mae sat in the back seat, leaning forward between the couple with her arms resting on her knees. "You know," she said, "it's not that I begrudge them the time together. I just wish she could remember I'm coming home on Saturday mornings."

"Are you usually at the Flambets' during the week?" asked Paul.

She flicked her eyes at Suzanne. "Yeah. She told you, huh?"

Paul flushed slightly. "I didn't know the Flambets even had a daughter, much less a nanny."

"Yes, little Eugenie. Poor kid."

He furrowed his brow. "Poor?"

"She's going to be so messed up from growing up in that family."

"Really?"

"Yeah. Think about it, the seven-year-old runs the family."

"That is scary," said Paul.

"It's scary, all right. Try working for 'em."

"I do, sort of." He grinned, and she returned it.

Suzanne tapped her steering wheel with her nails. "We all do. Do you have any other dirt on them? Paul's trying to do some investigative work."

"Well, let's see: Mac Flambet is going to be in court soon in a slightly different position."

Suzanne's face grew restless, though she smiled. "What do you mean?"

"His ex-wife—one of his ex-wives—is taking him to the cleaners."

"*What?*"

"Mm-hm. Evidently, he signed some paper giving her clear title to his condo. They had a joint interest in it before that. I guess he never dissolved it."

"So what does that mean? She's gonna be his landlord?"

"Girl, I think she'll throw him out on the goddamned street if she can. And I don't see anything to stop her."

"Cool!" Suzanne banged the steering wheel with one fist, laughing.

Paul grinned. "Suze, I get the feeling you don't like old Mac."

"That sonofabitch deserves whatever he gets. You know, if they had a picture next to the word 'leer' in the dictionary, it would be him."

"Leer?"

"Paul, the guy's been after me for months…almost a year. It's disgusting."

"I didn't know that. I just thought Cora was trying to get you interested in him. Well, at least he has good taste."

"I don't know, have you seen some of his bimbos? That's the most insulting thing about it. He'll jump just about anything with legs." She shuddered.

"I think I'm glad I didn't know about that," said Paul.

Suzanne smiled and patted his leg. "Don't worry, dear. He's not doing me any harm. I just don't like having him around."

"Well, neither will I, now."

"Oh, don't get all macho and huffy-puffy on me."

"I'm not. It just doesn't do much for me, thinking about him leering at you."

"Trust me, it doesn't do anything for *me*." They all laughed, and he relaxed a bit, sliding down in the seat and glancing out the window at a passing car.

Pamela Mae shook back her hair. "Why are you trying to get dirt on the Flambets?" she asked Suzanne.

"Actually, Paul's really trying to get information about Graham Woodcock. But that's pretty hard to do, so we figured we'd work on the Flambets, too."

"Who's Graham Woodcock?"

"He's the administrator for the 401(k) plan at Flambet," Paul answered. "He's like a senior vice-president."

"*And* Paul's boss," said Suzanne. "Can I tell her?"

He glanced over. "Why not? Just between the three of us, right?"

She nodded. "Paul thinks Graham's embezzling from the 401(k) somehow. He found these phony employee profiles Graham apparently created, and it looks like he may even be ripping us all off with some other scam."

"Whoa."

"He's my boss," said Paul, "so obviously I can't go to my boss. The only person above Graham is James Flambet."

"How well do you know James?" asked Pamela Mae.

"Not very. I don't know either of them well, actually. They're pretty remote."

Suzanne smirked. "Graham just had a birthday, and nobody in Paul's area even knew."

"Wow, close group. How did you even find out?"

"Mary, in human resources. Just in passing."

"You guys didn't even know it was his birthday?"

Paul shrugged. "Nobody knew. He doesn't talk to us."

"That's weird."

"He's a weird guy. At first, I thought maybe he just didn't like Americans. But I don't think that's it. That's just his personality."

"If you really think Graham's screwing you guys, you know who you should talk to."

"Who's that?"

"My friend Lakeisha."

Suzanne took her eyes off the road and made a face at Pamela Mae.

Paul said, "Who in the hell is this person? Everybody seems to know her except me."

"Her uncle Ned is a lawyer. A good one, too," Pamela Mae said.

Suzanne nodded. "You think he'd know anything about 401(k) plans or investigating fraud or anything like that?"

"Could be. And I bet he'd give you a free consultation, given the right references. You read me?"

"Loud and clear. Ned Bennefield."

"Ned Bennefield. I'll check for you to see if he's got a listing online, and if not, I'll run it by Lakeisha."

Suzanne adjusted her mirror and grinned. "Pamela, you're the greatest."

Pamela Mae grinned back. "I know," she said.

CHAPTER 27

NED BENNEFIELD PUT the profiles of Philip Banks and Dolores Buenas back down on his desk. He looked up at Paul and blinked through his bifocals. "And this is all you have, correct?"

"Afraid so." Paul pursed his lips, thinking how much trouble it had been to even get in to see this attorney. Now here was the question he'd most dreaded.

"Well," Bennefield said. "This kind of thing isn't my area of expertise, but unless you've got some way of retrieving these documents, I don't think you could make a case from them. They could have been generated anywhere."

"I was thinking the same thing."

"What makes more sense to pursue, to me, would be the issue of the 401(k) funds being somehow laundered or embezzled from others in the company. If I understand this story correctly, you think he's done some of that, too?"

"Exactly. In recent months."

"Well, that would be traceable. The only problem is wading through all the bureaucratic nonsense to get detailed fund information. You familiar with *Morningstar?*"

"No."

"It's a daily publication like *The Wall Street Journal.* You could track the exact progress of specific funds on a day-to-day basis for a period of several months. If you got back issues from the local library, or maybe even just checked their website, and found that the numbers substantiated your claims, you'd certainly have a case. You could use your own allocation of funds as an example. As I said, it's not my area of expertise—I deal with murder and mayhem—but I can put you in touch with someone who may be of some help to you. Let me just look through my numbers."

"I really appreciate it."

He leaned back in his chair and smiled. "Not a problem. Anyone who's a friend of my dear niece is a friend of mine."

Paul smiled back, embarrassed by how far he'd stretched the truth just to get the appointment.

"Here he is." Bennefield pulled out the business card and held it up. "Let me just write the number down for you." He scribbled across a card taken from a silver case and handed it to Paul.

Paul looked at the name. "David Gable. He doesn't happen to have a daughter named Cora, does he?"

Ned Bennefield's white teeth gleamed. "As a matter of fact, he does. You know Cora?"

"She works with us too."

"Well, I'll be damned. Small world." He leaned back, still smiling. "That should be a point in your favor, Mr. Panepinto. Yes, indeed, that should be a point in your favor."

Paul gave him a hopeful smiled in return, eyebrows raised, showing nothing. "Cool," he said. "I really appreciate it."

CHAPTER 28

"SO HE GAVE you the card, and you asked him if this David Gable has a daughter named Cora."

"Exactly."

Suzanne looked at the card again, then back at him. "And he said yes."

"He said yes."

"But how do you know it's the same one?"

Paul shook his head. "How many people you think there are in this town named Cora Gable? How many people you think there are in this *world* named Cora Gable?"

"It could just be a coincidence," she said weakly.

He laughed, and she sagged a little. "Okay," he said. "Maybe a coincidence, maybe not. But I'll bet you five bucks he's her father."

"I don't think I want to put that much on it," she said.

They both laughed in spite of themselves.

"Crap. Well, look, I'll call him up, right? 'This is Paul Panepinto calling from Flambet Insurance.' If he's her father, the company name should register, unless he literally doesn't know where his own daughter works. Which is unlikely, since he's a lawyer here in town, not in, say, Okskinaw, Michigan."

"And then we'll know."

"Exactly."

She poked the edge of the carpet with her big toe. "What do we do if he is?"

"Milk it for all it's worth. Explain that we think Graham's ripping *everybody* off, not just doing the Philip Banks and Dolores Buenas number."

"But oh, God, Paul. What if we have to deal with her? What if she joins the hunt, you know what I'm saying?"

"We'll have to keep her out of it as long as possible. Attorney-client privilege, right?"

"I guess. I don't know. I'm not used to dealing with lawyers."

"Me neither, but Ned Bennefield was a start. We'll just have to see."

"You're right. We'll wait and see. David Gable, huh?"

He grinned, and she kissed him, her jasmine perfume flooding his senses. "You know," he said, "it could be worse."

"How? How could it be worse?"

"He could have given me a business card for Mac Flambet."

CHAPTER 29

PAMELA MAE SWENSON sorted her whites into one pile and the colored clothes into another, thinking all the while about her last trip to Ybor with Lakeisha and one of Lakeisha's friends, an artist from Seattle who called herself Svelte. They'd walked up and down the strip for hours aimlessly, danced at Empire and Masquerade, but somehow the overall effect was numbing. After a while, it just wasn't fun: the music too loud, the people too phony, the bathrooms execrable. It made her want to curl up in a corner booth in the coffee shop, get wired on café con leche, and talk about music and art. More than anything, it made her homesick for Northampton.

She poured the detergent, shoved in the quarters, and headed back to the apartment. The phone was ringing. That could be Lakeisha, she thought, although she was actually expecting a call from Suzanne. She checked the caller ID: Unavailable.

"Hello?"

"Hi, Pamela?" A male voice.

"Who's calling, please?"

"It's Frank Brenkus. Is that you?"

Shit. "Yeah, it's me. Hi, Frank."

"How are you?"

Oh brother. "Okay, and you?"

"Fine, fine. Listen, I wanted to call and see if you'd like to check out The Red Zone in Ybor. Like, Saturday night?"

Pamela sighed. The Red Zone, really? Where the music was intolerably loud and the median age was twenty-one? Frank would look like a middle aged banker in a club like that. At thirty-eight, he'd be the oldest person in the place.

"Well, Frank, to be perfectly honest with you…I really like you as a friend and I'm only interested in you that way."

"I can definitely understand that. However —"

"Also, I'm only twenty-three, Frank. Remember?"

"Hmm? Oh, right. Well, but you're very mature for your age."

"Thanks but, again, no thanks. Maybe as part of a group, but not as a date. No hard feelings."

"Okay, okay. So, what are you up to these days?"

"Right now I'm in the middle of doing my laundry, and I was just about to check the yellow pages for a listing for an attorney for a friend of mine. Remember Lakeisha Bennefield? This is her uncle."

"Sure, I remember Lakeisha."

"And after that, I need to actually call Lakeisha."

"Ah. Well, don't let me keep you. I just —"

A beep in her ear cut him off a moment.

"Can you hold on, Frank? I have another call. That might be her."

"Sure."

She clicked over. "Hello?"

"Hey, Pamela Mae."

"Lakeisha! Guess who's on the other line?"

"I don't know. The President."

"Frank Brenkus."

Lakeisha chuckled. "Are you kiddin' me? He still after you?"

"Stop laughing. Hang on, lemme get rid of him."

Click. "Frank?"

"Heeyyy."
"Frank, I've gotta go. That's the call I was expecting. Okay?"
"Okay, I'll see ya around."
She smiled. "I'll see ya on the news."
Click.

CHAPTER 30

BEFORE THEIR MEETING, James considered the things he and Graham needed to discuss: the McDillon mess, finding better ways to get money from debtors, how to keep creditors at bay. Good God, he thought, asking an ice-cube like Graham to schmooze people for cash…it was almost unthinkable. He even considered discussing the 401(k) program. No doubt about it, the clock was ticking on Flambet Insurance. It promised to be a tense morning.

Graham crept into James' office with his sinister feline smile as James hung up from a conversation with his wife, Celia. "Eugenie has a toothache," she'd said. James had only grunted, tired of the catalogue of his pampered daughter's complaints. Sometimes, it seemed she feigned illness just to get their attention.

"Hey, Graham."

"Morning."

"Well, here's the deal – close that door, would you?" James waited while he did so. "We've got some shit going down here. We're at the point where I'm going to need you to cut loose a couple people just to shore up the foundations, if you know what I mean."

Graham cocked his head to one side. "Can we afford to lose them? With the current volume?"

"Well, we may have to. And, I hate to say it but, you know, lean on the rest of them to do more overtime. If they so much as hear the word *downsize*, they'll do it."

"Maybe, but it's a bloody good job market out there. If they panic, there may be a stampede out the fucking door."

"You're right. That's why I'm thinking just a couple people, not five or six. No more than three."

"Hmm. What about the margins? How serious is it?"

"Serious enough. Also, Western owes us about fourteen thousand. But then we owe Federal a hundred and twenty thousand, so what the hell's the difference?"

"Who are you thinking of giving the golden parachute?"

James laughed without humor. "I don't even know half the people by name anymore. You know that."

Graham nodded.

"We have a couple-three new processors. Still in their first ninety days, I'd guess. John Alsup or Alston or somebody. Mary something-or-other. They'll go quietly, and probably find something else with ease. Like you said, it's a killer market."

They both paused, as if sizing each other up.

"So, what else?"

"Well, okay." He wiped his brow. "The creditor/debtor thing. I need you to help me out with Western, and maybe some of the other major debtors. Call 'em up and charm some money out of 'em with that accent of yours. And call Jim Friel over at Federal and see if you can sweet-talk him into cutting us some slack on the hundred grand. What do you think?"

"Whatever."

James sighed. He knew what that response meant: I'll do it, but I'm not going to like it. "Thanks, Graham," he said. "Oh, were you able to work out that thing with the 401(k) company?"

"What thing?"

"That whole blackout deal. A couple people got concerned about not being able to monitor their funds for a whole month."

Graham tensed slightly. "All they'd have to do is check *Morningstar* or *The Wall Street Journal* to get an idea how they're doing."

"I know. Just a couple people were concerned they weren't getting their share."

He rolled his eyes. "They'll all get a quarterly report. And I could work up something in the meantime, if it's really —"

"No, no, don't worry about it. You've got too much to do as it is. Anyway, this whole McDillon thing has got me bogged down. I had Paul Panepinto look at it a while back, you'll remember, and he couldn't make heads or tails of it either."

"I remember."

"Well, we need to recapture the missing data somehow. Take a look at this." He pulled out the heavy stack of spreadsheets and spread them on his desk with another sigh. He knew it would be a long day.

CHAPTER 31

ELIZABETH FLAMBET SAT at the kitchen table with one hand on Mac's. His other hand covered his face, and a tear hung from his chin like a fat droplet of sweat.

How long since she'd last seen him?. How long since she'd touched his hand? She thought about it. Easily months since she'd seen him, likely almost a year. And since they'd exchanged so much as a hug? Years.

Almost as if he'd read her mind, he said, "You're the only one I can talk to about this, Liz." He wiped his face, then pulled his hand out from beneath hers. He'd tensed the hand first, as if to acknowledge that it had appreciated her touch.

"What are you going to do?"

He sighed. "I don't know."

He was silent for several moments, but he did not seem to be waiting for her to respond, and she hung back. The pause gave her more time to reflect. Of course he was right. Who else did he have to talk to? He spent a little time with James, but what of that? Liz knew how estranged they really were, probably better than they did. She knew what they talked about: Flambet Insurance, law firm trivialities. The weather. Professional tennis. It pained her to watch them play at being buddies, but she couldn't run interference for them. What could she say? Get real, guys?

And of course, Mother and Father were even less help. She knew what old man J.B. would say: "He's a hell of a lot more of a sonofabitch than I ever was. Serves him right!"

And Mother would fuss at him, turning to ice right before his eyes. Her denial was surpassed only by her apathy.

So Elizabeth could only leave all that alone and say, "What are you going to do?"

"I don't know," he murmured, and not once in the long pause that followed did he look at his sister.

But then he did, and the eyes pained her, not because his distress was so great, but because she saw the calculation behind them, the impersonal analysis he made at the deepest level. It pained her to know he might just be looking for a place to stay if it should come to that, or just another person to use on an as-needed basis.

Mac glanced away, as if he knew he'd been caught, and when he looked back again, the calculation was gone. Somehow, he'd summoned up another tear in each eye. He blinked and sniffled once. He wiped both eyes with the back of one hand.

"Jesus, Liz. Look at me. You know I've lived in that condo nearly ten years? That's what I told Steve that first day. Ten years. And now, sure as shit, I'm out of there. Lot of memories there, Liz. Lot of memories. Well, maybe it's for the best. Lot of bad memories there, too."

He barked out a little laugh. "And not only that, it's coming at a time when I really can't lean on James at all, with all he's got to contend with right now. You understand."

She blinked. "No, I don't. What about James?"

He looked at her, and her own eyes widened. Oh shit.

And then he said it. "You didn't know."

"Know what? Jesus Christ, Mac —"

"I'm sorry, I'm sorry. Well, for one thing, Eugenie's been sick a lot."

"I know that. She's going to be all right, isn't she?"

"Oh yeah."

"Well, what, then?"

He sighed. "Look, if I'm not supposed to tell you this, okay, whatever, but James is in the red."

"What?"

"Yeah. Please, if he brings it up, don't —"

"I won't, I won't."

"He'd probably never forgive me. I've pulled enough shit on him as it is. But yeah, Flambet Insurance is teetering on the brink of major fucking financial disaster."

She gripped the edge of the table. "Does Dad know?"

"Probably. I don't know. Christ, Liz, I've been such a basket case myself with this whole thing of mine, I don't know what's going on. If the old man does know something, he didn't get it from *me*."

"How serious is it?"

"Well, the banks sure as hell won't loan him any more money, and if it came down to it, I don't think the old folks could bail him out without seriously jeopardizing Dad's retirement. For that reason alone, I assume James hasn't told them."

"God damn, Mac."

"I know. I know. I'm sorry to lay all this on you. Some serious shit."

She looked at him, suddenly seeing the resemblance between them for the first time in a long while. She thought of their childhood vacations in Newport, the good old tennis days, Mac getting the Fulbright scholarship. She thought of how she'd refused to attend any more of Mac's weddings after his third divorce. "I'm not buying another dress," she'd said. And what could he say in response? Nothing.

"What kind of money are we talking about with James? That they owe but can't borrow elsewhere?"

"I don't know the exact numbers. I'd say definitely in excess of three, but probably less than four."

"Three *million?*"

"Yeah."

"Oh my God, Mac."

"I know. I know. It's serious."

She inhaled and felt her breath shake. Outside the house, the world no longer looked as solid as it had before he'd come in, and an anxious tension bloomed in her sternum, much more frightening than anything Mac's ex-wife troubles could cause.

"We need to talk to Mom and Dad about this," she said.

He paused, still brooding. "I don't know," he said. "I'm trying to stay out of it. Especially since I don't think they've got a clue. Besides, he may think of something. He may even go the old BK route."

"BK?"

"Sorry. Bankruptcy. A little legalese."

"Oh God. Bankruptcy?"

"Well, it would suck, but I've seen much worse scenarios. But to be honest, like I said before, I haven't really given it that much thought, I've been so caught up in this goddamn thing of my own. I just got blindsided." He stared out the window.

She studied him. "Bankruptcy, Mac?"

"Hm?" He turned back. "Oh. Yeah. Maybe," he said. "That may be the way to go."

CHAPTER 32

PAUL SIFTED THROUGH the mutual fund listings in *Morningstar* until he found April first: the first day of the second quarter and, of course, April Fools' Day.

How appropriate.

He used his own allocation of assets as one example, intending to use Suzanne's as another. It surprised him how much more conservative he was. While she didn't really have what could properly be called a portfolio—all her assets were invested in the company's "aggressive growth" stock fund—he'd spread his out among a whole range of blue chip, bond, growth and income funds in the hope that diversity would provide stability and good returns. Of course, he knew it would be easier to monitor Suzanne's fund for the time period, but it would also be almost too obvious a target for Graham, and he probably hadn't touched it because of the ease of tracing any problems. For that reason, Paul figured his own out first.

It took hours. One day the funds would be up a few cents, the next day they'd be down. In order to ensure accuracy, he figured the total portfolio per day based on changes in net asset value for each fund. When he reached the "blackout period" days, he found nothing unusual: just the daily ups and downs. Then he had to continue the calculations all the way up to the present date and check the current value against what it should have been according to *Morningstar.*

He came up short by about fifty dollars, but even this did not nail Graham, since Graham made the distributions to the plan on a bi-monthly basis. How to factor that into the equation became even more difficult, since no one but Graham could tell him exactly when distributions for any given payrolls were made. Quite possibly, the most recent contribution had not have gone through yet, and that would account for the fifty dollars. He decided to call the people at the mutual fund company itself.

"Well," the woman said, "you'd have to talk to your human resources director about when each distribution is made."

"That's the problem. They aren't made on specific dates, just twice a month, and I don't trust him."

"I'm sorry, sir, but since he's the person who manages the plan, he's the only one who can release that information."

He gripped the receiver. "Well, what if I think he's embezzling? What if I think he's ripping us all off? What recourse do I have then?"

"There are safeguards to the system, sir," she said mechanically, "but you'd still have to ask him about when the last distribution has been sent."

"Who's the supervisor there? I want to talk to somebody higher up."

"I'm the manager of the customer service department, sir."

"Great. And you're telling me there's nothing else I can do."

"Not for the moment. I'm sorry, sir —"

"Thank you." He hung up.

CHAPTER 33

THE ELDER FLAMBETS always told visitors that they knew Tampa like the backs of their hands. They knew where all the little out-of-the-way coffeehouses were—and "out-of-the-way" in Tampa meant not in the boondocks, but tucked away in the corner of some megalopolis-sized plaza, or down some quaint little side street—nothing visible to the naked eye from a major thoroughfare. They knew the best places to get bagels on Sunday mornings when most everything but the chain restaurants were closed, where to get the *New York Times Book Review* and tolerable sushi and a good manicure by a genuine Vietnamese illegal alien. They knew the shops in Hyde Park, which bars in Ybor City to avoid, and the best parks around Carrollwood.

As a result, they always smiled a bit indulgently whenever some poor transplanted New Yorker exclaimed, "I feel like I'm in Mayberry!" They resisted the temptation to pat him on the back and murmur, "Poor soul. Don't fret, you'll find civilization here, too, if you scout around a bit." Instead, J. B. only chuckled and said, "I love a town with an inferiority complex like Tampa's. It makes all the people from the Midwest feel right at home."

But it wasn't complaisant relaxation and banter every day: at times the tension at home was too much to bear, as evidenced by Alexis Flambet's comment to her husband after he'd just hung up with Mac.

"Jean Bertram Flambet, I can't believe you'd say such a thing about your own son," said Alexis. "Besides, you're calling *me* a bitch in the process."

"Well, I didn't mean it that way, Alexis." J.B. paused. "But damn it, the little bastard brought it on himself!"

She drew herself up. "Bastard is just as bad."

"Goddamn it, stop thinking about yourself for one goddamn minute and listen to me. Jesus Christ, at least I know where he gets his colossal self-centeredness."

"Well," she said, as if she were about to follow with, "I never." But she only shot him a killing look and returned her gaze to the painting she'd been working on before he'd come into the study.

"Listen." He was about to continue, but saw that she was going to ignore him. "Hang it all, can't you just listen for one goddamn minute?"

"I'm not going to be subjected to another tirade," she said. "If you can't keep from calling me self-centered, or a bitch, then you can expect to be ignored. And, I might add, deservedly so." Again, she returned her attention to the painting.

"Dear God," he said. "Never mind, then." He turned to his left, as a whirl of white flew past his hip. "Eugenie, darling. When did you come in?"

"Just now." The girl looked up at him, batting her lashes.

"Did you…did you hear what your grandmother and I were talking about?"

She smiled knowingly. "What were you talking about?"

He laughed, hard, and the laughter set off a spell of coughing. "Oh dear," he said, when it subsided. "Oh dear. Isn't she something? Alexis, did you hear her?"

"Yes," Alexis said, not turning. "Eugenie, you're your mother's daughter."

"Yes, yes," J.B. said. "Yes, she is that. Well, no matter. Eugenie, darling, you mustn't tell anyone if you heard any of what your grandmother and I were saying. All right?"

"Yes, Grandpa."

"That's my girl. Come give Grandpa a kiss."

She went to him and he kissed her on the cheek. She pulled back after he'd kissed her, as if it went without saying that his asking for a kiss meant only that he was allowed to give one.

"Sweetheart, would you excuse your grandmother and me for a moment? We need to talk privately."

"Okay, Grandpa."

"That's a good girl."

She turned and walked toward the door, then turned back. "Grandpa?"

"Yes, dear?"

"Was that Uncle Mac on the phone just now?"

He looked uneasily at his wife, then back at the girl. "No, dear, it was business. Why?"

"He just promised he'd call me today."

"Oh." He glanced at Alexis again. "Well, dear, I'm sure he'll call as soon as he has time."

"Okay." She bounced into the hallway, closing the door behind her.

"There you are," he said. "He just called to bitch about the condo, and didn't even remember his own niece."

"I heard." She continued to paint. "I'm not disagreeing with you on principle; I objected to your choice of words. In any event, what did your darling son say?"

"My darling son...." He gave her a dry look, then thought better of it. "He's going to court on Tuesday. Even with his attorney hanging by his side at every moment of every day, he hasn't got a chance, and he knows it. He signed the goddamn thing himself.

Nobody put a gun to his head. She's just going to say he recanted and throw him the fuck out."

"I swear your language is getting worse every day."

"Jesus Christ, did you even hear *what* I said, or are you just sitting there waiting to critique it while you work on that goddamn monstrosity of a painting?"

"Never mind," she said, standing. "I'll come back to my 'monstrosity' later."

She walked past him, and he looked at her as if she were on fire. But he said nothing, and the room remained silent even after the door slammed shut.

CHAPTER 34

FLUORESCENT LIGHTS GLARED above the executive desk where James stood with his hands clasped behind him, pausing in mid-pace behind the big leather chair.

Graham entered the office. "So, how's your brother these days?" he asked jauntily. "Haven't seen him dropping in for lunch much."

"Mac?"

"Yeah. Has he been incommunicado? Or is he just dropping in only when I'm out?"

James shook his head. "No, he hasn't been by for a while. He's kind of preoccupied with a case." He sat down at his desk and drummed his fingers.

Graham raised an eyebrow. "Really? Big case?"

"Personal, actually." James looked away. "Problem with an ex-wife."

"Oh?" Graham's eyes twinkled, though he did not exactly smile. "What sort of problem?"

"It's a property issue." He sighed and glanced up. "His ex's name is still on the condo, so he's going to lose it. Either that, or settle out of court."

Graham looked stunned. "What? That doesn't seem possible."

"Well, it was all a mistake. He signed something he shouldn't have signed."

"Really."

"Giving her clear title."

Graham shook his head. "Dear God, old boy. What'd she do, spike his tea with mescaline or something?"

James forced a laugh. "Ha. No, no. It's, uh…it's a long story."

"Well, that's an absolute bitch."

"Yeah. Ah, you know how it is. You know Mac."

Graham smirked. "Picked some winners, hasn't he? But that one—to pull a stunt like that. Bloody gargoyle from Hell, isn't she?"

"Hmph. Hey, what can you do, right?"

"Well, Christ, I should hope he'd win that case, at least. Where does a good lawyer find a good lawyer? His own firm?"

James cracked his knuckles, tiring of the topic. "He's actually retained a good attorney for years. Friend of the family, Steve Dawson."

"Hm. Well, wish him luck for me."

"Thanks, Graham, I will. You have a report for me?"

"Yes, I do. Here." He handed over a binder.

"Good." James looked at it, scowling. "Thanks."

CHAPTER 35

EULA YI AND JORGE Arce sat at the end of The Pier in St. Petersburg, looking out over the water. Jorge looked at his girlfriend from the corner of his eye and blinked. He scratched the top of his head with one hand, a parody of bewilderment. Asian women were only slightly more confusing than the average American woman, he thought, but then, that was really saying something.

What the hell did she really want? And why was she always talking about these other people he barely knew, Mac Flambet, Pamela Mae Swenson? Maybe he should just change the subject when she brought them up.

"So what did *Pamela* say about the case?" She glanced over at him, suddenly cold.

Christ, she asks him about Mac Flambet, and if he's heard anything about Mac's case. He says that he hasn't seen Mac, but that Pamela said something about it. Pamela overheard some comments. Just trying to answer the damned question, and now he gets, "So what did *Pamela* say?" He heard the tone, but when he looked over to confirm it, she showed nothing.

"Well, she didn't say much. You know how it is, I only bump into her here and there, when she's doing stuff for Eugenie. She just overheard some stuff."

"Yeah. So, is Mr. Mac gonna lose his ass, or what?"

"I don't know. I guess he was talking to his mother. Old Alexis. He said he hoped that even if he lost the case, that it would at least be over in a day. But it looks like it's gonna drag on for a while."

"What about the woman who put the paperwork in his chair? Ida or Ada, or whatever?"

"No idea, honey. No one mentioned her."

A brief silence, more uncomfortable than changing the subject. Before he had a chance to speak, she asked, "Do you think Pamela is good-looking?"

"Huh?"

"Pamela Swenson."

A horrible question. How could he think a stone fox like Pamela was not good-looking? He thought, too long, how he should answer. A flat-out *no* was transparently dishonest. A flat-out *yes* would almost guarantee a full evening or more of the dreaded Silent Treatment. But the pause alone was fatal.

"Never mind. The amount of time you took trying to think of a way out of telling the truth answers it."

"*What?* Why would I have to think of a way out of the truth? I mean, she's all right, she's not bad-looking, but why you asking *me* that?"

She crossed her arms around her middle. "Come on, Jorge. You know I don't like her, but you're always talking about her."

"I'm not 'always' talking about her! You asked me if I'd heard anything about Mac, and I ain't heard nothing, other than that one thing Pamela said. So I tell you, and then I get this 'So what did *Pamela* say?'"

"Well?"

"Well, what? Shit, girl, you want me to tell you what I heard only if it don't include Pamela Fucking Swenson?"

"Now you're just being rude."

He stood, wiping his brow. "Goddamn, I don't believe we're talking about this. There is nothing between me and Pamela Swenson. What's the big deal with her?"

"I never said there was anything between you. Where did that come from?"

"I'm just sayin'…the way you're actin'…."

"Why would you even feel you have to tell me that? Did I ever imply there was anything between you and Pamela Swenson?"

"Hell, I dunno. I guess not."

"Well, that just makes me wonder. Why would you have to deny something I didn't even suggest?"

"What the hell are you talkin' about?"

"Never mind. Nothing."

"Oh, Jésus y Maria. Okay, sure, whatever you say."

She folded her arms and said nothing. Sure enough, the dreaded Silent Treatment. For the rest of the evening, she would not speak another word.

CHAPTER 36

DAVID GABLE STOOD and stretched. The clock on the wall read 4:45, but it was only 4:35, an annoying company mannerism that never kept anyone there late or coerced anyone into arriving early, in any case.

In any case. An ironic word to be contemplating. The caseload was fatally low, almost the exact opposite of Mac Flambet's firm. If things didn't pick up, it would be time to hit the classifieds again.

He noticed the red message light on his phone, though he hadn't been on the phone in hours. Shit, a Friday afternoon, almost closing time, and he's getting voicemail. Five minutes in the bathroom, and there's a message on the goddamn voicemail. He sighed and picked up the phone.

"This is Paul Panepinto calling from Flambet Insurance?" said the voice. "Ned Bennefield referred me to you? I'm trying to crack a difficult case, I wondered if I might speak with you briefly. If you're available, you can reach me at home…."

David wrote down the number, then stared at it. Flambet Insurance. Cora's company. Trying to crack a difficult case? Christ, if it's anything to do with my daughter, I'm sure it's a difficult case. Pro bono. Wonderful. Well, fuck him, he can wait until Monday.

He loaded documents into his briefcase and stuck the phone number into his wallet. It was time to hit the fairway.

CHAPTER 37

"SUZANNE, IT'S ME."

"Hey there."

"How are ya, hon?"

"Doing okay, darling. What's the news? You still working on it?"

"Yeah, it's not getting me anywhere, although I did leave a message for that other lawyer, David Gable. Trouble is, Graham makes those distributions to the plan twice a month. And of course, nobody but Graham can tell me the exact dates distributions for each payroll are made. In fact, he's got *fifteen* days to make them, so unless he took a shitload of money, you can't tell. My account was short about fifty, yours was short about seventy-five, but the most recent contributions might not have gone through yet. We gotta find another way."

"That sucks."

"Tell me about it. Any idea how to break into the system?"

She laughed. "Nope, you got the wrong girl for that crime. You need to recreate your Dolores Buenas and Philip Banks stunt again, Sherlock."

"We may have to enlist someone else's help here. I hate to contemplate going to James. Don't you think he would automatically default to 'I'll discuss this with Graham' mode?"

"Could be. That's a dangerous game for you. You could be out of a job fast, dude."

"I almost don't care, at this point. It's not just that I need to nail the bastard. I don't think I can stand to stay there much longer, regardless of what happens with this."

"Why? Because of Graham?"

"Well, that's definitely a part of it. The whole framework is corrupt. But more than that, I don't want to keep doing this kind of work. It's so far from what I set out to be doing."

She sighed. "I hear that. What are you gonna do?"

"I may have to talk to James. If possible, I need to find out whether or not he knows the payroll system. That is, if I can figure a way to probe for that information without him getting suspicious. If he doesn't at least know the software, I think we're screwed."

"What if he goes directly to Graham to ask him?"

Paul paused, as if thinking about it. "Then I punt."

"Punt? You mean give up the chase, or give up the job?"

"Give up the job. Find employment elsewhere and investigate this on my own. It would almost be worth it, just to put Graham on the run."

"Well, you're braver than I am," said Suzanne. "Even if I do despise the bastard."

"It's a pretty good job market out there right now, from what I understand, so I'm not too worried. I'm more concerned about what's going to happen to us all, financially, if there's no way to determine what the hell he's doing." He paused again. "So what's happening later?"

"Later? You mean tonight?"

"Yeah. I need to see you."

She laughed again, a throaty sound, pure sexual self-confidence. "Dang, when did you get so aggressive, boy?"

"Mmm…I'll tell ya later."

On the way to her apartment, he had the sensation again, like he was hovering above a great emptiness, then falling into it, sweetly sinking. He didn't know if it was a loss of self or the anticipation of the long-overdue union with Suzanne, but it didn't scare him anymore. It felt like the prelude to a night of ecstasy.

And then he was in the distant past, remembering the pebble tossed into the air toward the shuttered window, the clatter when it dropped back to his feet, the fearful underhand toss, again and again. He felt the breeze, heard the long slow suspiration of breath, felt the enveloping warmth…it was all there again, the sounds of cricket and cicada, the scent of lilac, the cool backyard grass, all of it, and he looked out across the distances, beyond the reaches of time and space. It was not a longing for the time, nor even for the girl. Instead, he saw himself with Suzanne in that same situation, two innocents staring down the future, looking for a moment of relief in the midst of cold days in a colder world.

When he pulled into the parking lot of the apartment complex, he paused. He parked in one of the visitor spots, but didn't get out of the car right away. Instead, he simply remained in his seat and looked out beyond the steering wheel, seeing nothing, thinking nothing, still under the spell. What was it, after all? Nostalgia? Love? Fear? It could almost be a mixture of them all.

He walked up to her door and knocked.

"Hey," she said.

"Hey." He kissed her, distracted, already thinking, This can't go on like this much longer. I need to get seriously laid.

She led him to the sofa, a promising start. "Make yourself comfortable." She headed for the kitchen. "What do you want to drink?"

"Just water," he called, already thinking, I don't need anything to drink. That's not what I'm here for. That's not the reason I came.

She returned with the glasses and placed them on the coffee table, then settled herself close to him. After another kiss—a bit too subdued for his taste—he kissed her in earnest, and she responded with more and more fervor, moving against him passionately, almost frantically. He kissed her neck, and she moaned softly, pressing her breasts against his chest. He continued, pressing her tightly against him.

In no time, they were both disheveled, his shirt unbuttoned, as if the moment had finally come, after all this time. He had waited so long, he was so far beyond readiness. For an instant, he felt grateful the moment had finally, blessedly come.

But then she said it. "Paul…not yet, Not tonight. I – I want it to be…special."

He closed his eyes and sighed with unmistakable irritation. "What special thing has to happen first? We've been together for three months. I've prepared every bit of ground work I can imagine: romantic dinners, walks on the beach…."

"I know," she said. "And some of those nights would actually have been perfect, if you'd wanted to then. I felt like I was ready on several of those occasions, actually."

He stared, hard. "What? Why didn't you say anything?"

She laughed, clearly annoyed as well. "Uh, I gave you plenty of signs, Paul. Plenty. What was I supposed to do, some kind of hand signals, like in a goddamn football game?"

"Holy fucking shit." He stood and paced. "I can't believe it. I can't believe I'm hearing this. After three months…what the hell am I supposed to do, just keep trying every time we're together and getting rejected over and over again?"

"It's not a rejection of you, Paul," she said. "It's not even a rejection of sex with you. It's a rejection of sex at *that moment.*"

"Well, there have been plenty of *those moments*, that's for sure, including one just now," he said, pulling on his shirt. "I've been starting to feel like I couldn't get laid in a whorehouse with a fistful of twenties."

She stood and faced him, eyes flashing. "I didn't realize it was about getting laid," she said. "I thought it was maybe about having a little patience *and* a little persistence, and being ready to *make love* when the time is right. You know, maybe if you'd had the balls to just try again at the right time…. It's like this thing with Graham. If you had the balls to confront that situation, maybe it would've been resolved by now."

He sagged, and for a moment, he thought she had actually hit him. But it was merely the feeling in his gut that told him what she meant. He sat back down.

"Wait, Paul," she said. "I didn't mean —"

Too late. Too late. It hung in the air between them like poison, and he knew there was nothing more to say.

She heaved herself back down beside him, folding her arms, clearly as stuck in the silence as he was. They sat like that for a long time, side by side. Too long. He looked at their knees, lined up on the sofa like sentinels, and remembered that other time, when, sitting here in her place, she'd said *I think we'd better stop*. His pulse pounded almost audibly in the deadness of the room.

Eventually, when the silence grew unbearable, she stood slowly, went into her bedroom, and closed the door, leaving him to see himself out.

He spent the night there, though, sitting in the same position, wide awake, eventually hearing her soft breathing from the next room, or so he thought. He could not be sure what he heard in the night, colored as it was by the anger, the frustration…the shock of her insult.

Around daybreak, he left, closing the door silently behind him.

CHAPTER 38

ON MONDAY MORNING, Cora Gable looked across the ladies room at the mirror and sighed. "You remember Mercedes Eden, don't you?"

Jill Martin nodded. "Yeah, sure."

"Well, Mercedes and I were at this club last night in Ybor City, The Red Zone. And we were talking about Paul Panepinto. It seems Mr. Panepinto and our good friend Suzanne Beidertyme are officially doing the nasty."

Jill arched an eyebrow. "How do you know that?"

"He was spotted leaving Suzanne's apartment yesterday morning. Looked pretty tired, too."

"Jesus, Cora, are you *stalking* him?"

Cora sniffed. "Hardly. My friend Lakeisha just happened to be in the neighborhood, and she saw him leaving…early, like he was trying to sneak out before anybody but the old people were up. She told Mercedes, so of course Mercedes told me. She tells me about everything. Even her crush on the weatherman."

"The weatherman?"

"Oh, never mind that. We were talking about Paul Panepinto. Damn him."

"So, what are you supposed to do about it? Whack Suzanne over the head with something?"

Cora brought a hand down from her hair and stroked her chin. "Hm, not a bad idea, actually. I was thinking more along the lines of feeding her some antifreeze."

Jill shrieked. "You really are just too, too bad, Cora Gable."

"Well, you really are just too, too good, Jill Martin."

Jill left, and Cora prepared to apply the finishing touches to her eyeliner when Suzanne's unexpected entrance made her jaw twitch. "Hey Suzanne," she said with a smile.

"Hey girl." Suzanne showed nothing: no exultation, no warmth.

"How was *your* weekend?"

Suzanne seemed to withhold a sigh or a sneer. "Not the most relaxing one I've ever had." She stood next to Cora and tied her hair back. "What about you?"

"Oh, just hanging at The Red Zone with some of my posse." She laughed. "Looking out for some real men."

Suzanne scoffed. "Men. They can be real pigs sometimes, can't they?"

Cora pulled the eyeliner pencil away. "Oh? Trouble in paradise?"

"Fuck. I really don't want to talk about it, Cora."

"Whoa, my bad. I thought you'd be getting some serious carpet burns on the knees at this point." The trace of a smirk crossed and passed. "Paul not meeting your expectations?"

Suzanne pulled back from the mirror and eyed Cora instead of her own hair. "No offense, Cora, but it's really nobody's business but ours, okay?"

"Ah, the perils of workplace romance. I know them well. Too bad you never came across for Mac." She sighed. "Poor Mac. I bet you'd be willing to deal with the 'pig' issue for a few spins in that Jaguar and some nice dinners at Mise en Place."

Suzanne froze. "Oh no, you didn't."

"Didn't what, sweetie?"

"You didn't go there."

"Go where? To Mise en Place?" She chuckled.

"You know where. Mac Flambet."

Cora smiled broadly now. "Well, I don't know. Nothing wrong with having a couple men on the line at the same time, is there? I mean, they do it to us all the time."

"Cora —" But then she stopped, as if she was too tired to finish the thought. "Let's just drop the whole thing. I don't want to deal with this today." She leaned forward toward the mirror again, redoing her hair.

"Deal with what, sweetie? We're just talking."

"Sure. Sure we are."

"Well, you know, dare to dream and all that. There's more to life than sex appeal. And I guess Mac is a bit of a—a whatchama-callit—an alpha male. He must be doing something right, to get that many women to marry him."

Suzanne finished fixing her hair and stepped back again. "Sure," she said. "He must be doing something right." And with that, she walked out of the ladies' room and let the door close behind her.

CHAPTER 39

PAUL BROODED OVER the situation with James and Graham while he was licking his wounds from the evening at Suzanne's. He remembered saying that he'd have to find out whether James knew the payroll system without arousing suspicion. But how to broach *that* subject? He ran through the conversation in his mind, imagining all the responses James might have.

The most obvious question was why he cared. Why indeed? He couldn't very well just tell him the truth. The only way he could do that would be if he was ready to give notice. Ready to leave, if that's what it took. He knew the time was near. He had to make the move, even if it meant getting fired. He had been checking out employee classifieds online, emailing résumés, though so far without success.

He thought more cautiously about Graham. What if he was truly dangerous, and what if, facing the risk of exposure, he'd find a more serious way to retaliate? Who else knew how much was actually at stake here, or what Graham would do to protect it?

When he got home, he found a return message from David Gable on the voicemail. "Paul, David Gable returning your call," said the voice, terse and peevish. "Give me a call back here at the office on Friday, if you will." He'd rattled off his number and then hung up. No mention of Flambet Insurance. No mention of Cora. And he was putting Paul off the whole rest of the week.

Nothing looked promising, now. Not the job, not a way out of the job. Not the pursuit of Graham. Certainly not Suzanne. He had to find a way to make things, if not better, at least tolerable.

The following day, he went in and decided he would have to broach the subject of the payroll system with James. Just casually, nothing in-depth. If James asked why, he'd have to act like, as someone in Graham's department, he was just being ambitious enough to volunteer assistance if needed.

The morning was a typical parade of phone calls, email, more phone calls, paperwork. He hunched over his desk, drinking coffee from the old Federal Funding mug. God damn, it's always freezing in this place, he thought.

At 10:30, Graham strolled by his desk and paused, forcing him to put a caller on hold just so that Graham could announce, "I need to meet with you and a couple other people in my office this afternoon. One o'clock, all right?"

Paul knew *all right* meant the request was an order. "Yes sir."

At the appointed hour, he entered Graham's office, expecting a typical meeting with other drones in the hive: himself, maybe three or four of the people Graham most liked to recruit for extra busy-work. Instead, he found Graham leaning back in the big leather chair and, seated opposite him, John Alsup, the new processor from Claims, along with Mary Corwin, also from Claims. Paul sat down.

"Well, there's no easy way to say this," Graham began, "but I'm afraid we're going to have to let you three go, due to budget cuts." He split his gaze between John and Mary. "I know you two haven't been with us long, and I'm dreadfully sorry to have to do this. If I could have avoided it, I would have. You're both excellent, and it's nothing you've done. We just had to go by seniority, and of course, you two were the newest hires in Claims."

"Oh my God," said the woman. "Oh my God."

Graham ignored it. "Unfortunately," he continued, turning to Paul, "that didn't apply to you, Paul. I would have cut a third person from Claims, quite frankly, if I could have, but the company can't afford to lose more than two processors, so I had to look to our own department. It's really a damned shame to have to lose you, Paul, particularly after all your hard work on McDillon. But I had to choose someone, and I honestly think you'll bounce back quickly.

"On the bright side of things," he said, now addressing all three again, "your severance packages will be quite generous for a company of this size." He gestured to John and Mary. "You will each receive pay equivalent to half the amount you've already received for your service here, your two or three months or whatever it's been."

He swiveled his leather chair Paul's way. "Because you've been here the longest, you'll receive half a year's severance. Again, it's regrettable that we've had to take this step, but it simply can't be helped. I'll need your ID badges immediately, along with any keys you might have, and you may go as soon as you've gathered your personal items. Security will escort you."

With that, Graham gathered the badges and one key from Paul, then handed each of them an envelope. Paul took his carefully, as if afraid it would break. Or explode.

So that was it. Just like that, he was let go. But was it really that, or was he being chosen as a sacrificial lamb for another reason? Was he really just being fired at this conveniently "unfortunate" time? Had he gotten too close? Did Graham know something?

And then the realization hit him: what did it matter? He was *free*. Half a year's severance, not to mention unemployment to tide him over until he got something else. He could literally go to the Unemployment Office, file his claim, and live comfortably off the severance pay while looking for a job, putting in the obligatory weekly or biweekly interview, whatever they required. And he would be freer than ever to invesigate the 401(k), though no longer as an insider. He would have to call David Gable back first thing Friday morning.

He was free.

Dreaming, he walked back to his desk. Dreaming, he took down the calendar, dreaming, unplugged the little boombox. He decided to leave the Federal Funding mug there. Let someone else have it, it had no sentimental value. Nothing here did. Except....

What would she say? Would she even know he was gone? He had to tell her.

Or did he? It wasn't like he'd given two weeks' notice. He'd been dismissed, summarily let go like a telemarketer interrupting someone's dinner.

He thought about it. She would know immediately. John and Mary had both worked in Claims with Suzanne and, at the very least, they would go back, collect their belongings, and report that three of them had been laid off.

Before he could act, Graham himself solved the problem for him. "Right," he said, approaching Paul's desk. "Listen, hate to be a stickler about company policy on this one, but since you've been here the longest, I thought you might be tempted to kind of walk around and say a few farewells. Afraid I can't let it happen, my boy. Company morale and all that rot. I'll be happy to see you to the door myself."

"Oh, sure," Paul said, not much caring, but stung by the indignity nonetheless.

What a prick. Did James even know he was one of the three being sacrificed? He walked with Graham, his few personal items jostling around in a single cardboard box. Before he knew it, he was on the highway, heading home, listening to Aretha Franklin asking for a little respect. Fucking ironic, he thought.

And yet...he was free. Nearly two years in that place. He was glad he'd left the Federal Funding mug, glad he wouldn't have the awkward, blood-pressure-raising encounter with Suzanne in the hallway. He was gone, and for all practical purposes, that meant she was gone, too, unless she wanted to talk to him. She had his number.

Free, he thought. Free.

CHAPTER 40

MERCEDES EDEN AND Frank Brenkus almost never saw each other after the first time they'd met at the El Toro Sports Pub. He'd avoided her, and she, too shy and stricken with infatuation to actually pursue him, merely pined away for him like a spinster in an old Victorian era novel…if spinsters had painted their fingernails black and red or worn miniskirts on dance floors under flashing lights.

But there he was on a Tuesday night, back in El Toro with a group from station WRYY: Frank and his assistant Heather, nicknamed *Heather with Weather*; Don Adams from sports, balding and pudgy; and even local anchor Bill Laughlin, a distinguished looking gentleman of fifty. They all hunched in the corner over a large round wooden table overflowing with bottles of beer, wineglasses, and plates of food.

Across the bar, Mercedes sat with Lakeisha Bennefield, Cora Gable, Jill Martin, and a girl named Arlen Jameson from the Claims Department. Of the five, only Mercedes and Lakeisha weren't employed by the company, and even Lakeisha worked for James Flambet directly. The conversation centered around Flambet Insurance, but with Frank Brenkus so close by, Mercedes was in a state of nearly constant distraction.

"Uh-huh, I seen Paul walking out of her apartment last weekend," Lakeisha was saying to Arlen by way of explanation. "I told

Mercedes, Mercedes told Cora, Cora told Jill, and now you in the loop, too!" She giggled.

"What the hell happened to him last week?" asked Jill. "One minute the guy's there, looking like things are going well, and the next thing you know, Graham fires him *and* two other people. Has anybody heard why yet?"

"Not a word," said Cora. "Suzanne hasn't offered anything, and nobody seems to want to ask her about it. I may have to have a chat with her Monday. You know, 'It's a shame about Paul,' and all that."

Mercedes gazed across the room, no longer really much interested. Who cared, anyway? She watched Frank dig into a plate of nachos, his head back as he laughed at something Bill Laughlin just said. To think she was that close to their world. It was like going to an ordinary party and suddenly finding that you might be in the society pages of the local paper the next day.

She nodded and smiled at something Jill said, pretending to pay attention. But her eyes kept wandering to the table in the corner. An elderly couple asked for autographs from the group. Even Heather signed her name.

"That's Frank Brenkus," said Cora, and Mercedes snapped back to attention. The others all laughed.

"What did you say?" asked Mercedes.

"I said," Cora repeated, "that's Frank Brenkus over there with Bill Laughlin and Don What's-his-name from WRYY. You seem to remember Frank, Mercedes. Can't take your eyes off the old boy, eh?" She smiled archly.

Mercedes flushed. "I met him once," she said, trying to sound off-handed. "He was very nice."

"Nice?" Cora trilled. "You were crazy about him for weeks afterward. Looks like you still are."

"This isn't the part where you try to sell me on hooking up with Mac Flambet, is it?" asked Mercedes, and then it was Cora's turn for a scornful laugh from the group.

"Well," said Cora, unfazed, "I hadn't thought of it, but I don't see why not. You're still young and attractive. I'm sure Mac would do you in a heartbeat."

The others all laughed again, and Mercedes relaxed enough to laugh with them. "Bitch," she said.

Cora laughed. "Wait, wait, I think Frank sees us. Wave at him, and maybe he'll come over and say hi."

Mercedes shook her head. "Oh no, not me. I don't chase guys."

"I'll do it for you," said Cora, and before Mercedes could protest, she waved at Frank, smiling and familiar.

Frank saw her after a moment and waved back blankly. Wasn't that Cora Gable? Christ, and a whole passel of that crowd. Yup, with Mercedes Eden to boot. He waved again, trying to smile pleasantly enough.

"Who's that?" asked Heather with Weather.

"Some girls from another club. I mean, from a club in Ybor City. Nice bunch."

Don Adams chuckled. "Ybor City, eh, Frank? You mean nice as in 'that nice girl you'd take home to Mother,' or nice as in 'nice hooters, sweetheart?'"

They all laughed, and Frank looked nonplussed. But he acted slightly offended, as if on their behalf. "No, no, they're really a nice group of girls. Actually, the nicest of the bunch doesn't seem to be with them tonight," he added, noticing with a pang the absence of Pamela Mae Swenson.

"Well, Frank, you ought to be a gentleman and go over and say hello to these nice young ladies," said Bill Laughlin with a sneering smile. "Can't ever be too friendly with your public, you know." Frank nodded and looked back over at the girls.

"Yeah, I suppose you're right," said Frank. "I won't bring them over here, but I'll say hello. Maybe buy them a round or something. I'll do it on the way to the men's room, so I have a built-in excuse not to overstay my visit," he added, standing.

"Go get 'em, Frankie boy," said Don, and the group laughed again.

Somehow, the ridiculousness of it all relaxed him a little, bracing him for the ordeal of talking to Cora and Mercedes at the same time. "You guys are funny," he said. "Don't worry, I'm not about to go rob five cradles, Bill. One of them might be your granddaughter."

They all laughed again as he eased himself away from the table and headed toward the girls.

"He's coming this way, he's coming this way," Cora whispered. "You should invite him to join us," she said to Mercedes.

"No, no," said Mercedes. "Don't embarrass me anymore tonight, Cora."

"But really now," said Cora. "Maybe he likes you and he's just a little shy."

"A guy who makes his living on TV is shy?" she said, but by then it was too late, and Frank was nearly at their table.

"Evening, ladies," he said with a slight comic bow, his head looking small above the roly-poly body.

"You're Frank Brenkus from WRYY, aren't you?" said Cora, as if she didn't know. "I don't know if you remember me. I'm Cora."

"Sure, sure, I remember you," said Frank. "From Ladies' Night here, right?"

"Wow," she laughed, "you're good. And of course you remember my friend Mercedes."

"Sure," he said. "Hello again."

Mercedes looked up at him, then quickly away after saying hello.

"And these are our friends Lakeisha, Jill, and Arlen," said Cora, indicating each of them.

"Nice to meet you." Frank shook the proffered hands with feigned enthusiasm. He glanced at Mercedes again, but she was not making eye contact with him, and at that moment he remembered the fantasy he'd had about her in the newsroom that day. He remembered the cold, dead expression in her eyes, how he didn't like that, but then, beggars couldn't always be choosers either, could they? As long as they weren't gazing deeply into each other's eyes, he felt an urgent sexual attraction to her. She was a hot one, all right: more *model* hot than *girl-next-door* hot, actually. And her attraction to him had been undeniable.

"So how's the weather?" said Cora.

Frank heard himself say, "Well, it pays the mortgage." Secretly, it thrilled him that the girls were all laughing a bit nervously, but more than anything else, he focused on Mercedes, though it was a little too dark inside the bar to see anyone with perfect clarity. All cats are grey in the dark, he thought, and as the fantasy about her revolved in his head once more, her skirt hiked up, her legs flung wide apart, he felt himself getting aroused, and he knew he had to quickly sit or quickly exit.

"Well, you'll have to excuse me," he said, "I was just on my way to the facilities. Nice seeing you again. Nice meeting you," he added to the other three.

"Nice seeing *you* again, Frank," called Cora.

As he walked, he suddenly remembered what he'd intended to do and turned back. "I'll buy you a round on the way back."

The girls all tittered except Mercedes, who looked back and forth between Lakeisha and Cora as they grinned like mischievous children.

"He's going to buy you a round, Mercedes," teased Cora. "How about that?"

"I think he meant all of us," said Mercedes.

"Still sounds pretty promising, doesn't it?"

"Seriously, Cora, the guy has a certain attraction—after all, he's a public figure—but he really has never noticed me before."

"He's a *man*," said Cora with finality. "I guarantee you if you don't let him out of the bar tonight without you, he's yours."

"Well," said Mercedes. "I don't know. But I guess if I'm going to go for an older guy, it might as well be somebody like him, and not Mac Flambet."

"Oh, fuck Mac Flambet," Jill said.

"Cora would if he offered," said Arlen, and everyone laughed except Cora.

"Very funny," she said. "But given the choice between Mac and some of these little paupers, I'd say it's a no-brainer. Besides," she said, turning to Mercedes, "Frank's not that much older than you, is he? You're what, twenty-eight?"

"Something like that," Mercedes said.

"Well, there you go. Frank's not more than thirty-eight or forty. He can't go much lower than twenty-eight and get away with it, but it's not a huge gap."

Mercedes blanched, knowing what she meant and annoyed by the utter cattiness of it, but saying nothing.

"Hey, where's Pamela tonight?" asked Jill.

"No idea," said Lakeisha. "I thought she'd probably be here, actually. Maybe she working overtime for the Flambets this weekend."

Frank came back and sent the ladies drinks, and Mercedes realized that Cora might actually be onto something. At the end of the evening, Frank and Mercedes remained in the bar, talking idly, while the others said a discreet good night.

"You still have my number?" he asked her.

"Sure, Frank," she said. "We did go out once, remember?" She hadn't told any of the girls, not wanting to think it was going somewhere, since he hadn't called afterward.

"I remember. Seems like a long time ago now, doesn't it?"

She could tell he was slightly drunk. "Not so long ago," Mercedes purred. "Why don't you call me?"

"Give me your number again," said Frank, and she wrote it down on a napkin.

"Maybe we could see each other again before you have to call me," she said.

"I'm seeing you right now," he said, and they both laughed. "Want to get out of this place?"

She looked at him. Her and Frank Brenkus. They had both had a little too much to drink, she admitted to herself, but so what? He was going to take her home with him.

"Yeah." She smiled. "Let's get out of this place." And with one hand on his arm, she walked him out into the night.

CHAPTER 41

JAMES STOOD FOR just an instant in the middle of his living room, then resumed walking up and down in front of the great bay window.

"It's not like that, Celia," he was saying. "See, the thing with a business like Flambet Insurance is that it's almost guaranteed to lose money for the first three to five years. We've taken out a few… well, quite a few lines of credit, actually, in order to meet ongoing fixed expenses: rent, payroll, so on and so forth."

"But the bottom line," his wife interrupted, "is that you're standing here telling me we're fucking broke?"

"Not broke, exactly, because, you know, *broke* implies that it's *broken*, that it can't be fixed." He chuckled dryly, no longer smiling.

She bristled. "Goddamn it, James, stop talking in riddles and answer the question."

"Well, we just need to shore up the foundations a bit, and the first place we have to look is our personal spending. Now —" he raised a hand as she began to protest "— I'm not saying you're spending too much. What I *am* saying is that we need to find some areas to cut back. How many after-school activities is she enrolled in?"

She gazed at him coolly, her eyes showing nothing. "Your daughter has piano on Thursdays, ballet on Saturdays, and French

lessons Monday-Wednesday-Friday. But then, you knew all that…
or you would, anyway, if you were ever around to take her."

He ignored it. "Well, there you go, Celia. Does she really need
French lessons three times a week? The whole darned family's
French. She could learn from Mémé and Pépé, or from a CD set,
for that matter."

Celia recoiled. "A CD set."

He soldiered on, though he felt anything but sure of himself.
"Why not? She's a *kid*, they learn fast in any manner. Besides, isn't
that a lot of activities for someone her age? She ought to go out
and play, have some fun. Be a kid."

"Welcome to the twenty-first century, James. We're trying to
prepare her for a good university, not the local community college."

He winced. He'd gone to community college for two years
before transferring the credits to the University of South Florida.
"I know we are," he said, "but starting out in community college
hasn't put us in the poorhouse, has it?"

"Not yet."

Jesus. "Well, what do you suggest?"

Another long pause, and then she said, "Fine, we'll get her a
hundred dollars' worth of CDs, and a thousand dollars' worth of
French lessons will have gone for naught. Anything else I should
know?"

"Well," he continued, "what about all the help around here? Is
there anything we can do in that respect? You tell me."

She glared at him as if he'd just implied that her parentage was
questionable. "What do you expect me to do: fire Lakeisha and
Pamela? Or how about Jorge? I suppose I can cook meals for the
whole family seven days a week?"

"I didn't say to fire anybody. I'm just asking a question. You've
got to understand, this week I had Graham lay off three of our
own people and offload their work onto other employees just to
tighten up payroll."

"Well, you can hardly compare that to our own home. We're talking about our cook, housekeeper, and nanny. They're all we've got."

"I know, but what about their quarters? Pamela's got a place of her own in town, doesn't she? Maybe we could rent out her room."

She gasped. "A boarder? Are you serious?"

"Okay," he said. "Okay, okay. I'm just thinking out loud. We've got to do *some*thing."

"Well," she said, "make it something else. For Christ's sake, James."

He looked around the room at the décor: grand piano, track lighting, Ethan Allen furniture. You could still smell the leather of that sofa and love seat set. Hadn't they been content once, less driven, more or less able to relax and drift a little? "I'm working on it," he said vaguely.

"What about your brother?" she asked. "Couldn't he provide some help, even if 'Mémé and Pépé' can't, or won't?" She leaned on the names, heavy with sarcasm.

"Mac?" He appeared to snap out of something. "No, he's not in a position to do anything. He may be looking at having to rent an apartment soon, with his situation. They're meeting about it today, remember?"

She sneered. "Oh, come on. You really think Angela's just going to throw him out? She doesn't need that place. She'll just take the thing over and make him pay rent. It's easy money, and the pleasure of humiliating Mac is probably so valuable to Angela, I doubt she'll even raise the rent on him…at first, anyway."

James looked at her steadily. She almost seemed to exult in his brother's misfortune, and though he could see that, objectively speaking, most people would find Mac an unappealing character, it stung him to think his own wife felt that way.

"Well," he said slowly, "I'm still hoping they're going to settle out of court, but I'm not really that optimistic."

"So, are you going to give me the numbers, or what? Not on Mac's deal—I could give a shit about that. I'm talking about the company."

He took a deep breath, let it all out. Should he? She might find out the truth some other way if he didn't. It was best not to risk it. "Just a little over three," he said.

"Three?" Her face fell. "Three *million*?"

"Right."

"Jesus H. Christ, this place isn't even worth much more than two million, James." She waved her hand, indicating the whole house. "What the fuck?"

"Honey, Flambet Insurance itself would be worth at least ten if we paid all the debt down and balanced the books, maybe more. But right now, we're in the red to the tune of about three mil."

She shook her head, not looking at him. "I can't believe it. I can't fucking believe it. And when you were going to tell me? When they foreclose and start carting shit away?"

"It's not like that," he said gently. "I didn't want you to be as worried as me. But bottom line, we have to cut some expenses. I know you don't balance the checkbook, but I can tell you that if you did, you'd see I haven't drawn a salary myself for almost three months. We're living off savings. And I'm sure I'm going to have to cash in a CD or two. In fact, I was thinking second mortgage, if it comes to it. Since we refinanced not that long ago, the house payment is pretty high now, so I've wanted to avoid it, but...."

She stared at him, her face a mask of indignation, bewilderment, terror. He saw, clearly enough, the main thing concerning her was the potential loss of discretionary income, the cold fact that she might have to give up a charge account, curtail her spending. The business, the debt, was *his* problem. No more Saturdays at Saks, he thought grimly.

"All right," she said, as if they'd just settled something. "All right. We'll talk about it later." And with that, she left the room.

CHAPTER 42

ACROSS TOWN, MAC Flambet was getting in his own share of male-female conflict in Superior Court. As the judge listened with an expression of complete and abject boredom, Steve Dawson detailed how Ida Stephan placed the memo in Mac's big leather chair, how Ida knew that Mac barely glanced at such items, how Ida knew that he trusted her unquestioningly. It was all Ida, Ida, Ida, and by the look on the judge's face, it was safe to assume that he felt a repetitive rhetorical device did not necessarily make a Sermon on the Mount or "I Have A Dream" speech out of a weak defense. Mac glanced over at Steve periodically and felt the air slowly going out of the room.

"Mr. Dawson," said the judge with unutterable weariness, "Mr. Flambet signed this document in his own hand, without witnesses, in the privacy of his own offices. Correct?"

"Yes, Your Honor. However —"

"However, instead of merely acknowledging his mistake and, at the very least, employing the arbitration process to work this out with Ms. Foster—an option of which he would certainly have been well aware, as an attorney—he has instead chosen to spend his hard-earned money to have *you* take up the court's valuable time with this matter."

"Your Honor, I must protest —"

"Save it for the TV cameras, Dawson. I'm going to dismiss this as summarily as I wish I could have dismissed even hearing it." He swiveled his chair around toward Mac. "Mr. Flambet, I'm going to allow you and Ms. Foster to work this out between yourselves without so much as another word from Mr. Dawson. She is now, in effect, your landlord, and the two of you may come to terms with that in whatever way Ms. Foster deems satisfactory. If you and your counsel do not find her terms agreeable, whatever they may be, you are most certainly financially capable of securing other accommodations. Case dismissed."

And with a bang of the gavel, Mac's fate was sealed.

He walked across the steaming parking lot toward the Jaguar in silence. Steve Dawson jabbered by his side, but the word *landlord* echoed in his head like a basketball bounced in an empty gymnasium and drowned out everything else. A profound and bitter sense of déjà vu overcame him, remembering that other day, almost exactly the same—unbearably hot, sick to his stomach, lurching toward the Jaguar thinking, My ex-wife is my fucking landlord. My landlord. Then he remembered the most gut-wrenching and ugly part of that day: Dawson driving past him on the highway in the baby blue Porsche, cell phone in hand, head thrown back in laughter. Having a great day. Suddenly, Mac wheeled on his attorney and grabbed the lapels of his sport coat with a viciousness that he himself hadn't imagined possible. "Motherfucker, how the fuck can you talk like this is just some damn case? He said *Landlord*. He actually said *Landlord*."

Steve tried to pull back, terrified. "Jesus, Mac, take it easy. Just calm down. We'll work on it. We can go through arbitration, just like the judge said —"

"God fucking damn it, what do you think this is, Steve? You want me to sit down with the fucking devil and negotiate to continue enjoying the privilege of living in my own goddamn residence? Is that what you're saying?"

Steve sighed. "Well, what I started to say before you called me a motherfucker was that we are going to appeal, of course. You and I both know it's not the end of the line. Now, come on, Mac. Will you please let go?"

Mac released the lapels slowly. "Jesus H. Christ. That cocksucker told you to save it for the TV cameras like he knew you were gonna have a fucking press conference. We're not doing it, Steve. We've got no comment, and I don't want you even talking to the press. Any of them. All right?"

"Of course, of course."

Mac glanced around them and then sighed. There was no one from the press present. No one gave a shit about this except him. It wasn't a big enough story for page thirteen, *Local Attorney Hosed By Ex-Wife Out of Condo*, and the pettiness and absurdity of the whole situation infuriated him more by the second. He knew it would be fucking hilarious to them both if it was anybody else but him, and he hated to admit that it probably was still funny to Steve in his private moments.

He slammed the door of the Jag. "And Steve?"

"Yes, Mac?"

"Do me a favor. Don't call me this weekend. I don't want to talk, I don't want to play golf, I don't want to go out for a drink. I don't want to do anything. Got it?"

"I understand. Listen, Mac…no hard feelings on my part." He raised one hand, as if he were being sworn in. "Seriously."

Mac sighed and closed his eyes. "Jesus." *Like I give a shit.* He opened his eyes again. "I'll see ya," he said, and maneuvered the Jaguar out of the parking lot.

CHAPTER 43

JAMES AND GRAHAM sat across from each other in the large sunlit office, James with his back to the tinted window, looking ironically comfortable, master of his fate. He leaned back in the chair and nodded benignly, as if Graham were his best friend.

"So how did it go last week with the—what did you call it—the 'golden parachute' situation?"

"Oh, they went quietly, as expected," said Graham with little expression. In truth, though he acted nonchalant, his heart raced a bit, knowing James might not be pleased to learn Paul was one of the sacrificial lambs.

"Who did we lose again? I know we'd mentioned Claims...."

"Yes, John Alsup and Mary Corwin from Claims, and then Paul Panepinto from Servicing."

James's brow furrowed. "Paul Panepinto? What did *he* do to get fired?" His expression turned from complacent to annoyed so quickly that Graham had to slow his breath to remain calm.

"Well, it wasn't anything he'd done or not done," said Graham, avoiding eye contact. "Truth is, we really couldn't afford to lose more than two from the Claims side, and I figured Paul hadn't been here that long. I'm sure he'll land on his feet. In fact, I told him so."

James shook his head. "Yeah, but Graham, wasn't there anybody else?"

"Not really. We've got a couple girls in Servicing who started around the same time as Paul, but of course their salaries are smaller, and in fact, they're faster on the keyboard than Paul." He looked James square in the face. "All things considered, I thought it best to save the money *and* keep the productivity."

James glanced away, looking more downcast than angered, as if he himself were the one being fired. "Christ."

"Would you like me to fire someone else? I can call him up, offer him his job back." He maintained a serious expression, though the suggestion was pure sarcasm.

"No, no. I just feel bad, that's all. I liked the kid. All right, well, that's the way it is, then, right? And you say you think he'll land on his feet pretty quickly?"

"Remember what a good severance package we've got here, old man. He'll do just fine." He smiled his sinister smile, and James nodded again.

"All right," he repeated. "Well, maybe I'll just give him a call later, let him know I appreciate the work he did here."

Graham nodded without replying, and they returned to their discussion of the company's finances, pausing only for incoming calls from James's secretary. Once finished, Graham returned to his own office and James was left with the prospect of calling Paul Panepinto. He got the number from his secretary.

"Hello?"

"Paul, James Flambet."

There was a pause on the other end. "Hey, Mr. Flambet."

James drummed his fingers on the desktop. "Paul, I wanted to call you personally to say I'm sorry about our having to let you go. I know you and I talked a while back about the fact that we were trying to get some things done with creditors and so forth, but we really didn't expect to have to let people go. Graham felt you'd be the most likely candidate from the department to land on your feet quickly, and I have to say he's probably right."

"Did he tell you *that's* the reason he chose me, or was there some other reason?"

"What do you mean?"

Another pause. "Well, I'd like to use you as a reference, if I may," Paul said, his tone changed, "but I did have a concern that there may have been something else going on. I don't want to burn any bridges."

"You can use me as a reference any time, Paul. I'd be happy to recommend you, and you can give out my phone, my email, whatever you please. Matter of fact, I'll give you my cell. What's on your mind?"

Paul took a deep breath. "I'm really not comfortable talking about it over the phone, to be perfectly honest."

James sounded surprised. "Is this something concerning Graham?"

"Yes, it is, as a matter of fact. And it concerns quite a few other people in the company as well."

James cleared his throat. "Can you be a little more specific?"

"Actually…I'd really like to speak with you in person, if possible. Could we get together sometime when you're free? I can meet you whenever your schedule allows."

James looked out the window across the lawn to where the fountain shot a high arc of spray above the manmade pond. "Sure, Paul, not a problem. Let me have Jeanie call you and schedule an appointment here. No, wait, skip that. Your security clearance is already revoked. Tell you what, let me buy you lunch and we can talk then, if you're comfortable with that."

"Sure. Thank you. I'd rather do that than come by the office, actually."

"Well, Jeanie knows my schedule better than I do, so I'll have her call you and get it set up. You like Thai food?"

"Definitely."

"Okay, sir. I'll talk to you soon, probably early next week."

"Thanks for calling, Mr. F."

They hung up, and James Flambet sat looking at the phone for a few moments before he picked up the file folder on his desk. He wondered what that was all about, but he knew it would have to wait.

CHAPTER 44

TWO DAYS LATER, when David Gable finally called him back, Paul was not at home. When Paul retrieved the voicemail, he listened to it anxiously, then returned the call at once. Mr. Gable was out of the office. Paul left another message, but he continued to call back without waiting for a response. At last, after two more days, he reached him.

Gable answered his line as if he didn't know who was calling, although his secretary told Paul she'd let him know he was on the line.

"David Gable."

"Mr. Gable, this is Paul Panepinto."

The voice warmed almost imperceptibly. "Yes, Paul. What can I do for you?"

"I don't know if you remember, but I had left a message before mentioning Flambet Insurance…."

There was the sound of tapping a keyboard; Gable was obviously working while he talked.

"Yes, I've been getting your messages. Sorry I haven't tried you back more than once. Big case." He did not sound sorry.

"That's all right. Well, I work there—at Flambet Insurance—that is, I did work there. I was just recently fired."

"I'm sorry to hear that."

"That's all right. I wasn't sure how familiar you were with the company."

"Not terribly," he added, "although my daughter Cora works there."

"Yes, I know Cora."

"Really? What did you say your last name was again?"

He hesitated an instant. "Panepinto. Paul Panepinto."

David Gable repeated it. "Well, I think she may have mentioned the name," he said at length, noncommittal.

Shit. "Really?"

"Possibly. Anyway, how can I help you, Paul?"

He told him about Flambet Insurance's 401(k), about Dolores Buenas and Philip Banks.

"How long has it been since you were fired?"

"It's been a few weeks now," said Paul.

"Have you cashed out your 401(k) money or rolled it into some kind of Individual Retirement Account?"

"Yeah, I've got it converting to a Roth IRA, actually."

"Good boy," he said, sounding like a professor pleased with his student. "Well, at this point you're out of there, so they really can't screw you on your severance or your 401(k). I take it you've already deposited the severance check?"

"Yessir."

"Okay, well, then *you're* safe. I'd suggest you simply go to the police with it."

"Just with the Dolores Buenas and Philip Banks thing?"

"Sure. There's nothing I, or any other attorney, can do for you at this juncture since this Graham Woodcock, as you said, is the sole administrator of the plan. In fact, if he's confronted by way of affidavits or even some type of attorney-to-attorney correspondence, he might bolt...take the money and run, if he's able to cash it out. Even though *your* funds would be safe, you might be putting everyone else's funds in jeopardy, depending on what kind of access he has as administrator."

"Can the cops solve something like this, based on what I've got? I've always thought it was pretty flimsy, since it's just a piece of paper."

"If they think it's enough to warrant a warrant—pardon the pun—a search warrant, why, then, sure. The sheriff's office will either use their computer forensics unit, or they'll farm it out to the FBI. They just confiscate the hard drive and decode every goddamn thing he's ever done on there. From Dolores Buenas to Hot Chicks In Bondage."

Paul laughed. "Well, okay, thank you very much."

"Thank you," said Gable. "My daughter has some money in that 401(k), too, I'm sure, so I'll let her know she ought to drop out of it. But don't worry, I won't let her know about our conversation. I'll just tell her the stock market is too risky right now, and she'll do whatever I suggest. She may be my daughter, but I'm cognizant that she's not the brightest bulb in the box."

Paul laughed again, just barely, not wishing to give offense by agreeing too strongly. "Oh, I was going to talk to the company owner about it as well, just to sort of let him know what's going on. You think that's advisable, I mean, if the police are involved?"

"Flambet? Well, as long as you make sure he knows that he can't tip Woodcock off. You need to tell him that, for practical purposes, it would be illegal for him to do so. It's very important that you reassure him it's not him or his company that's being investigated, only his employee."

"Well, thanks again."

"You bet. Keep me up to date, if you would."

"I will."

CHAPTER 45

J.B. AND ALEXIS Flambet sat on their giant overstuffed leather sofa in the great room, which was rich in reds and blacks, like a parlor from a novel by Stendahl or Balzac, a monument to old world class and taste. Great Turkish tapestries hung from the walls, the chandelier glittered, although J.B. saw that it was dusty. That fucking maid, he thought—Lakesia, Shaniqua—whatever the fuck these people named their kids—Christ!

Strikingly different paintings hung on the wall opposite the stone fireplace. It was a model of eclecticism, this room, with its original Gainesborough, a Matisse lithograph, and something that looked almost as though it could have been done by Arshile Gorky, one of what J.B. called "the Alexis monstrosities." Splashes of abstract paint blotches called up nightmare images of city back alleys, barnyard slaughter, and serial killer crime scenes.

"What do you think we ought to do?" Alexis asked, her chin high, as though she were posing for a post-op plastic surgery ad.

"Well, it's that fucking Angela," he said. "She's got all the cards now. You heard the judge."

Seated in the courtroom in the row behind Mac, he and Alexis had listened to the words that fell on them like stones through the heavy recycled air. J.B. knew he'd been right all along, though it was hardly something he would gloat over: she would throw Mac out on his ass.

"I know," Alexis said wearily. "I just don't know what we ought to do for him. Probably nothing for now, at least, though that scarcely seems adequate. I hate to even trouble him with a greeting card in his state."

"Look," he said, and for a moment the two drew nearer, as if truly married in the most profound sense of the word. A sorry illusion, he had to confess. "We can't do shit for him, and really there's no need to. He's going to be *the* senior partner in another five years at most, when I retire, and in the meantime he's not exactly hurting for cash. Unless he's spending it all on some whore."

"*What?* For God's sake, Jean …."

"You know his history," he began, then changed his mind and decided to cover for him, not wanting to divulge details of Mac's more remarkable dissolutions, only some of which he knew. "I mean," he added, "he's not exactly big on long-term celibacy. He's been known to find a new floozy before the ink on his latest divorce papers is even dry. He's not seeing anyone regularly now, as far as you know, is he?"

He knew the answer in advance and felt pleased at how considerate he was being to his wife by essentially lying to her.

"No," she said, distracted by the spectre of actual whores cavorting with her son. "He hasn't mentioned anyone to me."

"Well, he's going to have to bear up as best he can. He doesn't have to pay her alimony, and his other ex-wives hardly get anything worth mentioning. I don't think he's sending out more than three grand a month to the lot of them. If he doesn't want to rent from Angela, or she decides to throw him out, he can swallow his pride and find another condo…or buy a house, for that matter. He can't be that goddamned attached to the place."

"I rather think he is."

"Well, one can't always afford to be so sentimental," said J.B., not saying it as harshly as he felt it. He was too tired to spar with her today. "By the way," he added, shifting his bulk in his seat, "has James mentioned anything to you?"

"About what?"

"He said he wanted to get together with us, and Liz as well. Not to exclude Mac, but he didn't mention him. Probably thinking he's too preoccupied with the case."

"No, he hasn't said anything about it to me. He wants to bring the family here?"

"He didn't say, though I'd supposed he meant here. Just you, me, Liz, and him. Family meeting, on some level. Strange, the way he brought it up."

"No," she said, still distant, distracted. "No, I haven't spoken to him, actually."

"Maybe he wants to ask the same question you just asked… help for Mac and all that."

"Maybe," she said. "Well, go ahead and call Liz, if you like. At least two of my children can provide me a modicum of contentment."

CHAPTER 46

LAKEISHA BENNEFIELD HAD a single ally in the world run by white women. Cora Gable ran circles around the competition when it came to neighborhood, company, and inter-acquaintance gossip, although Lakeisha was certainly a sufficiently dependable carrier of gossip of her own. What Cora didn't know, Lakeisha might, and if that didn't make her entertainment enough for Cora, then nothing would.

It probably didn't hurt, as Lakeisha well knew, that Cora had no other close friends. And although that might not exactly be flattering to *her*, it was entrée enough into the white bread world for Lakeisha, who, in any event, had plenty of friends of her own race. Though, truth be told, those friends didn't really care one way or the other how many friends she could claim in the white bread world.

Of course, there was always Pamela Mae Swenson, but she wasn't really a confidante in the style of Cora Gable. Pamela was more a colleague, a co-worker, dealing with little Eugenie Flambet while Lakeisha struggled mightily with dust bunnies and debris or whatever mess Jorge Arce left in the kitchen the previous evening. It was baffling how much of a mess that boy made.

Thus Lakeisha pondered, both on her bus ride back home from the Flambets and on her way to the Dunkin' Donuts where Cora promised a lengthy coffee and donuts session, then back home again for a short night's sleep before returning to begin another glorious day of indentured servitude with the Flambets.

Cora began talking even before the door closed behind her, and Lakeisha held her breath, almost as excited by Cora's story as Cora was, though her own news was far more interesting.

"Wait 'til you hear this shit," Cora began, oblivious to two little old ladies sitting at the counter looking up disapprovingly as she entered, perhaps at the curse, though just as likely at the too-small halter top and short skirt. "You're not going to believe it. Guess who called my father at his office."

"Who?"

"Paul Fucking Panepinto."

A darker scowl from the little old ladies.

Lakeisha's head darted forward like a cat sniffing the air. "Are you serious?"

"Serious as a missed period. Can you believe that? It's too bizarre."

"Why is Paul Panepinto calling your father?"

Cora shrugged. "Paul thinks someone is stealing from Flambet Insurance, probably Graham. Trying to get some legal advice. He didn't know I was his daughter, actually—just a coincidence—but *still*. Dad said the whole thing is confidential, attorney-client privilege and all that shit. Which is bullshit. Paul can't afford to take on my dad as his attorney, but whatever. You know how my dad is."

"That's some weird shit, girl."

"Tell me about it. I got all goose-pimply just thinking about him calling my dad."

"You really like that boy, don't you?"

"He's cute. He's always been cute. And you know he's not seeing Suzanne anymore. I always thought the office romance thing would kill it, so I wouldn't have gone after him there anyway, myself. But now that he's out of there, who knows? I mean, with Suzanne out of the picture, I could still have a shot. I can't call him, though. He'd run like a fucking little girl." She laughed through her nose.

"Speaking of guys you'd be interested in, guess what happened at the Flambets?"

"What?" Cora leaned on the table.

"They havin' this family meeting about Mac."

Her eyebrows shot up. "What about him?"

"You know he in trouble with one of his ex-wives, right? How he was going to court and all?"

"I may have heard something about it." She smiled.

"Well, apparently he signed over his condo to his ex-wife, and now she got the rights to the place. From what they were say-ing, he didn't even know he done it, some kind of accident or misunderstanding."

"That doesn't sound right. Maybe he's doing coke or some-thing." Cora laughed. "You know some of those fucking lawyers, they've got more money than sense."

"Yeah, well, it turns out the ex-wife is throwing him out. They were trying to figure out what to do for him."

Cora shook her head, taking it in. "The ex-wife booted him out? Did they say why? I mean, I heard she was a bitch—from Mac himself, obviously—but I don't see why she wouldn't want to milk him for rent as long as she could."

"She *selling* the place, and she wanted him out of there as soon as possible, so she could redecorate it and have real estate agents show it and whatnot."

"You're shitting me."

"Nope. You shoulda seen it. You woulda thought the damned baby died or something. They was cryin' and carryin' on like nobody's business. Worst thing ever happened to 'em, I guess."

Cora rolled her eyes. "Jesus. Big fucking deal. All he has to do is get another place. I think he's a partner in his father's law firm, and with that Porsche, I guarantee you he's making some coin. He must be more of a pussy than I thought."

"They sounded like he was really depressed. Said he hadn't come out in days, and was supposed to be moving his stuff out but hadn't done any of it yet."

She thought about it. "Well, if he ever needs a place to stay, I wouldn't kick him out of bed for eating crackers."

Lakeisha laughed. "You crazy, girl. I'd stay away from that one, if I was you. He got like four ex-wives, I think."

"That's all right. It just means he's probably gotten pretty good at fucking, 'cause he's had a lot of practice."

Lakeisha laughed again. "Crazy," she said. "You really crazy."

CHAPTER 47

THE APARTMENT LOOKED worse than ever, and Paul knew
it. He stared at the television by the hour, drained of energy, thinking only of the 401(k), of Dolores and Philip, of the supposedly
robust job market. Of course, it didn't matter yet, he still had thou-
sands in the bank, but he had to look for work in order to qualify
for unemployment compensation. And eventually, he would have
to find a new position.

He hated the Unemployment Office, hated its outdated computer system and outdated listings of crappy jobs. Most of all, he
hated their lax attitudes toward helping people find work. So he sat
in front of the television, hour after hour, not yet admitting that he
was, in fact, depressed.

The free legal advice from David Gable had been so skimpy
that Paul still wasn't even really sure what to do, or what he would
say, but waiting was no longer an option. He had to meet James the
following afternoon, and then at least he'd know whether or not
he could really move forward and go to the police. He'd decided
that much.

He had to run it by James first, rather than trying to get someone to go in there with a search warrant or something. Stuck in
the middle position between inaction and possibly too-aggressive
action, he'd decided to make a decision only after he had talked to
James. It felt cowardly to wait, and yet he didn't think he could just

go ahead with contacting police, filing a report, whatever might be required, if he didn't at least let James know that that might be necessary.

Beyond that, he was preoccupied with Suzanne, the one person he didn't want to think about at all.

It had been weeks since they'd spoken, and he knew she had to be well aware he was gone. It would have been all over the office. He didn't really expect her to call him, but he wasn't entirely ready to let go. On some level, he still wanted her, in spite of what happened, in spite of what she'd said.

He thought about it—his responsibility to her, to the company's other employees, to himself. He felt now that he was the only one who could save them from Graham, if anyone could. It was up to him alone. Freedom from employment meant freedom to pursue the case, if he could call it that yet, but he had to admit it also meant more responsibility than he'd ever had or even wanted. The fear of failure was never far away, and he had to admit that, too.

He spent a restless night before he went to meet James at the Thai restaurant. He wandered around the apartment, shut the TV off, tried to read. Distracted by his own thoughts, he turned the TV back on, then read and watched TV at the same time. Nothing worked. The thought that somehow he would have to finally face up to the truth and gird himself for battle was inescapable, rolling around in his mind continually. Anything he did to try to drive it out only made it that much stronger.

How had it come to this? He thought of the long and sometimes idle days at Flambet Insurance, watching the slow arc of spray from the fountain, listening to Muddy Waters or Horace Silver on the old boombox. Two years, he thought. Hard to believe he had gotten away with so little work and done such a menial job—it was almost a résumé-buster, and would have been, truly, if anyone knew just how slack things really were in that office. The thought served as a reminder that he needed to update his résumé.

Before he went to bed, he headed out for a walk through the neighborhood, an old section of Tampa that he hadn't taken time to even notice recently. He needed to get some air, clear out the cobwebs. He slipped into his old worn running shoes and headed into the night.

Typical Florida weather awaited him, muggy with a slight breeze, the sky overhead revealing only a handful of stars. He walked past the houses on Himes Avenue, then changed his mind and headed toward Armenia and the Vietnamese, Filipino, and Chinese neighborhoods. The houses, painted in oddly sedate colors, made him feel like he was in New England—pale blues, grays, off-whites. Not one had a classic "Florida" color, those shell-pinks and yellows and greens so popular in the established beach neighborhoods in Clearwater and St. Pete, or, farther down the coast, in Sarasota and Fort Myers.

He noticed that a few of the houses had been recently painted different colors, and some of the old live oaks in the front yards had been cut down, presumably to keep them from growing too close to power lines or telephone wires. The storefronts that sprouted up just past the edge of the subdivision flickered like worn-out Christmas lights: Aimco, La Seña Gun and Pawn, Mick's Auto Repair. No doubt, it was pretty much a shit neighborhood. Mi barrio, he thought ironically.

He walked on, thinking of Suzanne. It hadn't ended well, but neither had anything else for quite some time. The job at Flambet, the long on-again off-again fling with Inocente Madrigal Fuentes. He wondered how she was doing. It had been a good six months or more since they'd talked, and she'd been in a treatment center at that point. *Coke,* he remembered her saying, *was what brought me to my knees.*

He knew he couldn't go back there, knew she wouldn't be ready, for him or for anyone else. She'd told him as much and he'd said he'd understood, and they'd parted amicably enough. How odd that he was even thinking of her, especially because Suzanne was so much different—more refined, he thought, more sophisticated. But it was the sex, he was forced to admit. That was the real draw. Goddamned celibacy, he muttered, and laughed, in spite of himself. The moon hung higher in the sky now, no longer harvest orange. Almost white. He turned and walked back toward the house, his mind blessedly empty at last.

CHAPTER 48

JORGE ARCE WONDERED whether he was going to have to look for part-time work. Cooking for the Flambets wasn't the worst job in the world, he knew; he'd been a short order cook, and this was much better. The pay was only slightly more, of course, but after all, the Flambets were a family, not a full-service restaurant.

Still, he couldn't help acknowledging the superiority of the surroundings: a beautiful home, well-manicured lawn, even living quarters for the household staff. And the house was generally peaceful, quiet. It didn't elevate him to a better lifestyle, but it was a nice enough place to work.

But now things suddenly looked bleak. He'd heard rumblings around the house about The Market, which he presumed meant the stock market, and then there was the whole mess with Mac. Jorge knew Mac had lost the case, the whole family talked about it almost incessantly, and every time Jorge overheard Celia Flambet talking to Pamela Swenson or Lakeisha Bennefield, it was either about reducing household expenses or, worse, the possibility of cutting their hours.

Bringing it up with Eula was out. She had enough to worry about, and besides, she was trying to get him on the marriage track. The mere mention of a possible loss of income would be an unwelcome intrusion into their relationship, which had, most recently, grown positively nerve-racking.

The only place he could take his worries was the priest at confession, which he did not want to do. A lifelong Catholic and member of the mostly Latino Santo Domingo church in north Tampa, Jorge went to Mass religiously every Sunday, and knew most of the regular sections by heart as a result. *We believe in one holy Catholic and apostolic church. We acknowledge one baptism for the forgiveness of sins. We look for the resurrection of the dead, and the life of the world to come. Amen.* And when he thought about what to say and what to do, he merely supposed he ought to pray for prosperity for the family. In any case, he'd leave Eula out of it unless he actually had something to tell her.

As if on cue, he heard Eula's key in the lock. She entered the apartment, laden with groceries: cheap mangoes from the Oriental food store, strange drinks with grass jelly or basil seeds in them, exotic-looking fish, bitter candies. Her face was impassive as a statue.

"Hey," he called, hopeful.

"Hey," she said. She unpacked the groceries briskly.

"What you got there?"

"Food." She sounded peevish, as if the question were a stupid one.

"Need help?"

"I think I'm good. How was work?"

"Not bad," he said.

"Oh yeah?" She smiled. "What's new in Flambetland?"

He laughed. "Is that like Disneyland?"

"More like Crazy Person Land, from what you tell me." Her voice sounded a little softer, and so he rose, chuckling, and walked out to the kitchen to kiss her hello.

"It's always the same at the Flambets," he said, "pretty boring. How's your day?"

She handed him a grass jelly drink. "Same old shit. Boss lady on the rag, boss man trying not to piss her off." She smiled briefly and rolled her eyes.

Jorge drummed his fingers on the countertop, looking distracted. "You ever think about quitting?"

She stopped unpacking the groceries and looked at him with narrowed eyes. "Only every day. Not seriously, though. Can't neither one of us afford to quit our jobs. How would we pay the rent?"

He nodded. "I know. I'm just sayin' maybe you could find something else?" He winced inwardly; he was the one who should be thinking about a job change.

"Well," she said, "I don't know. I mean, I'm glad you're paying part of the rent, because then I can work that cheap-shit job and not stress about keeping a roof over my head, but I don't think I'm gonna find better unless I go back to school. Maybe if you moved in here full-time and left the 'Flambet servants' quarters' behind, you could take care of the place while I'm out looking for my new job or going to school or whatever …."

She'd begun massaging his shoulders during this last bit, abandoning the groceries for a moment.

"The only problem," Jorge said, "is the transportation issue. I mean, it's fine for me to be over here a few times a week, but driving all the way over to the Flambets and back twice a day is almost fifteen miles one way, and with gas prices…." He let it trail off.

The pressure on his shoulders ceased. "Yeah, but fuck, man. How long are we gonna do this?"

He turned around and looked at her, then glanced away when he saw the look in her eyes. It was either anger or hurt, possibly both. Against his better judgment he asked, "Do what?"

"This part-time relationship shit. You being here only when it's, like, convenient."

"Can we not talk about marriage tonight, please?"

"Who's talking about marriage?" She turned her back to him and loaded cans of food into the cabinet. "Hell, I'm not even mentioning you not putting a ring on my finger or anything like that. I'm just talking about shacking up. Living in sin."

"We already do that, don't we? Just not *every single day*."

She laughed bitterly, turning back to him. "Yeah, you pay some money for what ends up being like the cheapest motel room in town. Never mind, forget I brought it up."

After a moment he said, "It's going to be one of those nights, isn't it?"

"Don't feel like you have to stay out of obligation," she said. "I didn't know whether you were even going to be here tonight anyway, so I didn't buy food for both of us."

He looked at her levelly, expressionless and furiously silent. "Fine," he said, turning. "I'll talk to you later."

Just before he closed the door, he heard her burst into tears. He'd intended to exit quietly, but somehow the sound made him slam the door.

CHAPTER 49

WHEN PAUL WENT to meet James at Sabai Thai the following day, he still retained a remnant of the previous night's nervousness, still not exactly sure what he would say. Reviewing the possibilities in his mind brought him no nearer to a solution. Every opening gambit sounded too glib, too timid, too dull. He was more than nervous—he was afraid.

But when the two were seated and had ordered drinks, he suddenly felt as though the ordeal had already ended. He looked across the polished wooden table at James Flambet and saw no longer the slightly intimidating presence of a boss but instead the somewhat rumpled figure of a former employer, a man with troubles and problems of his own. Paul was not there to accuse James or to give him more problems, but to help him.

He realized he'd had nothing to fear all along, and a great sense of relaxation suffused his entire being. It would be all right, whatever the outcome of their conversation, and he would not burn any bridges. He would still retain the reference from James, he was sure of that much.

The waitress returned with their drinks and asked if they were ready to order. Paul sipped his water with lime, deferring to James.

"Chicken with mixed vegetables," James said.

Paul handed back the luncheon menu. "I'll have the red curry with coconut milk," he said.

"How spicy you want?" the waitress asked.

"Not too spicy."

They sat back and relaxed, sipping their drinks. After a minute of small talk—questions about what Paul was planning to do next, whether he'd had any good job offers—James leaned forward, elbows on the table, and asked, "So, what was it you wanted to talk to me about?"

"Well, Mr. Flambet —"

"Please, James...."

He took a deep breath. "James. I made a...discovery when I was still working there that I need to tell you about, but it's more a story than just an incident."

"Okay."

"That is, I have to explain it to you in some detail."

"All right."

And he told James about Dolores Buenas and Philip Banks. He'd pulled the documents from a red file folder and explained what happened under Graham's sign-in, how he'd gotten to the records accidentally and didn't know how to get back to them, how he'd tried to research the résumés and found the information inaccurate. He told James his suspicions about the 401(k), how he'd searched Morningstar, called the company, gotten nowhere with customer service, how they'd merely referred him back to Graham.

James perused the documents as Paul spoke, his brow furrowed. At last, his face cleared and he asked the one question Paul had dreaded hearing: "Why didn't you tell me about this before?"

But Paul was ready. "Well," he said, "to be perfectly honest, I was afraid you might take it to Graham himself. And that looked like a recipe for getting fired." He sipped his water. "In fact, I wondered whether Graham suspected I knew something, because I found it pretty strange he just happened to choose me to fire out of all the people in the department."

James nodded. "Understandable," he said, then looked away.

"Also, I was thinking there might be some kind of connection to that whole McDillon thing. I don't know, but I was definitely looking for a connection when I went through those spreadsheets, though I never found one. Graham looked at me funny, in sort of a patronizing way, when he found out you'd asked me to work on McDillon. He looked like he was gloating when I said I couldn't explain the missing fields. Like he knew I hadn't gotten him."

James folded his hands on the table.

"Well, quite frankly, Paul—and I can confide in you on this because you're no longer an employee—Graham's accounting practices have been something of a mystery to me since we got this newest software system. I don't know if I've just been too trusting, or if you're barking up the wrong tree. But if this is true, then I'm all for having it investigated, of course. I want you to let me know if there's anything you need, and you have my word that, obviously, I'll accommodate you any way I can."

"Thank you," said Paul, nodding. He searched James's face, still wondering whether he'd made a mistake. He didn't think so, but he had scarcely begun. "There may be a need to bring the police into it," he added. "I don't know everything yet, but I consulted an attorney —"

"Really?" James looked stunned, but Paul wasn't sure if he was impressed or wounded. Perhaps he was already thinking of bad publicity, the effect on creditors and customers.

"Well, just a brief conversation, actually. The attorney wasn't an expert in that area, he said, but he suggested going straight to the police. He also suggested I tell you that it would be illegal to let Graham know about our conversation, as well as impractical, of course. He told me I should emphasize that neither you nor the company would be investigated, just Graham. And anyone else who might have had access, obviously, like the computer guys.

Anyway, I figured I had to at least run it by you before I do anything. Like I said, I don't want to be burning any bridges."

"No, no, of course not. And you're not burning any bridges with me. Don't worry about that." He tapped his fingertips on the table, the old abstracted look on his face. "Sure, go ahead and contact them. Let them know you spoke with me, and see what they say. I suspect they'll suggest the company investigate it internally, in which case I'll need to get other people involved, but let me know what they tell you before they take any kind of action. I don't want a surprise police visit at the office."

"Absolutely. I understand it's your company. I'm just trying to help."

"I appreciate it." James looked at him, unguarded, and Paul knew he had not made a mistake. James's eyes conveyed the regret even before he said, "You know, I'm sorry we had to lose someone like you, Paul. But maybe that's the only way I would have found out about this situation."

Paul nodded. "I suppose so."

"Let me know what the police say, and keep me updated on your job search as well, if you would. Depending on how things work out, we may be able to find a place for you again if you'd be willing to consider an offer."

Paul smiled graciously. "Thank you," he said.

CHAPTER 50

FRANK BRENKUS STOOD on his balcony at the top of Crump Tower Tampa, fifty-two stories above the Bay, naked but for a pair of neon orange swimming trunks. He wavered high above the tiny sunbathers, one white pudgy fist in the air, shouting down at them in drunken fury.

"You're not kidding anyone, you know. You'll all be old and ugly someday. You're not helping anyone down there."

Frank was awaiting the arrival of Mercedes Eden, having spent that fateful night with her on a different drunken whim. Now he wasn't so sure it had been a good choice. He hadn't used protection, and in his stupor, he hadn't asked Mercedes whether or not she was on birth control. An ill-advised move, he realized now. He had to find a tactful way to ask without pushing her to make a scene, and especially without jeopardizing his opportunity to get laid again…assuming, of course, that he remained sober enough to perform.

The doorbell rang, and Frank lurched toward it, splashing part of a 25-ounce Foster's Lager onto his New Zealand wool carpet. "Just a minute," he called, realizing he couldn't manage the door with a beer in one hand and the iPod in the other. He set down the Foster's can, plucked the ear buds from his ears, and swapped the iPod for the beer can on his way to the door.

The bell rang a second time.

"Be right there," he called, though nearly at the door by now.

There stood Mercedes, a vision in red and black. Her eyes were still not quite right, thought Frank, but what the hell. All cats are grey in the dark, he reminded himself, and besides, they hadn't exactly spent every moment face to face the last time they'd gotten together. In fact, he thought, he'd like to be looking at the back of her head in about an hour if he could manage it.

"Hey, Frank," she purred. She leaned up and kissed him demurely on the cheek, still unsure enough of her position to go for the lips. Frank saw this, and a self-congratulatory thrill rushed through him. It was good to be the weatherman.

"Hey, babe," he said nonchalantly, though he kissed her on the lips as if to make up for the casual tone. "That's no way to kiss your daddy," he said. "It's gotta be on the lips."

"Daddy?" she said, misunderstanding the intent. "Why daddy?" She did not look amused.

"'Who's your daddy? Who's your daddy?'" He slapped her on the ass.

She laughed, though hesitantly. "You men are all alike," she said.

"Especially us weathermen," he said. "Today's forecast: very horny, with a slight chance of a golden shower."

"Ewww."

He laughed. "Wasn't sure you'd even know what that meant, but don't worry. I'm just kidding."

"I'm not that naïve," she said. "I know all about that stuff: water sports, bondage, you name it." She paused and studied him. "I'm just not freaky like that. I like a little romance, like most women do." She sat on the white leather sofa and crossed her legs primly.

"Most women?" He tried to hold on to his bantering tone. "You know *any* women who don't bother with romance?"

"If I did, I wouldn't introduce them to you." She recrossed her legs in the other direction.

Frank laughed. "I'm not that bad, am I?"

"Well, why don't you come sit by me and we'll talk about it?"

He realized that he was still standing in the middle of the room, not even particularly close to her. "Be right there," he said. "I've gotta use the facilities real quick. Drink?"

She looked around, at a loss. "Sure, what do you have?"

"Fully stocked liquor cabinet," he said, waving over his shoulder. "Help yourself, or if you want a mixed drink, I can fix you one soon as I come back. I warn you in advance, though, I make 'em strong."

Now it was her turn to laugh. "No doubt."

He left the bathroom door ajar as he pissed and continued the conversation with her from afar. "Did you ever hear any more about that little love triangle you were telling me about last time?"

She chuckled again. "No, not really. It's not really a love triangle, though: Cora Gable likes Paul Panepinto, and Paul dated Suzanne Beidertyme, but Paul and Cora have never actually hooked up."

"Ah," he said, nodding seriously. "I see, said the blind man."

"Paul's free now, but I still don't think he would ever actually go for Cora."

"Understandable." He flushed and began washing his hands.

"That's mean."

Frank laughed. "On the other hand, if he could manage to get them both together, I'm sure your pal Paul would go for some threesome action there. Any man would, even though it's Cora." He returned, flopped down on the sofa beside her.

Mercedes laughed. "Well, no, Cora and Suzanne hate each other, so it's not like they'd ever do that…unless they were drugged."

He frowned. "Now, *that* might not be a bad idea."

"You pig." She slapped his arm weakly. "I can't believe you'd think that."

"I'm just kidding," he said. "So what about you, you wanna fuck?"

Mercedes blanched. "Jeez, Frank, you get right to it, don't you?"

"Hey, when you get to be my age, every minute counts. You don't want to miss out on any opportunities."

"Well, try to stay a little sober and I'll catch up with you, okay? Then we can build up to it. How's that?"

"Anything you say, babe."

"Maybe we can go out first."

He looked around, then leered at her. "Or maybe we can go out afterward," he said.

It was a battle she was willing to lose, knowing she hadn't really hooked him yet with the sex and that, in the end, even sex might not be enough.

Later, after the drinks and the inevitable sex (again he'd neglected to ask her about birth control, forgetting about it completely a second time), they lay together just like real lovers, drifting on a wave of post-coital contentment. Mercedes said, "I'm really kind of freaked out about this whole thing with Cora."

Frank chuckled. "Cora. What a piece of work. You said her father told her Paul Panepinto called him about what?"

"Paul thinks his old boss is stealing from Flambet Insurance, and he called Cora's dad looking for advice about it. I'm not supposed to know about it. And neither are you, for that matter ."

"Like I give a shit."

"I know, I know, but it's the principle."

"I went to school with James Flambet, actually."

"Really?"

"Yup."

"Wow, Frank, you're old."

He laughed. "Not that old."

"Anyway, Paul told Cora's dad he thinks Graham Woodcock is embezzling from the company somehow, and then Cora told me."

"Graham Woodcock."

"Don't even say it."

Frank cackled hideously. "I don't have to. Some jokes write themselves. Fucking Woodcock."

She poked him in the ribs. "Anyway, don't say anything about it to anybody, okay? I'm seriously not supposed to know. I don't even know Paul personally. And there may be a police investigation, for all I know."

"Yeah, an investigation of the Wood Cock," he snorted, laughing again.

"Shh," said Mercedes. "Shh."

CHAPTER 51

GRAHAM LIFTED A Manhattan to his lips and drank deeply. It was dead summer in Tampa, ninety-five degrees and climbing, and so he thought of London and his last few days of cool freedom before he'd embarked for the home of the brave and the land of the not-exactly-free. He pictured the tiny flat he'd stayed in that last year, how he stood at the window and stared blankly across the rooftops of the great city through falling snow at the beveled tops of industrial buildings and whole neighborhoods squatting like great square mountains, hunkered down in the shroud of mist and fog, white clouds, snow and sleet. On days like those, he'd played cassette tapes endlessly, setting up one after another and changing the music rapidly, urgently, a metaphysical deejay striving to create and sustain a mood, a sublime and gentle melancholy as funereal and beautiful to him as an autumn rain, lulling him into a dreamy longing at once intangible and elliptical.

He was slightly drunk now, and thinking of London made him remember the prostitute—Donna? Lana?—in the Plant City bar, years ago. Back before he'd become second-in-command at Flambet Insurance, he'd gone there with a co-worker, long gone now, who asked him, "So, how do you like working for what's-his-name?"

He'd thought about it. "Well, apart from the fact that he walks around sucking his teeth and humming such great musical compositions as the theme from *The Addams Family*, I have no problem at all."

The co-worker had laughed sharply and told him on the way to the bar, "I'm gonna get you laid tonight."

The prostitute stood at the bar beside him and sized Graham up coolly from the corner of her eye. She'd looked like anything but his idea of a hooker: shorter-than-average hair, regular features, pretty only to a point. An average-looking young woman at best, not too thin though with no excess fat on her either. She was dressed shabbily, like a factory worker, jeans and plain Jane shoes.

"You need a date?" she asked.

He looked at her and looked away, surprised she had spoken to him and still not completely sure she was what he thought she must be. She looked too normal. No lipstick, no visible makeup. Nothing fancy, even, about her hair.

"Yeah," he said, not meeting her eyes. "Yeah, I need a date."

"Forty dollars, half and half."

He gave her another furtive glance, so out of his element he felt almost panicky in spite of the Yukon Jack he'd been drinking. "Half and half?"

"One blow, one fuck. Forty dollars." In the background, the jukebox was playing *The House of the Rising Sun*, an irony not lost on Graham.

"Sure, sure. No problem." Though her blasé tone astonished him, the low number was almost a relief. He had little money. But then, it was incredibly low. Frighteningly low.

"Whenever you're ready, baby," she said flatly. Clearly a business transaction to her. Still, he felt she was pleased somehow, at the very least relieved, to have a trick who wasn't fat, or an old man. He wondered with embarrassment whether she thought he would prematurely ejaculate, a "two-stroke joke," as his college friends would have said. He'd never had that problem. By the time I'm done, he thought drunkenly, she'll want to pay *me*.

But then they were back in her shitty hovel of an apartment, and he felt increasingly more fucked up, almost to the point where the room would begin to spin. They fell onto the bare mattress on the floor, the whole thing a grim experience, shockingly raw and without any merit whatsoever. Her vagina was cavernous, far too large for his average-sized cock, and although he was horny enough to fuck, and plunged into her again and again, he was too drunk and too sickened by the whole scene to actually come, too worried about venereal disease, AIDS, whatever.

He had not carried protection, and she had not even brought it up, and so he plunged into her joylessly, repeatedly, for what felt like an eternity, sweat dripping from his forehead, while she lay supine, making no sound other than her somewhat labored breathing, her eyes studying the ceiling, expressionless, far away from him and the forty dollars and the dirty grey mattress. He wondered whether she was thinking anything at all. Maybe she was going to go cop drugs afterward, and was just counting the minutes.

When he'd finished—stopped, actually, as he never did achieve an orgasm, the combination of alcohol, fear and disgust having made it impossible—he lurched out into the street and hitched a ride from some grinning maniac drunk enough to pick up a hitchhiker in the city in the middle of the night. Somehow, the grinning maniac let him crash on his couch, which sat in the center of a living room space in another shitty apartment, this one filled with overly friendly poodles. In the morning, he came to, intolerably hung over, covered in and stinking of dog hair, and feeling as though he'd given, not sold, his soul to the devil.

CHAPTER 52

THE NIGHT BEFORE Paul called the Tampa police, he drove to the department store to look for a wedding present for an old friend and former colleague. David Johnson from the Flambet Insurance Underwriting department had been a workout partner until Paul switched to a cheaper gym, and the two had shared the occasional beer and inevitable commiseration about the single women in Tampa. When Paul received the wedding invitation, his heart clenched momentarily. It was hard to believe old Dave had found the love of his life in just the past eighteen months, while Paul was still slogging his way through the dating scene.

With Suzanne gone and no one on the horizon who might attend the wedding with him, he would have to go stag. A casual dating situation would not lend itself well to a wedding, even if he found someone else. Of course, he was glad for his friend, but not really all that thrilled about attending *any* wedding at this point, especially without a date.

There was no getting out of it, though. Everyone knew what had happened with Suzanne by now, and with the severance package from Flambet he couldn't very well claim the status of the poor unemployed schmuck who can't afford a gift. Not that he would have done that—Dave had asked him to be a groomsman in the invitation.

So he prowled the aisles of the only reasonably priced place the couple registered, trying to find something appropriate but not too showy. The only thing worse than being the single guy at the reception was being the one who attracted a lot of attention. He glanced at the list of potential items and then continued on his way, searching for the best option. The air conditioning in the store had made the temperature glacial, and he shivered slightly as he walked.

When he looked up and saw Suzanne in the bed and bath section, his brain did not register it at first. It was too outrageous, too improbable, as when a child sees one of his teachers outside of the classroom and cannot believe that this individual could possibly lead an existence apart from school. How could she defy the rules of logic and reason and appear in front of him at this moment in their shared history like a deus ex machina, or better yet, demon ex machina, in some cheesy romantic comedy? For if there was one thing of which Paul was sure, it was that his life, far from being comic, was essentially tragic.

All this flashed through his mind in less than a second, far too little time to self-censor what immediately came to his lips, or rather, under his breath: "Fuck."

Suzanne had undoubtedly spotted him first and taken time to compose herself silently before he'd even seen her. With scarcely a glance in his direction, she replied, as if he'd spoken to her directly, "Not exactly a welcoming reaction to someone who was once close, but I suppose I shouldn't be surprised." And she turned on one heel and slowly walked away.

The entire incident took all of five seconds, but for Paul, time virtually stopped. He saw it with the slow-motion horror of a fatal shooting or car accident, and as he stood rooted to the spot, he felt the perspiration on his forehead and a flush that spread across his face. He followed her before he even had time to think what to say, and without any more thought than he'd been able to give the curse, he called, "Suzanne."

She glanced back over her shoulder and slowed, but kept walking. She did not pause until he said one last word.

"Wait."

Even when she'd let him catch up with her, her face and manner gave no encouragement. Not the slightest bit flustered—unlike him, with his burning face and relentless perspiration—to the contrary, she stood cool as dry ice and gazed at him with the kind of slight inquisitiveness she might have reserved for a marginally unpleasant salesman or an elderly man asking her to help him find his car in a bewilderingly large parking garage.

"Listen," he said, still sticking to the one word theme. He took a deep breath and fought to form a full sentence. "I'm sorry, I just…I didn't expect to see you, of all people, here —"

"I do shop," she said with just the trace of a smirk.

"— I know, and…it's good to see you, Suzanne —"

"So good that you just can't help saying 'fuck.'" She looked away.

"I'm sorry," he said, painfully aware he'd just apologized twice within the same minute. "I – I should have called you."

She stiffened, and her expression changed from mild inquisitiveness to something he couldn't read: blank, not especially sympathetic. "Called me?"

"I mean it's been a while since we talked at all—since before I got fired —"

"Yes, I was sorry to hear about that." She did not look or sound sorry at all as she glanced away again.

"Well," he said, at a loss. "That's all right." He looked down. "I wanted to call you to tell you, but somehow I just couldn't do it then. I guess I was still kind of pissed off."

"*Were* you?"

He looked up again, but still read nothing definable in her eyes. "Yeah," he said, "sure I was. You must have been, too."

"Oh, I don't know." She looked at something on the shelf beside them and absently fingered it. "It all seems like a long time ago now, doesn't it?"

His eyes followed her movements as she turned away yet again, his heart still in his throat. Her perfume annihilated him. He wanted some encouragement, but if she'd given him any, he'd missed it. He didn't even really know what else to say, but then he realized that she'd asked him a question, however rhetorical. He nodded, serious. "Yeah, it does seem like a long time ago. How have you been doing?"

It was the first direct question he had asked her, he suddenly realized, and she warmed exactly one iota. "Fine. Found another job?"

When their eyes met again, he saw that they'd regressed so far back even small talk was awkward. "No," he said, "no new job yet. You're still at Flambet?"

"Of course," she said, with mock enthusiasm.

He wondered whether he brought out the sarcasm in her, or if she'd always been like this, and he remembered telling her she had always been reserved before they had gone out, even distant. She was distant now, in another time zone.

"Listen, Suzanne…I —" he touched her arm lightly.

She recoiled. "Don't."

It was all she had to say. The movement, the expression, told him everything he feared, and more than he'd wanted to know.

"I gotta go," she said.

"I know, me too. I've got a present I need to buy for some people."

She looked at him, less hurt now, maybe, less angry. "See you later."

He grasped at this as if it were an invitation. "Okay," he said. "I'll…I'll give you a call sometime."

Again, she looked at him blankly. "Yeah," she said. That was all, and then she was gone.

CHAPTER 53

ALTHOUGH STILL YOUNG enough to be somewhat caught up in the club scene with her other women friends, Pamela Mae Swenson found herself increasingly isolated by the demands of being Eugenie's nanny. Naturally, there were the occasional trips to her actual apartment—punctuated periodically with an inevitable *coitus interruptus* of her roommate Sarah and the hapless Ron—but more and more, she had to stay at the Flambets to take care of tasks that fell far outside the normal requirements of a nanny's station.

First, there was the grocery shopping. To Pamela, it would have made far more sense to have Jorge purchase whatever food the family needed for their ongoing needs, since he was their cook. But somehow, Celia Flambet decided it was Pamela's job to "shop for the baby," *a seven-year-old baby*, and of course, Celia was not to be questioned. Taking Eugenie to school was an understandable nanny task. But having to fill in at parent-teacher conferences or student activities when Celia needed new hair extensions or facial peels was simply too much.

Then there was the tutoring. Although Eugenie was perspicacious in a social setting, and had a facility with words, she was nearly hopeless in the areas of math and science. And so it fell to Pamela to tutor her in both, a responsibility she found almost as cumbersome as Eugenie herself found the subjects.

Small wonder, then, if Pamela couldn't stand to face Saturday morning after a Friday night in Ybor City or, the newest thing, going to The Pier in St. Pete for a night of body shots, loud music, and the fending off of drunken idiots. She rolled out of bed at 6:00 a.m. after only three hours' sleep, threw water on her face and applied fresh makeup, then headed straight to the Flambets, eating an energy bar in the car and arriving at the house at 6:30 with a pounding headache that didn't feel much better even after a half liter of bottled water. Almost tempted to make herself a Bloody Mary in the kitchen to see if it really worked as a hangover cure, she'd never taken a drink in the morning and decided she wasn't about to start now. She could live with the pain.

The scene at the Flambets was annoyingly chaotic, with Lakeisha in the living room cleaning the large bay window, Jorge in the kitchen cooking, and, inexplicably, Mac Flambet lying unmoving on the floral-patterned Ethan Allen sofa, one forearm flung casually over his brow, as if he'd slept there. He leered as Pamela passed, his eyes blinking like a lizard's, and she pretended not to notice him.

Along with Jorge, Pamela found a bleary looking James in the kitchen, dressed in his bathrobe, a cup of coffee in his hand. Eugenie was already up, too, eating cereal and drinking orange juice. She made a face each time she took a sip of her juice.

"Hey, Pam. She's up early today with Daddy," he added by way of explanation.

Pamela smiled formally and spoke directly to Eugenie: "You're having an early breakfast, huh?"

"This juice is sour," Eugenie said.

"That's because your cereal is very sweet," said Pamela.

"Thanks for getting here so early," James added. "I've gotta run." He took a last sip of coffee and rose to exit. "Another thrilling day at the office."

Pamela smiled again with forced warmth, though she really did like James well enough. "See you later."

James left and Pamela talked to Jorge about the day's menu. Before she had a chance to take Eugenie upstairs to get her ready, Mac slouched into the kitchen, looking even blearier than James. "Still got some coffee left, Jorge, my boy?"

"Sure, Mr. Flambet." He served it as if they were in a restaurant. Pamela seethed inwardly, though she was much too hung over to think about it long.

"Pamela Mae Swenson," said Mac, turning his leer upon her again.

"Good memory."

"Certainly," he said, and grinned.

"I'm surprised to see you here," she said neutrally.

His expression turned serious again. "I'm off this week, moving into a new place, but half my stuff is still in storage." He sighed.

"Ah. I knew there had to be a reason you weren't up and out early like James."

Mac raised an eyebrow. "I wake up at five every morning like clockwork, whether I want to or not. No point getting up today, though."

She began to clean up Eugenie's place. "Mm," she said.

"Well, see ya later," Mac said. "I'm gonna catch a shower."

"See ya," she said.

CHAPTER 54

THE TAMPA POLICE Department's 24-hour information line answered Paul's call in the traditional manner: with an automated attendant. After listening to a bewildering menu of choices, he decided it sounded like the correct line would actually be the Hillsborough County Sheriff's office, so he hung up and called them. But when he told them why he was calling, they asked for the address of Flambet Insurance, and after he gave it, they referred him back to the police, and their Non-Emergency Dispatch line. He hesitated. He'd already made two phone calls, and now he would have to make a third, and he knew it was the right line now, yet he hesitated. He felt the same as he'd felt the night before he talked to James, the finality of it. Once he made that call, there was no turning back. He would be in it as deeply as if it were *his* business, *his* company.

What business was it of his, really? Sure, he'd been fired, but possibly not even for the nebulous reasons he thought. And with that fat severance check sitting in the bank swelling his checking account, he didn't have to look for work right away. He was, compared to his entire past history, relatively well off whether it was related to Graham or not.

For a moment, he even considered just blowing the whole thing off, letting it slide. And when James called him to follow up, after a week or two of hearing nothing, what then? What would he say? Well, James, you know, I've been thinking…maybe it's not really any of my business after all. Maybe it would be best if you called the police yourself. Here's their Non-Emergency number. Sorry about all that.

Still, he dialed the number. It rang seven times before the recording began.

You have reached the City of Tampa Police Department. All of our operators are busy with other callers at this time. Your call will be answered in the order it was received. If you have an emergency, hang up and dial 911. The entire message then played in Spanish before beginning again: *You have reached….*

After a third repeat of the message, a live voice came on and said, "Tampa Police 622 on a recorded line."

"Good morning, this is Paul Panepinto calling. I had a question about surveillance and computer forensic analysis."

"Let me get you downtown to our Info Counter. They might have somebody down there who can help you."

He was transferred automatically and then listened to a variation on the same message.

Thank you for calling the Tampa Police Department. If this is an emergency, hang up and dial 911. Normal business hours for most operations of the Tampa Police Department are nine a.m. to five p.m., Monday through Friday.

For information in English, press one. Para información en Español, oprima el dos.

This last bit played in a loop: *For information in English, press one. Para información en Español, oprima el dos.* Then the message said, *For more information, press star.* Then came a longer pause before he heard, *Goodbye,* and the line went dead.

"Fuck." He called the same number, which miraculously delivered a live human being on the first try, a female voice.

"Tampa Police 91, this is a recorded line."

He tried a different tack. "Good morning, this is Paul Panepinto. I'm calling for information on who to talk to about someone embezzling from a company."

"Is it an employee that's embezzling?"

"Right."

"How much have they embezzled?"

"Not actually sure," said Paul, wondering if he were really expected to know that.

"How are they getting to the money? Do they have access to the account?"

"It's through a 401(k)."

There was a pause. "Oh."

"The administrator of a 401(k) account," Paul explained.

"Okay." Another long pause. "I can give you a phone number to Delayed Reports and Information. They'll file a telephone report for you, and then whatever information you have, I guess they'll turn it over to a detective."

She gave him the number, and he hung up, then dialed again.

You have reached the Tampa Police Delayed Crimes Investigation Unit. For quality assurance, your call may be monitored or recorded. If you need instructions in English, press one. For instructions in Spanish, press two.

Paul thought it odd that the message did not say, *Para información en Español, oprima el dos,* but then the entire message repeated in Spanish.

After the Spanish version, he heard, *The next available agent will assist you. If you are calling to report a crime that's occurred outside the city limits of Tampa, please call the law enforcement agency in whose jurisdiction the crime occurred. We cannot investigate crimes that occur outside of our jurisdiction.*

The message continued: *At any time during this call, you may go directly to our voicemail system by pressing nine, or you may bypass this message and go directly into our call queue by pressing zero. Our office hours are eight a.m. to seven p.m. Monday through Friday, nine a.m. to seven p.m.*

Saturday and Sunday. Please choose one of the following options or remain on the line to hold for the next available agent: if you're reporting the loss or theft of a cellular telephone, press one; if you're reporting the theft of a motor vehicle, press two; if you're reporting a lost or stolen motor vehicle tag, press three; if you're reporting that someone is using your name or identity numbers to steal from you or someone else, press four; if you're reporting a runaway juvenile or missing person, press five; if you're reporting an insufficient funds or account closed check, press six; if you're reporting a burglary, press seven; if you're calling for general information, or to see how to get a copy of a previously written report, press eight.

While thinking about the depressing fact that missing persons was not a higher priority than number five on the menu—perhaps they were in order of popularity, he thought—Paul decided that general information was probably what he was seeking, and pressed eight.

Thank you for calling the Tampa Police Department. If you have an emergency, hang up and dial 911. Normal business hours for most operations of the Tampa Police Department are nine a.m. to five p.m. Monday through Friday. For information in English, press one. Para información en Español, oprima el dos.

Jesus H. Christ.

He pressed one.

If you are calling to report a crime, press one; if you need to obtain a copy of a previously filed police report, press two; if you need to speak to a specific detective, and you know the detective's name, press three; if you are interested in becoming a Tampa Police Officer, and need information on how to apply, press four; if your vehicle is the subject of a police seizure, and you need to speak to someone in the forfeiture unit, press five; if you need to schedule a residential or commercial security check on your property, or if you need information about Neighborhood Watch, school, or civic organization programs, press six; if you have questions about paying a traffic ticket, please call the violations bureau; if you need information on persons in police custody, or for Non-Emergency police information outside the city limits of Tampa, please call the Hillsborough County Sheriff's Office. For all other police-related matters, or for general information, remain on the line or press nine.

He remained on the line while the menu repeated and then said to him, *For more information, press star.* He paused, too long, and then heard it again: *Goodbye.*

And again he punched in the number, his blood boiling.

You have reached the Tampa Police Delayed Crimes Investigation Unit. For quality assurance, your call may be monitored or recorded.

This time he merely pressed one immediately.

The next available agent will assist you. If you are calling to report a crime that's occurred outside the city limits of Tampa, please call the law enforcement agency in whose jurisdiction the crime occurred. We cannot investigate crimes that occur outside of our jurisdiction.

At any time during this call, you may go directly to our voicemail system by pressing nine, or you may bypass this message and go directly into our call queue by pressing zero.

He had not paid attention to that option before, and so he immediately pressed zero. A male voice came on the line.

"Tampa Police."

"Good morning, this is Paul Panepinto calling. I wanted to get information on who to talk to about somebody embezzling from a company. Can someone tell me if the police would have the resources to do surveillance in that kind of a case?"

The officer sounded confused. "Surveillance? What do you mean? There has to be a report originated before they can start to do anything."

"Okay," said Paul.

"Who is it doing this?"

"Someone high up in the company. We think he's embezzling from the company's 401(k) account."

"Okay...."

"An attorney suggested that I go right to the police, and the owner of the company said I should do that and keep him posted."

"The person taking the loss needs to report it, and he needs to bring in proof that this is going on."

"So, the owner himself needs to file the report."

"Yeah, it's going to be the victim. Whoever the victim is in the case."

"Well, before the owner files the report, are there steps he should take, to determine whether this particular employee is involved in this embezzlement situation?"

"Whatever he wants to do. If he wants to set up surveillance and use that as evidence, he can do it."

"Is that something that the local police department can do, or would he need to hire a private investigator?"

The officer stuck to the original point. "The first thing he needs to do is originate a report."

"Okay, sure," said Paul.

"We get that done, and then we ship it to our detectives. They decide if they want to do surveillance or whatever the case may be. They'll contact him, talk to him, find out what's going on, and if they want to do some type of surveillance, it's up to them."

"Can they do computer forensic analysis, or does that get farmed out to some other agency?"

"What kind of forensics are you talking about?"

"Like taking the hard drive and having somebody analyze it. Like look at every keystroke."

"I don't know. We ship the reports to our detectives, and what they do is up to them. I don't know what to tell you on that."

"Is it possible for me to actually talk to one of the detectives, or are they only allowed to talk to you once they're on a case?"

"Like I said, the report's got to be initiated, and it's got to be shipped up to them. If you're not the victim in the case, we really need to be talking to the owner. Where is the business located?"

Paul told him.

"Okay, well, that's within the city limits."

"Right," said Paul. "I just wanted to find out what kind of resources the police would have, or if this would require a private detective."

"If somebody is stealing from the company, that's a crime. If they want to involve a PI to get more evidence on the case, have at it. But usually people do that if a PI can obtain evidence somehow where we couldn't."

Paul thanked him and hung up. His shirt was soaked through.

And now, after all that, he had to call back James with the news.

CHAPTER 55

JAMES FLAMBET LISTENED, dread washing over him as Paul told him on the phone what the Tampa Police Department said. He felt almost ashamed at his own lack of courage, feeling it bordered on cowardice. Certainly, Graham intimidated him.

Fortunately, Graham was on the other side of the state, doing Flambet Insurance work on the Atlantic coast, so there was no chance of him strolling into James's office as he made the call.

You have reached the Tampa Police Delayed Crimes Investigation Unit. For quality assurance, your call may be monitored or recorded.

As Paul had instructed, James pressed one, then immediately pressed zero. He looked up at the painting on the wall, a scene from a Mediterranean island, and wished he could be there: a cool drink in his hand, Celia and Eugenie in the background…better yet, just him, free of the responsibilities of matrimony, parenthood, the business —

"Tampa Police."

He cleared his throat. "Yeah, hi, James Flambet here." He paused, but at first there was no sound on the other end.

"Go ahead, sir."

"Y-yes. Thank you. My name is James Flambet, as I said, and I run an insurance—I own an insurance company here in town, Flambet Insurance."

"How can I help you, sir?"

"Well—okay—here's the deal. I think my second-in-command is embezzling from me. I had an employee, a former employee, actually, who came forward with some information indicating that my VP of Operations, who administers our company 401(k) program, may be stealing from it, as well as stealing through some kind of fake employee records he appears to have created."

"Fake employee records?"

"Yeah, I think he created these records. To be honest, I don't remember these people—it's a fairly big operation, a few hundred people, and you don't get to know—that is, I don't always really get to even meet all my employees, and you know, people come and go —"

"This employee, this VP person, he handles the accounts?"

"Yes, yes, he does. I'm the owner, and I oversee the entire operation, but we don't really have a formal accounting department per se, and I've let him handle much of the financial side of the business for some time now."

"You'll have to come in and file a report, sir. How much has he embezzled from your company?"

"I—I don't honestly know. I was given —"

"Do you have some sort of evidence to back up the allegation, sir? Because, if not, I'm thinking this is something you could possibly handle internally."

"I have a document from the employee, the former employee. Actually, I had him contact the police already, but they told him the victim—that is, me, since I'm the owner—they said I'd have to file the report."

"Yes, sir, you'd need to come in to your local precinct to file it. You need to bring whatever documentation you have. You mentioned a document."

"Yes, I have a printout of these employee records from the VP's computer. It's like they're on the payroll for retirement funds—stock options, the whole nine yards."

"The business is located within the Tampa city limits?"

"Yes."

"Okay, well, we're here from nine a.m. to five p.m. Monday through Friday, sir, so come in whenever you can and file the report. You need to be here in person because we need a signature on the paperwork if you're going to press charges."

"Press charges. Right." He almost laughed at how surreal this was. Would he actually have to press charges against Graham? Fire him first? Fire him after pressing charges? He had no idea. "At this point, I really don't know what I'm doing," he said. "I guess I just have to file the report first and go from there. Your office investigates this sort of thing?"

"Yes, sir. You just have to file the report."

"Right, right. Okay. Okay, I'll be down later."

"All right, sir. Nine a.m. to five p.m. Is there anything else I can help you with at this time?"

"I don't think so, no. You've been very helpful, thank you."

He hung up the phone and looked back up at the painting, thought about the local news and what they would do with this story. Majorca, that's where that was. The Spanish island of Majorca. He looked from the painting to the green, green lawn outside, and felt for a moment the way he imagined an animal in a cage must feel.

CHAPTER 56

PAUL'S CALL TO Suzanne was neither as tentative nor as awkward as he anticipated. After their disastrous encounter in the department store, he'd expected to find himself seriously dreading even picking up the phone. But he'd also realized that their relationship had most likely been permanently and irrevocably shattered anyway, and one phone call wasn't likely to make things either better or worse. Anyway, he thought, it couldn't make them any worse.

He dialed the old familiar number early on a Friday evening with no expectation, hoping only that he wouldn't reach her voice-mail and feel obligated to leave a message.

She answered on the second ring. "Hello?"

He was surprised she answered, and even more surprised to find an internal calm that matched the level of casualness in his tone. "Hey Suzanne, it's Paul."

"Hi," she said without inflection.

"I know I said I'd give you a call when we bumped into each other, so...here it is."

"Yes. Can you hold on a moment?"

"Sure."

She was gone for a good two minutes, and he wondered what she was doing—stalling for time, thinking what to say, an excuse why she couldn't talk? For a moment, he moved beyond calm and actually felt bad for her, if indeed she was going to create some lame story about a sick relative or a flood in her apartment. Well, it wasn't his problem.

"Okay, I'm back."

"How are you?" he asked.

"Fine," she said, still pure neutrality. "How about yourself?"

"Pretty good. How's Flambet Insurance these days?"

"You miss the place?"

It was the first spark of personality in the conversation, and he paused to actually think about it, realizing he missed only her, not the place. "Sometimes," he said slowly. "I guess it wasn't as bad as I made it out to be when I was there."

"I told you that a while ago."

"Yeah," he said, "I guess you did. How's old Graham doing without me?"

"I don't know, actually. I don't get over that way much these days. I'm doing a lot of overtime since they laid you guys off. I don't know if you knew this, but the other two people were both from Claims."

"That's right, I remember. I guess their being gone would make a lot more work for all of you, now that you mention it."

"Exactly." The old mock enthusiasm was back in her voice, that bantering tone he knew so well. Was there anything worth salvaging here? Yes, of course there was, but was it possible? Or was there too much baggage from the past? He hesitated, unsure where to go next.

"So what's up, Paul?" she asked.

He knew what she meant: "What can I do for you, Paul? What do you want?" He decided to evade the question by answering it directly. "Not much," he said. "Just wanted to say hello." He knew he'd have to ask about more than just Flambet Insurance and Graham Woodcock to keep her on the line, and so he took the chance of getting a little more personal. "You still managing to spend time with any of the old gang there, or are you too swamped?"

"Well," she said, "I've got to admit I'm not that crazy about some of them. Cora drives me nuts, so I never go out with her, of course. Sometimes I go to that El Toro bar with Arlen Jameson from Claims, though. You know her?"

"No, I don't think so."

"She's friends with that girl Mercedes Eden who's going out with the TV weatherman, Frank Brenkus."

"Really? I've seen him."

"Yeah, I guess she chased him until he caught her. Something like that."

Paul laughed. It was strange to hear Suzanne gossiping, something he associated more with Cora and her crowd. "So you're hanging out with some celebrities now, eh?"

"No," she said, "I haven't actually met the guy. I just know of Mercedes through Arlen. No big thrill, he's just a local weatherman."

Paul didn't know where to go with that, and it didn't seem as though she intended to elaborate further, so before things stalled even more, he took another tack. "I guess you're probably wondering why I called at this particular point in time."

"A little."

"Well, I wanted to talk to you."

"About…?

"Nothing special. Just wanted to hear your voice."

"Paul —"

"I know how that sounds. But I'm not asking you for anything or telling you I'm going to do anything, or…or anything, really. I'm just saying hello."

"Hello," she said.

"Exactly."

He was just about to return to neutral ground, to the latest in the situation with James Flambet and the police, when she said, "Listen, I hate to be rude here, but I've got to get going. I'm expecting company —"

"Oh, sure." It stung to hear the same urgent need to get away he'd seen in the store, and he knew by the fire in his chest that he hadn't let her go at all. "Well," he said, "I'll be seeing you."

They said goodbye, and when he hung up, he stared out the window into the darkness of evening. Flambet Insurance was in the past, the 401(k) problem was firmly back in James's hands—where it belonged—and now Paul had nothing to do, nowhere to go, no one to see. He looked across the room at the long-abandoned ghost of a painting and the dried paintbrushes surrounding it. He could admit it now, feeling as empty as he ever had: he was utterly without purpose.

CHAPTER 57

"SO, WHAT DO you want to do, Mr. Flambet?" The policeman looked at James with sheer apathy, as if asking whether he'd prefer to pay a traffic ticket by check or credit card.

James took a deep breath and heaved it out, then looked down and to his left and right. "Well, I'm not sure, really, what I *should* do at this point. That's why I came down here and filed the report."

The officer, who appeared to James to be about twelve years old, tilted his chair back and examined his fingernails. They needed cleaning. "Oh, it's up to you, you know," he said. He looked up at James again. "It depends on a few things. One thing you said is that you want to avoid negative publicity for your company, correct?"

"Right," said James. "If at all possible."

"Here's the thing: if you determine you've definitely suffered a financial loss from this employee, you can file a civil action or you can pursue criminal prosecution. Either way you go, that kind of filing is a matter of public record. Criminal prosecution probably wouldn't cost you as much, but like I said, either way you go, you're looking at publicity. How big is the company?"

"About three hundred employees."

He whistled. "I see."

"But instead of doing either—for the time being—can I get some kind of action from the police to investigate? Surveillance or something?"

"Well, I'm sending your report upstairs, but I don't know what will happen then. I mean, the detective will call you, but beyond that, I can't say what direction they'll want to go."

James felt himself sag. "So at this point, I just have to wait for the call."

"At this point, you just have to wait for the call. It's a very busy unit, sir."

He thanked the officer and walked to his car, looking with vague discomfort at the lot full of police cruisers. The sun beat down on the back of his neck, stinging, and he thought about his brother Mac. Suddenly, nearly everyone had the law in their lives, and it was not a pleasant experience.

CHAPTER 58

THE FOLLOWING DAY, James got the call.

"Mr. Flambet?"

"Yes?"

"Detective Mark Fletcher, Tampa Police."

"Yes, sir." James got up from his desk and closed the door to his office.

"Your complaint has been forwarded to me at our Delayed Crimes Investigation Unit, and for the time being, at least, I'm handling your case. Can you tell me a little more about what's going on there?"

James told him about Dolores Buenas and Philip Banks, and about the 401(k) issue.

"You have a human resources department or hiring manager?"

"No," said James, "Graham is pretty much it, aside from myself."

"Graham being the perpetrator?"

"Pardon?"

"Graham Woodcock is listed here as the perpetrator. You say he created these files for fictitious employees?"

"I believe so, yes."

"Have you seen any other records on them other than the document referenced in your complaint?"

"No," said James. "I don't remember these people, but frankly that doesn't mean they *didn't* work here."

There was a pause. "Sir, with all due respect, are you saying there may be people in your employ whom you haven't ever met?"

James flushed. "Well, it's possible. Our employee records were kind of disorganized for a while when we transitioned to computer file maintenance. People come and go, and a company this size…I'm in and out of the office a lot, and it's possible I could overlook a person or two, yes. We've got several I can think of off the top of my head whose faces I know, but I can never remember their names, and —"

"Mr. Flambet, I think we need to establish first that the crime, the alleged embezzlement, has taken place. Have you considered other suspects in addition to, or instead of, Mr. Woodcock?"

"Not really, no."

"Okay, let me ask you this: is there anyone else who might have access to these files or programs? Another administrator, a computer person, someone like that?"

"Possibly. Graham—Mr. Woodcock—has passwords for these various programs, but we have a couple of computer guys who have access to everything. I trust them, though. Hell, I trusted Graham implicitly until this came along."

"Well, sir, the first thing you need to do is identify all employees, at any level, who have access, or may have had access, to these records and monies. What about this Paul Panepinto, the man who alerted you to the matter?"

"He's a former employee, actually."

There was a pause. "Any chance he's a *disgruntled* former employee? Could he have had more access than you were aware of?"

James shook his head, as if answering in person. "No. He told me he found out about it by accident, and anyway, he wouldn't have access to any company funds. The computer guys wouldn't, either, unless they were doing something they shouldn't have been, obviously."

"Still a possibility at this point, no?"

James had to admit that it was a possibility.

"Okay, well, after you determine all the employees who could be involved, or could have been involved at some point, you really need to determine whether or not there has actually been a loss at all. Who else can determine that, other than Mr. Woodcock?"

He thought about it and sighed. "Me."

"You can do whatever accounting will be necessary to determine the loss, or potential loss?"

"Seems like I don't have much choice," said James, "unless I pay an outside auditor."

"From what you've told me, the 401(k) thing will be harder to determine because funds are distributed on a biweekly basis, and he could just always be a couple weeks or even a month behind. As far as these employees, Dolores and Philip, that should be much easier to determine."

"I agree."

"Once you find that out," he continued, "you should have a timeline as to when the loss, or losses, in your case, occurred. You need to take each employee who had access and interview them individually, and find out their activities on the days and times in question."

"Okay."

"Ask each employee for a written, signed statement of their recollection of the facts on the dates and times in question. Make sure you interview all of them on the same day, so they don't have a chance to get together and talk about it."

"Okay," said James again.

"Also, you need to make sure that all of them are informed that the meeting is confidential and that any discussion of the meeting with any other employee is grounds for immediate termination. Even if this Graham Woodcock is a manager, you're still the sole owner, correct?"

"Correct."

"Well, good. You can't mess around with any of these people at this point. You can be polite about it, but you need to get everything in writing. There's no other management people besides you and Woodcock, with or without access to company funds?"

"Nope. It's just me, and he's my second in command."

"Good. After you get their written statements, you need to follow up with an oral interview with any employee whose statements don't match. Your computer guys, for example. They may all tell the same story, and Woodcock may be your man, but you don't know that yet."

"True."

"If any of them fail to cooperate, get belligerent on you, change their stories during your investigation or whatever, I'd advise either placing them on immediate leave, or simply terminating their position without notice. You can do that if you have to, right?"

He drew in his breath. "If I really have to, yeah."

"Fair enough. If you determine a definite economic loss, and you want to press charges, by all means, contact us."

"What about doing surveillance or something like that?"

"If you're talking about a substantial loss, you may want to rely on a private investigator to help you with things like polygraphs or surveillance. Unfortunately, employees have a lot of rights under ERISA, the Employee Retirement Income Security Act, so if you're trying to recoup funds, even if they were embezzled, you may not be able to get them from the employee."

James sat silently for a moment, absorbing it. "Are you serious?"

"Serious as a heart attack. The employee would have to pay it back *voluntarily*."

"Jesus Christ."

"Yeah, it's freaking ridiculous how the laws are written. On the other hand, you could always sue the guy, and in a court of law, you'd have a good chance of winning enough damages to cover the loss anyway, at least if he hasn't already spent it all."

"This is terrible. So at this point, I have to really try to find out from him if he did it without scaring him into running off with any funds he may have embezzled."

"If you can. Whatever you do, don't make a deal with this guy. If he really did it, he may know that you can't force him to actually pay the funds back from his own retirement account, so he may not even try to run. On the other hand, if you're going after him, or anyone else for that matter, you'll need to retain counsel, and you'll probably need to retain the services of some sort of computer data specialist to get all the information, especially if he worked alone and hid it with encrypted passwords or something."

"Okay. Well, it sounds like I've got a lot of investigative work to do on my own."

"I wish we could help more, Mr. Flambet, but unfortunately the department just doesn't have the resources to throw at a company crime like this, unless you have the evidence *and* you're going to press charges. Even then, it would mostly just be a matter of arresting him, due process and all of that."

James thanked him and hung up. He sighed. He was going to have to hire a PI.

CHAPTER 59

AFTER HER PHONE conversation with Paul, Suzanne quickly realized it would have little effect on her. She had not, in fact, entertained any visitors on the night of the conversation, and felt guilty for lying as an excuse to get off the phone, but the simple fact was that she wasn't ready to talk to him yet. Even though there was no one else in her life, for today at least, Paul was going to have to be out.

Since his absence, the Flambet Insurance grind was worse than she'd let on when she talked to him. The loss of John Alsup and Mary Corwin had brought more than just longer hours and more work for the Claims Department; it brought mandatory overtime on evenings and weekends. Suzanne reached the office every day by 7:30 and more or less strapped herself to her desk, where she frequently ate a joyless lunch in between phone calls, until at least 5:30. She then dragged herself in again each Saturday from eight until noon. The additional hours meant more income, but it also meant more taxes on that income, so it was hardly worth the loss of free time and energy. In her own mind, she had no life.

So it was with bleary eyes and a heavy heart that she pulled her car into the parking lot the following Monday morning and ground to a halt. She listened to the radio for one last moment before turning the key in the ignition and dropping the oversized key ring into her purse. She felt bloated and crampy, and having only Sunday to recover hadn't done anything for her, so the Monday morning bleakness felt even more pronounced than usual.

Things instantly went downhill after she swiped her security card and entered the building. Across from her cubicle, not more than twenty feet away, Mac Flambet and Graham Woodcock were drinking Starbucks and chattiing away like old pals. It was 7:25 a.m.

As far as she could remember, she hadn't seen Mac since the *pussy is pussy* comment he'd made to Graham the last time he'd been in the office. She wondered what in hell he was doing there and avoided eye contact with both him and Graham. She settled herself at her desk, expressionless, her jaw set.

"Yeah, it's a bloody shame about your condo," she heard Graham say. "James told me about the gargoyle from hell, and I've got to say I sympathize, old boy. They can really get you by the short hairs."

Suzanne put on a pair of headphones and plugged them into her mp3 player as she booted up the computer for the long day ahead. The conversation between Mac and Graham grew faint as the music took over, but she saw Mac occasionally glance at her while he and Graham talked.

At 7:35, the conversation appeared to end, or at least be temporarily suspended by a phone call. Even through the earphones, Suzanne heard the announcement—*Graham Woodcock line three, Graham line three*—and she typed faster, trying to look as frantically busy as possible while Mac Flambet, suddenly left to his own devices, looked around for something to do.

And like one of those days when the car breaks down, the dog dies, and lunchtime brings food poisoning to the salad bar, Suzanne's Monday got even worse. Mac stared in her direction with such undisguised lust that she wouldn't even have been surprised, really, if he had dropped his drawers and rubbed one out right on the spot.

She only glanced his way for one horrid moment because she felt his eyes on her, then returned to typing more furiously than ever, but apparently that was still incentive enough for Mac. He strolled over, hands rummaging around in his pants pockets as if giving himself one thorough adjustment. Suzanne's cramps came back, and she swallowed, nauseous. She suddenly felt seriously unwell, and she began to perspire.

"Hey, how's it going?" His voice was loud enough to penetrate through the earphones, and several people at nearby desks turned to see who had spoken.

Suzanne nodded and smiled grimly.

"How's life in the Claims Department these days?" he asked just as loudly, and she saw there was no getting around it. Since he was the owner's brother, she had to talk to him.

"Hey Mr. Flambet," she said as she removed the headphones. She typed again, feverishly, only glancing up at him as she spoke.

"Oh, please, please," he said, "call me Mac. Looking pretty good over here, Suzie Q. What's happening in Claims?"

"It's busy," she said, not looking up from the keyboard. "Real busy."

"I understand you lost a couple people not too long ago," he said.

She glanced up and his eyes bored into her. The feeling of being violated swelled higher, ebbed and flowed. "Yes, it's been quite the challenge," she said neutrally, fingers flying.

"I also understand your pal Paul is no longer employed here."

She paused, mid-keystroke, and looked at him with undisguised malice. Then she smiled, though her brow was still furrowed. "Paul?"

Mac laughed without humor. "You can't fool me, Suzie Q. I know all about Paul Panepinto. It's all right, these kids come and go like the night." He looked at her appraisingly, as if sizing up a cut of rump roast, but then he turned serious. "You okay? Not feeling well today?"

"Got my period," she said and began typing again. "I'm having a dysmenorrhea."

Even that didn't cool him off. "Oh," he said, "sorry to hear that. Sounds complicated," he purred. "Well, you know you're not pregnant then, right?"

"No, I'm not pregnant."

"It's good to know everything's working properly."

"Yeah, right," she said, her fingers hammering the keyboard.

"Listen, Suze, I don't know if you're interested in dinner the-atre, but I've got a couple of tickets to this murder mystery thing coming up on Saturday. Maybe you should come along with me. You might even get lucky."

"Sorry, Mr. Flambet, I've got to work," she said.

"On Saturday night?"

"Well, I'm here early Saturday morning, so I'm not usually up for Saturday nights out," she said without looking up. "Besides, I just got my period, so Saturday will probably be a heavy flow day. I'll probably just go home and sleep afterward. Thanks for the thought, though."

"Sure, sure," he said, edging away from the desk. "Take care, Suzie Q."

"You too." Still not a glance in his direction.

"Feel better," he said, but she did not acknowledge it.

CHAPTER 60

GRAHAM GLIDED DOWN the hallway to his office and shut the door. Within minutes, his door swung open again and he called, "Felix."

Felix Nash poked his head around the side of his cubicle. "Hey, Graham."

"Why do I have a new computer?"

"That's right, you weren't here this weekend, were you?"

Graham gave him a withering look, not bothering to conceal his annoyance. "I try to avoid this place outside my usual six to six schedule Monday through Friday. What happened this weekend?"

"James brought in new computers for all of us on Saturday. He even set them up himself, which I thought was pretty cool. Weird, but cool by me. I don't have any shortage of things to do."

Graham looked stricken. "Who else did he do that for?"

"Just us IT guys and you. Don't worry, boss, you've got all your stuff on there. I saw him configuring it himself. I offered to help, actually, but he told me he was all set."

"Where are the old machines?"

"Not sure," said Felix. "James took them with him. I don't know if he was donating them or what. Also, when you check your email, you'll see he sent all three of us a message about meeting with us when he gets back from Dallas on Friday."

"Right. Thanks, Felix."

Graham closed his office door again and dug through a small box for a thumb drive. When he found what he was looking for, he rebooted his machine, then went through the series of commands which brought him to the employee profiles for Philip Banks and Dolores Buenas. Everything was still there. He burned what he needed to the thumb drive, deleted the files, and removed the software program completely before slipping the drive into his briefcase. It looked like he was still safe, at least for now.

There was a knock at the door. Mac Flambet wanted more company.

"Come on in, Mac."

"Hey, I was starting to tell you before, but then I got sidetracked by that little Suzanne number coming in. You know James's nanny, Pamela, right?"

"I seem to recall a rather attractive young lady employed in that position, yes. Your brother has a knack for picking out good-looking nannies, doesn't he?"

"He sure as shit does. I'd like to dress that one up in a French maid uniform and bang her senseless. She is *hot*."

"Right, right…might be trouble for you there, though, Mac, fooling around with your niece's nanny like that."

"Well, Pamela hates my guts, so no danger of that happening anyway. I had the damnedest conversation with her the other day, though."

Graham began to go through some papers, losing interest. "Really?"

"Apropos of nothing, she asks me, *How's that embezzlement problem working out for James?*"

Graham blanched, though he recovered quickly. "Embezzlement?"

"That's what I said: embezzlement? Then she said she must have gotten James's place confused with a place her friend works, or some shit. But she turned a little red when she said it. So is

James hiding something from his family here, buddy? I figured, if anybody would know, it would be you."

Graham had already gone back to shuffling paperwork, avoiding eye contact. "No, nothing like that here. Of course, I'd be among the first to know if he'd found any evidence of impropriety, being management and all."

"Of course. Well, maybe the kid is just easily embarrassed."

Finally, he looked back up. "Maybe so. Or maybe she's just overwhelmed by your charm, Mackie, old boy."

He laughed. "No, no, I'm serious when I say she hates my guts. Well, I've got my track record going against me."

"Oh yeah?"

"Yeah, unfortunately, my history with women has been kind of like my history with cars: there have been some real beauties, but they turned out to be a lot of trouble, and then there have been some real lemons, too."

Graham chuckled. "How *is* the old Jaguar running these days?"

"Pain in the ass," he said and launched into a story about the car and a bad mechanic. In fact, he did not even notice when Suzanne Beidertyme walked by and made eye contact with Graham momentarily through his office window as she headed for the lady's room, her purse strapped as tightly to her shoulder as the holster of a gun.

CHAPTER 61

JAMES HIRED THE first private investigator he interviewed. He'd quickly become frustrated by how little the police could do with their limited resources, and decided that a combination of surveillance and computer forensic analysis would be just the thing he'd need to determine whether there truly was a loss and, if so, how much it was. The discussion with Detective Mark Fletcher had convinced him of that.

Freddie Wilson, the PI, worked out of his home in the central Tampa neighborhood of Seminole Heights. Offices were expensive, Freddie explained to James on the phone. The house was pure old Florida, a shabby bungalow the color of broiled salmon, and James Flambet felt infinitely awkward and overdressed as he stepped out of his Mercedes C55 AMG and headed past the carport to the front of the house.

An African-American man of about fifty answered the door. "Mr. Flambet?"

"Yes sir," said James, smiling gamely.

"I'm Freddie. Come on in." He swung the outer screen door open and held it for James, who stepped across the threshold gingerly, as if entering a homeless shelter.

"Sorry about the mess," said Freddie, shaking hands with his right hand while, with the left, he indicated a tangle of old clothes, piled up plates and bowls, and yellowed newspapers. "I'm in and out a lot with this work, and never been much of a housekeeper, 'specially since my divorce."

"Oh," said James, "I'm sorry to hear about that."

"Well, I wasn't sad to see her go until I saw how bad she cleaned me out. Look at that fucking TV." He sighed and gestured toward a 25-inch tube TV of a brand James did not recognize. "We had a 50-inch flat screen, and the bitch took that with her, along with a whole lot more. Anyway, enough about me. Sit down, sit down. Tell me about your situation with your company."

James perched on the edge of the sofa and told him.

"Listen," said Freddie when he had heard enough. "I've been in this game a long time, and I can tell you straight up, surveillance is a good way to go. You may think people are gonna notice they're being followed, like you always see in the movies, but believe me, they don't. Even a lot of hardened criminals are pretty damned oblivious when they're going through their daily routines. The key is *how* you do it. You never get too close, and if they notice you at all, you back off and try again another day. You feel me?"

"Sure."

"So, you believe this guy is embezzling from you?"

"Yeah, and in fact, I took the computers and replaced them with new ones. I need forensic analysis done on them."

"Well, PIs don't do computer forensic work, but I know a guy who can do it cheaper than most. You let me know if you want to check him out and I'll give him a call."

"That would be great."

Freddie Wilson cupped his jaw with one hand. "Is there a way we can surveil this guy while he's on the job? I mean, you can put some kind of spyware program on his computer, but if you just gave them new computers, he may be suspicious and only make these illegal transactions on his laptop. You said he's got a laptop, right?"

"Yeah, I couldn't switch that one out. He takes it home on weekends. You think I should confiscate it, or would he get too suspicious?"

"Let him have it. I'll see if I can pick up what he's doing on it while I'm surveilling him."

"Okay."

"We can set up a mini video camera there?"

"In the office?"

"Yes sir."

James shrugged. "Sure, I don't see why not. As long as he won't see it."

"He'll never see it. He has his own office, right, not just a cubicle?"

"Yes, he does."

"Does he have any plants in there? Like large ones?"

"Yes."

"Perfect. When you're ready, I'll go in with you and take care of it. There a timeframe when he's definitely not ever going to be there, like an evening or a weekend?"

"Weekends are good. I'd have to wait until the end of this week anyway, because I'm supposed to be in Dallas all week. I'm leaving tomorrow, actually, but Graham thinks I'm gone already."

"Good call. You let me know what day is good and we'll set up a time. Meanwhile, I can surveil him outside of the office and see what I pick up."

James gave him Graham's address and the office address before he shook hands and left. He still felt uneasy about the whole thing, afraid of Graham finding out he was being surveilled, and afraid of him bolting if he did find out. Definitely afraid of the bad publicity if the case went public. He fiddled with the car stereo as he turned back onto the highway, wishing he still smoked.

CHAPTER 62

PAUL CALLED SUZANNE again much sooner than either of them had expected, only ten days later. He made his second call on a Tuesday night, a little later than he would ordinarily have felt comfortable calling, except that he knew she worked until at least 5:30 and then most likely headed for the gym. He waited until nine before he finally picked up the phone, and only had to let it ring three times before she answered.

"Hello?"

"Hey, Suzanne, it's Paul."

She responded first with the same ominous silence as last time. "Hey, Paul," she said at last.

"How are ya?"

"Doing fine," she said. "How about yourself?"

"I'm all right. I wasn't actually planning on calling you again this soon, but I wanted to let you know what was going on with James."

"James Flambet?"

"Yeah. Just between you and me, I was still working on the whole Graham-embezzling thing after I left the company, and I finally ended up bringing it to James."

She paused again. "Really?" she said.

"Yeah. Since you and I talked about it quite a bit when I was still there, I wanted to tell someone what happened, and you're the only one who knows all the details."

"What happened?"

"Well, James is interested in pursuing an investigation but, obviously, no one in the company is supposed to know."

"Obviously."

"But, of course, I figured I can trust you to keep it to yourself."

"You know I will. So what's happening at this point?"

"Well, James was really blindsided when I told him. And then when I went to the police, they instructed me to have James file a report if he planned to pursue it. I haven't heard back from him yet, but I'm assuming he's investigating."

"Do you think Graham's really going to get caught?"

"I don't know, but you may see some kind of shit go down there. I'd really like to pursue him myself, but I guess I have to stay out of it completely now, since James is on it."

"Sure." She paused, took a deep breath. "Well, I may need to go polish up the old résumé after all, in case something really does go down."

"Yeah, that was the other reason I wanted to tell you. It probably wouldn't hurt to have a Plan B."

"Thanks for the warning. Pretty humanitarian of you, I'd say, since you can't possibly have an ulterior motive at this point."

Now it was his turn to pause, unsure whether she was serious or not. He took the chance. "What do you mean?"

"I'm sorry, did that sound sarcastic?"

"Possibly...." He chuckled, and she laughed with him, the sound like a mutual sigh of relief.

"Well, I know I can be pretty sarcastic sometimes, but I didn't mean it that way. I just meant that, since we're no longer an item, your motive in telling me must be, uh, altruistic."

"I'm not sure what my motive is at this point," he said slowly. "Paul...."

"No, I'm serious. I haven't really sat down and analyzed it."

She paused yet again. "Hmm, so maybe you *do* have an ulterior motive."

"I just don't want to see you get hurt, Suzanne. I think that's it. But I don't know, I mean, maybe deep down, I wanted you to think I'm some sort of grand fucking hero in this thing, even though we both know I'm not. I just wanted to talk about it, and I knew I could trust you, and if hearing about it helps you protect yourself in some way, then...well, I really think that's it."

"Okay," she said gently. "Thank you."

"So we're cool, right?"

"We're cool," she said, and the smile was in her voice again. "I wasn't trying to upset you."

"I'm not upset," he said. "I just didn't know...anyway, I guess you've gotta do what you've gotta do, and I've gotta do what I've gotta do."

"Well put."

"Look, don't be a stranger, all right? Just because I'm no longer working there...."

"Okay," she said. "Take care, Paul. It's good talking to you."

"You too."

They said good night and hung up. He sat still for a moment, wondering what had just happened. He had to admit he did not know, but it didn't feel like much.

He crossed the room to a large stretched canvas—abandoned, surrounded by dried paintbrushes and his old palette. He picked up one of the brushes and began to clean it; first idly, then with a vague, half-formed intent. Soon, all the brushes were clean and ready for use. He cleaned the palette. Then he mixed colors, something he had not done in a long time, longer even than he'd realized, too long to count the time.

He felt no urgency at first. He was enjoying himself, playing, the way a child plays in a room of familiar toys, absentmindedly. He realized in a sort of distant way that he wouldn't mind putting brush to canvas again after all, just for the hell of it, not with an actual sense of direction. He began to paint.

At first, the colors did not look quite right, and so he mixed them more: a little burnt umber, more cadmium yellow, a bluer blue than he'd mixed in a long while. He didn't have a specific picture in mind, or even a feeling he could identify. He merely mixed and painted and mixed and painted, and before long, he was slashing the brush across the canvas with abandon, creating shapes, altering them, putting into an abstract form the jumble of feelings he'd swallowed since he'd talked to Suzanne, maybe even since before they'd fought. He kept it up, relentless, pausing only to mix again when necessary, and he did not stop until the painting was finished and it was nearly dawn.

CHAPTER 63

GRAHAM WOODCOCK PUNCHED in the account number and listened for his results. It had been a good couple of months, and since the Dow Jones Industrial Average had passed the 17,000 mark, certain mutual funds had grown exponentially in value.

"Your total portfolio value is forty-six…thousand…seven hundred…."

He hung up and hit redial.

"Your total portfolio value is thirteen…thousand…six hundred…."

He added the figures absently and hung up again. Dolores Buenas and Philip Banks had yielded a total of sixty thousand dollars. Not bad. It wasn't much, at least not in America, but in a Third World country, it would last a long, long time.

If he took it all—he could count on the entire forty-six thousand from Philip Banks, who was "retired," and about eighty percent from Dolores Buenas after taxes and penalties for early withdrawal—he would have about fifty-seven thousand. Add to that a possible thirty more if he sold his car on the black market, a distinct possibility thanks to a certain connection. He figured, if he cashed out of the condo and took all the equity, he'd get about two hundred thousand for his trouble

That money, plus the sixty in mutual funds, thirty for the car, plus the twenty or so he had in the bank, he figured he could walk with three hundred grand easily, even without cashing in his own 401(k) contributions, which would draw suspicion if he touched them. Enough to live superbly well in Belize or Guatemala for the rest of his life, assuming an average lifespan. He'd wanted to retire to Nova Scotia for as long as he could remember, but it looked like a Third World country would have to do.

The problem was getting it all done without raising any suspicions and then transferring all the cash into offshore accounts that couldn't be touched by U.S. authorities, federal or otherwise. Maybe in the Cayman Islands, or the Isle of Man. He'd have to check that out.

For all he knew, the FBI would be the agency trying to track him down after he left Flambet Insurance. He'd need an alias, false passport, the works. Once he'd liquidated his assets and transferred the funds—wiring them from one bank to another to confuse authorities, then cashing out and opening the offshore accounts under his new, assumed name—he'd have to disappear and not come back. In fact, he might even have to live on the run to truly stay under the radar, moving from country to country.

Belize sounded good for starters. He'd vacationed there when he was much younger, just a couple of years after the career at Flambet Insurance had really taken off. He thought about the little bungalow by the beach he'd bought then, which he still regretted selling. It was just a little bungalow, really; but it was a rustic, lovely, dingy bungalow, with sand coming in at the seams and great palm fronds hanging lazily over the doorway. It had been a place he could relax and enjoy himself, a place for comfort and expansion…not like those bloated monstrosities of the American suburbs, shiny new façades that sprang up like great rectangular toadstools surrounded by fields of sharp crabgrass.

Always inhabited by insurance salesmen or land-rapers—"developers," they called themselves—every one of them had the same cookie-cutter look as the last, an almost insufferable ostentation of style and form that seemed to announce, "Here I am. I'm big and new, and I have no history. My innards are a museum of shiny modern appliances, and I am peopled by soulless drones who proudly define their lives by cataloguing those shiny appliances."

Horrible. He shuddered, thinking again of the unassuming little bungalow by the shore in Belize. Maybe he could buy a smaller version, something less expensive, not as close to the water. He could search one of those websites in advance, *Escape from America* or *Retire Wealthy Abroad*, maybe even scout out a property or two before he cashed out and went on the lam.

In a country like that, cash was king. Nobody gave a shit when you paid cash. They were just happy to have it. *Gracias, señor,* and that was that. He remembered that the people in Belize spoke Spanish. Fucking great, he thought. It'll be just like I'm still in Florida, only cheaper.

CHAPTER 64

"PAUL PANEPINTO?"

The line crackled. "Yes?"

"James Flambet."

There was a moment of dead air and a few moments of *Hello? Hello?* Then the connection was reestablished and Paul could hear him again. "Mr. Flambet?"

"Really, Paul," James chuckled, "you can call me James now. You say 'Mr. Flambet' and I look around for my dad." He laughed that same conspiratorial buddy-to-buddy laugh Paul had heard so many times in the past two years.

"Sure enough, James. How's it going?"

"Pretty well, pretty well. Listen, I wanted to let you know I filed the police report on Graham, but at this point, no one else is aware of this thing except you."

"Okay…."

"Well, you and a private investigator I've hired, that is. He's going to be surveilling Graham for the time being. I've got to head to Dallas for a conference, but I'll be back by the end of the week. I appreciate everything you've done, Paul, and just didn't want you to think that this had fallen through the cracks."

"Thanks for letting me know, James." The name still sounded awkward to his ear. "If there's anything else I can do…."

"Actually, there is. I may be bringing everyone in for a polygraph on Friday, if I can arrange it. Just the people who had access to the records. Of course, as a former employee, you're certainly under no obligation to participate, but it could help our case in court, if it comes to that."

"Sure. I've got nothing to hide."

"Thanks, Paul. We may need you as a witness, you know. Anyway, I'll keep you up to date as things progress."

They hung up, and Paul looked around the apartment. It felt surreal to be talking about Graham Woodcock and mutual funds and embezzlement when there were paintbrushes and half-painted canvases propped on easels all around him. He was absorbed in a world of color and motion, and the colorless problems of Flambet Insurance held little interest now.

It was late autumn, growing cool outside, and he wore a t-shirt beneath his long flannel shirt, which was untucked and unbuttoned, hanging loosely around him. He sat back in the chair and surveyed his work. Three paintings in as many days, and he was beginning to look like an artist again, too—he hadn't shaved in a couple of days, a look quite different from that of the disaffected insurance company employee of just a few months ago. It had much more to do with his art than with anything Graham might have done. Though he had to admit he'd still like to have something to do with bringing the bastard to justice, if it should come to that. Well, he thought, maybe it will all play out in court.

He picked up a brush and approached the canvas again, a large abstract that looked like nothing he had ever done before. He quickly forgot about Graham and James and Flambet Insurance, and the world around him dropped away. He felt like his heart was on fire, and he painted with renewed fury, as if more depended on it than even he realized.

CHAPTER 65

IT WAS UNUSUAL for a true family meeting to take place at the home of J.B. and Alexis Flambet, but any such meeting inevitably excluded James's wife Celia—a fact Celia resented, and for which she would ultimately punish him by way of several thousand dollars' worth of dresses from Saks. Occasionally, she wore one of the dresses to an event as if she'd just bought it that day, and James simply looked on helplessly, afraid to bring it up.

The most momentous aspect of the present Flambet family meeting was that everyone would be there for the first time in years: J.B., Alexis, and all three of their children. Mac and Liz had gotten together more recently without James when Mac had told Liz about the possible implosion of Flambet Insurance.

James's original idea for the meeting, which took place just hours before his departure for Dallas, was to discuss the Flambet Insurance situation, and perhaps to confide in his family something they already understood only too well: that relations with his wife were, to put it mildly, somewhat strained. He would not discuss the embezzlement issue, as the rest was already burdensome enough for the family to absorb.

As always in their family meetings, everyone arrived with their own agenda. J. B. and Alexis both wanted to discuss Mac's condo situation, and Liz wanted to talk to Mac about fixing him up with someone. Like a dog scenting blood, Mac sensed this, and, not wanting the family to focus on him *or* his love life, determined that he would use the occasion to confront James, however diplomatically, about the problem of Flambet Insurance. Perhaps it wasn't too late to make James a junior partner in Flambet, Flambet and Weisenstein, if he was willing to go back to school.

And, as always, the meeting was something midway between a party and an expensive business luncheon, since the elder Flambets spared no expense to make their children feel indulged. Dishes catered by Donatello covered the countertops, along with some large fruit trays that Alexis had rather frugally purchased from her neighborhood Publix supermarket the previous day. The bottles of Grey Goose vodka, Hennessy X.O, and Armagnac Lapostolle, Mac's favorite, were a testament not only to a hearty appetite for fine spirits, but also to the Flambets' thoughtfulness regarding their children's tastes. They remembered what the children liked to drink, and were sure to supply plenty of it.

Mac leaned against the counter as if it were a bar, Armagnac in hand. "Ah yes," he said, contemplating his glass. "Living la vida loca, eh, Liz?"

His sister chuckled softly, looking across the great room at her parents, who strutted on the lanai like pelicans ruffling their feathers. "Well," she said, "it's better than a poke in the eye with a sharp stick. By the way, what is keeping our dear brother?"

"I'm beginning to wonder whether he's going to make it or not," said Mac. "You realize you and I haven't been in the same room together with James since I was, like, eighteen?"

"No shit. I've gotten together with him, and you've gotten together with him, but —"

"— But somehow he always manages to sneak out of town whenever you come to Tampa. Why is that, sister dear? Why does James feel a need to keep you all to himself?"

"I might ask you the same thing."

Mac gave a hollow laugh. "Well, I may be the little brother, but somehow I always feel like I've got to look out for the big lug. Take his cunt of a wife, for example —"

"Mac...."

"You know what I mean, Liz. Look in the dictionary under *ballbuster*, and you'd see a picture of Celia holding a Louis Vuitton purse in one hand and James's ballsack in the other."

Liz laughed at the image, shaking her head. "You'll never change, Mac."

"God willing."

J.B. came back in from the lanai, trailing Alexis and brandishing a great bottle of Hennessy as if about to christen a ship. "What in hell is the matter with red?" he was saying. "It's a goddamn primary color, isn't it?"

Alexis shook her head. "Well, of course it is, Jean, but it's *garish* on a car. For goodness' sake, you're a little old to be having a mid-life crisis."

J.B. nodded to his children, a gleam in his eye. "Your mother seems to think I'm having a midlife crisis because I like the new Alpha Romeo in red," he said with a grin, then turned serious again. "I've always liked red, and I don't see what's wrong with buying what I like at my age."

"'At your age.' That's exactly the point. And by the way, I don't think you're having a midlife crisis. I think you're having a twilight-years crisis."

Alexis pulled a sour face, and J.B. turned even redder, but their progeny roared as if they'd just heard the funniest of jokes.

"Laugh all you want, children," said J.B., "but don't be surprised next time you're here if you see a brand new Alpha Romeo in the driveway, and your mother isn't speaking to me."

J.B. was spared further abuse from Alexis by James' timely arrival. He announced himself at the front door with a knock and halloo. "Anybody back there?"

"We're all back here," Liz called. She and Mac crossed to James and they all exchanged awkwardly formal hugs.

"So," said James, when they settled themselves at last. "The reason I wanted to talk to everyone together is because I've got a couple things going that may keep us from getting together like this for a while. I may be spending too much time in the office to be able to do this again any time soon."

J.B. crossed his arms. "Well, let's have it."

"Let the boy speak," Alexis said crossly.

"Here's the deal," James continued. "Flambet Insurance is at a crossroads. We've got a considerable amount of outstanding debt, and if I don't sell the company, I may have to declare personal bankruptcy."

There was a moment of silence. One corner of Mac's mouth curled up for an instant, but no one noticed. James hung his head for just a moment, and J.B. and Alexis simply gaped as if they couldn't believe their ears.

"Well, Christ," said J.B. "I hardly know what to say. I'd loan you the money myself, my boy, but at this point retirement funds are pretty much all I've got. What are we talking about here, cash-wise?"

"About three million."

J.B. puffed out a cloud of cigar smoke. "Fuck me, that's serious." Alexis poked him in the ribs with her index finger, but he ignored her. "Very serious. What do you mean to do?"

"At this point, I've got some big checks due, which should tide us over a bit when they clear. It's a little like bailing water out of a leaky boat right now, Dad. I'm sorry."

"Your father started that company for you, James," said Alexis, "but if you have to let it go, we're certainly not going to be upset with *you*."

"Things are also a little dicey with Celia, as you can well imagine, which was the other thing I wanted to talk to you about."

Alexis furrowed her brow. "What's wrong with Celia?"

"She's taking this thing with the company pretty hard. Not keeping her in the lifestyle she's grown accustomed to—which is a possibility down the road—well, I don't know where that might lead. I think we need to be prepared for anything."

"If she tries to screw you on alimony and child support, we'll have Steve Dawson down on her like a fly on shit," said J.B., and Alexis poked him again.

James didn't flinch. "It hasn't come to that, but I did want you all to know that things are looking a little rocky right now. It's been one hell of a tough year."

For another moment, there was silence. With the exception of Mac's ex-wife troubles, it was a good year for everyone else in the room, and no one wanted to bring that up, nor offer any solutions to James. Indeed, perhaps there weren't any. Mac was visibly relieved not to be on the hot seat about his love life, but none of the family paid him any mind, which was fine by him.

James poured himself an Armagnac and downed it in one gulp. "Well, I hate to break up our party so soon, but I've got a plane to catch."

Everyone hovered round him like mourners at a funeral, but still there came no tangible offer of help, nor even of concrete advice. James said his goodbyes to them all, and was off. After a few moments of commiseration with their children about the situation, Alexis and J.B. made their way back to the lanai and sat back down, looking somewhat deflated.

"You know," said Liz, "I was planning to talk to you about fixing you up with someone."

Mac grinned. "She'd better work for an escort service," he said. "These days, I'm only doing the hotties."

Liz frowned and jabbed him in the ribs, much like their mother had done to their father a few minutes earlier, and Mac laughed. It wasn't turning out to be such a bad day after all.

CHAPTER 66

THURSDAY AFTERNOON, THE caller ID showed a strange area code and the word *Unavailable*, but Paul picked up anyway on a hunch that it was James in Texas.

"Hey, Paul."

He was right. "James, how are you?"

"Good, good. Still in Texas."

"That's what I thought."

"Listen," James said, the cell phone crackling, "if you're available tomorrow, I'd like you to come in and join us for that polygraph. I had to make a few calls to the PI to get it arranged, but we can do it in the afternoon if you're free."

"Okay." His voice must have conveyed some uneasiness about the idea, because the next thing he heard was James's humorless laugh.

"Don't worry, Paul, I know you weren't involved but I need you there for two reasons: first, to establish that any access you had to these records was strictly through Graham; and second, when Graham sees you there, his reaction should tell us a lot about what's really going on."

"Sure, sure. Just as long as I don't have to talk to him."

"I've thought about that, and for that reason, I'd like to have you be the first person on the polygraph. When you come in, Jeanie will bring you directly to my office, and when you're done, you can leave and Graham won't even see you until you walk out of the conference room on your way out of the building. I'll make sure of that, and he'll be next, then the computer guys. I think we all want him to see you there, but not long enough to talk to you."

"Got it."

They set the time for two o'clock, and when Paul hung up, he looked around the room as he had recently after a different phone call. He looked at the mess of the room and of himself, and he realized he had to at least clean up a bit and put on good clothes to go into the old office. It wouldn't do to treat it too casually.

CHAPTER 67

THE NEXT DAY, promptly at two, Paul entered Flambet Insurance for the first time since his firing. It felt strange to be led in by a security guard and escorted to James's office, even stranger to pass his old department without stopping to speak with anyone there. A few people looked up when he passed, unsure who they had just seen.

James's office sat next to the conference room, and Paul was ushered in to see James and Freddie Wilson side by side in plush leather chairs at the conference table. There was a large glassine area to the right, and people walking by could see into the room as they passed, but few employees had cause to be in that part of the building at that hour.

The interview was predictably uneventful. Paul filled out some paperwork documenting his story and detailing everything he could remember, even answering a few questions that hadn't been asked directly, then they hooked him up to the polygraph machine. He was nervous, although he knew he had nothing to fear, but the polygraph indicated that he'd told the entire truth about Dolores Buenas, Philip Banks, and his phone calls to National Fidelity to inquire about the 401(k). The three men talked for a few minutes about the test results, and about what might be expected from the other employees, and Freddie mentioned that the weeklong surveillance of Graham Woodcock revealed nothing of use.

As if on cue, Graham himself walked by the conference room and glanced through the glass at the three of them. Paul's eyes met Graham's. He saw the eyes widen, and then the face hardened, expressionless. Graham glanced away as he made his way down the hall.

"Well, Paul," said James, breaking the momentary silence. "I think that may have just told part of the story right there. Freddie, would you mind waiting here for just a moment? I'm going to walk Paul back out to the lobby."

"No problem, Mr. Flambet."

The two walked quickly out to the front desk, James talking in a low tone the entire time. "Now, listen," he began, "don't worry about Graham. If he should call you—I doubt he would, but you never know—just remind him you don't work here anymore, and refer him to me if he has any questions at all. You don't have to tell him a thing, and in fact it's best if you don't. I'll let you know how things go, and if I have any more information for you, I'll call as soon as I can. Fair enough?"

"Sure."

"Thank you, my friend." He paused with Paul at the front desk and shook his hand. "I appreciate what you've done for us here, Paul, and like I said before, I won't forget it. We'll be in touch."

CHAPTER 68

JAMES STRODE BACK into the conference room and buzzed Graham to come in next.

Graham entered stiffly, his face expressionless as before, seating himself across the table from Freddie and James. "What's all this about?"

James introduced Graham and Freddie, and the two nodded to each other, then he turned to Graham and stood, pacing behind the chairs. "Graham, we've got a problem here, and you're one of the people we're looking to for answers. Do you remember an employee named Philip Banks?"

Graham furrowed his brow and looked away, then looked back at them. "Not particularly. Retired, I'm guessing?"

"That's one of the things we're trying to ascertain. Did he work here, and if so, when? I didn't find him in the old employee records files, but you know how badly we kept those before they were converted from paper to the database."

"Yes, well, hard to remember all the people who've come and gone in this place. It was quite a revolving door for a while. Anyway, what about Mr. Banks?"

"Well, there are two employees we need all the records on: Banks, and a Dolores Buenas."

Again Graham's brow creased, and again he assumed a look of curious indifference. "All right. What else?"

"Mr. Wilson here is assisting us in an investigation of some missing company funds. Since you're my second-in-command, we need to speak frankly, and in strictly confidential terms, about this situation, along with —"

"Well, bloody hell, James, I'm doing all the accounting here, and I'm not aware of *any* missing funds. Can you elaborate for me?"

James stopped pacing and glanced at Freddie Wilson, who shook his head.

"Here's the thing, Graham. We found these employee records related to these two employees, and I'm not sure they ever worked here, or ever even existed." He weighed his words, remembering how cautious he had to be in order not to violate any of the Employee Rights laws. "It's possible that one of the computer guys may have created these records and, well, they may be embezzling from the company. Someone may be. What we need to do is get a statement from everyone, and we're doing a polygraph with them, and with you, of course, strictly as a formality. All perfectly confidential. And that's where Mr. Wilson comes in."

Graham glanced at Freddie in much the same way as James had, asking a silent question. Freddie returned Graham's gaze, expressionless.

"Well, all right, then," said Graham breezily, "let's get on with it." He smiled amiably, and took the pen James handed him, apparently ready to do whatever he could to help.

CHAPTER 69

GRAHAM DIDN'T WAIT for the polygraph results. He left the office immediately after the interview, telling the secretary he was taking a late lunch. His condo was now a dead loss: he could never sell. He'd have to abandon it like a fucking rat, emptied of everything but the living room set and the contents of the fridge.

He could transfer the sixty thousand dollars from Dolores and Philip to one of his bank accounts immediately, but he could not access the funds he had taken from the Flambet Insurance employees themselves. The McDillon fiasco had netted him a cool thirty grand. He could get maybe another thirty grand in cash for the Lexus from his black market connection, and he had just over twenty thousand in savings. He hadn't cashed his last paycheck, so that gave him another fifty-five hundred.

He added it all up in his head on the way to the car: sixty, thirty, thirty, twenty…a total of a hundred and forty-five thousand dollars. Not enough, not enough. And somehow, he would have to live on that for the rest of his life, unless he bashed in somebody's head for—for what? Jewelry? Cash? Or worse, he'd have to work a menial job in some Third World backwater, a dying gringo bent double beneath the weight of whatever load they wanted him to carry.

Knowing that Freddie Wilson was still in the conference room back at Flambet Insurance, polygraphing the computer guys,

Graham sped home, hurried inside, and logged on to his personal computer. If Wilson had been surveilling him at home, that game had just come to an end.

He made transactions frantically, foregoing the laptop because of any evidence he might have left behind. Evidence! He didn't know fuck-all about computer forensics, but he knew enough to wipe out everything on this goddamn hard drive, at least.

He dumped it all, then decided to just sell the damn machine. He could have the entire drive wiped clean, and then sell it to the same guy who did the work. The machine could be identified by its serial number eventually, if they came looking for it, but by then it would be too late. It would be as clean as a baby's ass. He decided he'd do the same with both the laptop and his own PC.

He pulled out drawer after drawer of receipts, records, personal effects. No bleeding idea what to pack. He opted for the largest amount of decent clothes that he could carry, vowing to sell them for credit or cash at one of those high-end consignment places. He packed his casual clothes in a separate suitcase, ready to wear. He had to keep a low profile. Then he filled a small shaving kit bag with nothing but watches and rings, all for the pawn shop, all lost forever. No matter, they were his to do with as he liked.

He found all the documents he had on the McDillon file, and ran them through the shredder. Fucking McDillon could bring him down faster than either Philip *or* Dolores. He packed paper and plastic bags, boxes, suitcases, with everything he had. He boxed up the audio equipment, the smaller TV, even the lamps. The place would be empty, nothing but furniture and the big flat screen.

He filled the trunk of the Lexus with the bags and suitcases, loaded the back seat with boxes, and then moved on to the front passenger seat. When there was no more space anywhere, he ran back to see what he would have to abandon. Though mostly personal items, at this point they would have to stay. He let the cats out, never to be seen again, and said goodbye to them without much emotion, mostly just despair about the abandoned condo—more than a third of his assets, after all, wiped out in an instant. Finally, he eased the overloaded car slowly into the street, ready to cash the paycheck, see his computer guy, and hit the pawnshops.

CHAPTER 70

GRAHAM DID BETTER than he'd anticipated. Five pawnshops and a used computer dealer later, he had unloaded the newly cleansed computer equipment, all the audio and video equipment, and the jewelry, and was three thousand dollars to the good. The big TV he'd abandoned had been worth as much, but three grand would go a long way if he traveled light.

He checked into a motel on Bay Avenue, paying cash under the name Jay Mercer, and rose on Saturday morning to a sunny day wherein he was able to sell all of his best clothes at consignment shops and add a couple hundred more to his wallet. Again, he knew he was being thoroughly fleeced, but at this point it didn't matter. He was already in a Third World country in his mind, and cash was king.

He found his black market connection at the auto body shop he frequented. It was questionable whether Angelo actually worked, there or anywhere else, on the right side of the law, but Graham didn't care. He coolly negotiated thirty-five thousand for the Lexus, noting all the extras. The car was worth fifty, easily.

"For you, Graham, no problem." Angelo twirled one end of his mustache. "You're an old friend, and I know you'll send me some good business if I do you right, right?"

Graham laughed. "Of course, Angelo, old boy. You know that."

"So why you want to sell her so fast, eh? You got money troubles?"

"No, no, I'm just going out of the country for a little while, and by the time I'm back, I'll be looking for a new one. Good exchange rate right now on American dollars."

"Oh yeah? Where you going, back to Thailand? See some of them little chinky chinky bitches?"

Graham laughed again, loosening up. Fucking idiot. "No, no, I'm going to be heading to Chile this time. Business trip."

"Chile, huh? Well, hope you like spicy food. My wife's chili would give you the shits for a week."

The two laughed and settled up.

"Listen," said Graham, pocketing the cash. "You know someone who can do passports and birth certificates, that sort of thing?"

"Sure, I got a guy over in Oldsmar," said Angelo. "You need him?"

"Yeah, I'd be interested in seeing what he could work up, in case I run into any trouble. South American countries can be a little dicey sometimes."

"Don't I know it." He gave Graham the contact's address and phone number. "Tell him I sent you, and he'll give you a discount, maybe."

"Thanks, old boy."

"Hey, you leaving the car now, right?"

"Yeah, let me just get the plate and sign the registration over to you."

"No problem. How you getting home? You need a ride?"

"No, I'll call a cab," said Graham. "Thanks, though."

"Sure. You heading straight to the airport, or you gonna see my Oldsmar guy? You may need to call first, make sure he's there. He don't like surprises."

"Actually, I thought I might stop off at a friend's," Graham said, noncommittal. "I have a few things I need to take care of before I leave town."

"I know how that is. Phone's in the back, if you need it."

Graham used the phone to call the taxi, then called Tim, the Oldsmar connection, from his cell phone on the way. Tim was there, and using Angelo's name helped allay suspicion, but did not grant an immediate appointment.

"I've got someone here now I'm doing some work with," said Tim. "Can you come on Monday?"

"What about tomorrow?" Graham asked.

"Can't," said Tim, "the soonest I can do is Monday morning." He did not elaborate.

"All right, I'll call you then."

So now he had the whole weekend, and he was officially on the run. The meter was ticking. Graham had just over a hundred and forty-five thousand dollars at his disposal, forty-three of it on him, but it was going to have to last him the rest of his life. He decided to take a ride.

"How much to drive me from here to Winter Park?"

The cabbie craned his neck around. "Winter Park? That's over an hour away, buddy. Thought you just wanted to go to Oldsmar."

"Change of plans. Tell you what. How about a hundred dollars just to take me there and drop me off?"

"Off the meter? I can't do it, sir. Cab's owned by the company. I've got to charge whatever it takes to get us there."

"How much you think that would be?"

"Hard to tell. Probably closer to a buck fifty. You could take a bus a lot cheaper, to be honest."

"No, no, that's all right." He looked out the window, resigned to just spend the money. "Let's go."

The cabbie hesitated. "You got that much cash?"

From beneath hooded eyes, Graham looked at the man with utter contempt, but he still knew he needed to reassure him. He was not dressed fashionably anymore. He pulled a hundred and a fifty from his wallet and snapped them into the front seat.

"Okay, okay. No offense. Here." The cabbie tried to hand them back.

Graham looked at him without blinking. "Just drive."

CHAPTER 71

BECAUSE IT WAS a Friday afternoon when James gathered the employee statements and Freddie conducted their polygraphs, it did not truly register until Monday morning, when he called Graham at home and got his voicemail right after he'd called in sick, that the man might be gone.

"Freddie, James Flambet."

"Morning, Mr. Flambet. No news yet. Graham's car's not here."

"Really."

"No sir. He doesn't seem to have come home at all this weekend."

James gripped the receiver tighter. "Well, he just called in sick this morning, so if he's not home, he's calling in from somewhere else."

There was a pause. "He's bolted."

"I don't know, buddy." James thought about it. "Does that condo look like something *you'd* just walk away from?"

Another pause. "Not me, but you know him better than I do. I'm still waiting to hear back from the computer forensics place, so right now we don't know for sure whether he could have accessed those monies and taken off with them anyway. Can you call and get information from your mutual fund company?"

"Sure. If he did take off, I'll have to resume the responsibilities of overseeing our plan's administration anyway. I can't imagine he'd actually do that, but I guess all bets are off at this point."

"All bets are off."

"It doesn't seem like he'd be able to live on whatever's in there, no matter how much it is. He'd have to sell his place, too, and that's not going to happen in a day."

"Better safe than sorry, though."

James considered it. "All right, I'll call National Fidelity and check it out, and I'll get right back when I have an answer. Can you stay there and watch for him?"

"If you want. You call back and tell me he's taken those funds out, then I'll know he's gone, and it's on to Plan B."

James drummed his fingers on the desk. "Which is?"

"I find him."

Once National Fidelity confirmed that both Philip Banks and Dolores Buenas had cashed out their 401(k) accounts a year earlier and had them rolled into IRAs, James knew that there was no way, at least for the moment, to track the funds. His next question was a pointed one: "What is the current status on Graham Woodcock's account?"

"Well, sir, balance information is confidential to the accountholder," began the representative.

"Don't give me that crap," James snapped. "I'm the owner of the company, and the money that went into that account came *from me*. The only reason Graham Woodcock was the administrator is because *I* appointed him as such. He's no longer with the company, so *I'm* the current administrator."

"I apologize, sir. When did Mr. Woodcock leave the company?"

James paused. "Friday."

Now there was a pause on the other end of the line. "This past Friday, sir?"

"Yes. Now, I need to make sure he hasn't cashed out the funds in his own name, as I believe he was embezzling from the firm. There has to be some way to put a hold on any transactions for at least the next thirty days, correct?"

"I'm not sure, sir. I'm going to need to speak to the manager."

"Can you get him on the line?"

Another pause. "Well, I'm not sure whether she's in the office yet, sir."

"Fine, I'll hold. Please see if you can get her."

"One moment."

James drummed his fingers harder on the desktop while on hold. There had to be a way to deny Graham access to his 401(k) money if he was on the run. Unless he'd previously cashed it out, there had to be a way to keep him from doing so.

After several minutes on hold, a female voice came on the line. "Dana Hollander."

"Dana, James Flambet, Flambet Insurance."

"Yes, Mr. Flambet. I understand you have an employee who's looking to roll over his 401(k) into an IRA?"

James shook his head, growing more aggravated. "No no no. Is this—are you the customer service manager?"

"Yes, sir."

"All right, listen. My administrator, Graham Woodcock, is no longer with us, and I need to put a freeze on his account until we get some things sorted out. I'm taking over as administrator."

"Well, sir, we can't put a freeze on his account, but if he's no longer with the company, then of course no more contributions will be forthcoming from you."

"Wait, what do you mean, you can't put a freeze on it?"

"He has to roll it into an IRA within ninety days. He can't just let it sit indefinitely."

James almost chuckled through gritted teeth. "Maybe your underling didn't make it clear what we're talking about here.

Graham Woodcock has been embezzling from my company. If we are to recover some, or all, of the assets he's embezzled, we're certainly not interested in letting him roll anything over into an IRA."

"Oh my goodness. I apologize, sir, I was not aware of that information."

"Well, you are now. Are there still funds in his account?"

"We'll need some more information from you, sir."

He provided the necessary information: his own social security number, and a special code he'd been given when Graham had originally set up the program.

There were funds, although James could have no way of knowing that Graham had actually taken a loan against them, and the manager did not scroll down far enough to see those notes on the system, so what was there did not truly represent the balance of Graham's account. Still, James felt slightly comforted by what information he was given, and after the manager agreed to put a hold on the account for the next thirty days pending an investigation, he finished up with her and called Freddie Wilson.

"Well, Freddie, we're kind of screwed here," he began. "Graham rolled over the Buenas and Banks funds a year ago, so no idea where they are, or even how much was lost there. His own funds are still untouched, and I've got a hold on them for thirty days, but that doesn't get us any closer to finding out whether he's left town or not. If he contacts them, they're going to let me know."

"Meantime, you want me to watch for him, or try to track him?"

"How long can you stay there tonight?"

Freddie weighed it out in his mind. "I can stay all night, as long as I've got coffee."

"Why don't you wait there tonight, and if there's no sign of him by tomorrow morning, then look elsewhere."

"Sure thing, Mr. Flambet. Any ideas where he might have gone? Friends, family?"

Now it was James's turn to weigh it out. "None of the above," he said at length. "I'd like to get into his place and see what's what, but we'd have to have the police get a warrant and I'm not even sure we can do that with what we've got."

"Right, at least not until the computer forensics report comes in. I can get in there if you want me to…probably wouldn't take anything more sophisticated than disabling a security system."

"That's not legal, though."

He chuckled. "Hardly. But if you want an answer quick…."

"No no," said James quickly. "Give it the night, and then we can figure out more without breaking in."

"Fair enough. I'll call you on your cell in the morning?"

"Okay, Freddie. Thanks."

CHAPTER 72

FLAMBET INSURANCE FADED further into the past as Paul's painting absorbed him more and more. He began his days now with a bowl of cereal and the morning paper, and after those first few minutes of war headlines and political scandals and human interest stories, he always felt sufficiently disgusted with humanity to set aside the paper and begin another grim abstract. Soon, great slashes of yellow and cadmium and vermilion, vivid as wounds, stretched across finely pixilated canvas. A long way now from the days of the tossed pebble and the midnight backyard romance, he was also a long way from the corporate grind, and that held some satisfaction.

It was strange to consider how much he enjoyed painting these cruel, harsh images, just as it was strange to think that, a short time ago, he'd been stuck at a place like Flambet Insurance. He reflected about it occasionally, with a kind of bitter nostalgia for the job he'd had before Flambet, with its crushing responsibilities, and then he drifted even further back, to Penn State and the days when he'd painted what seemed to him now the most ambitious works of his life. There in the linen closet they sat, gathering dust, stacked against old stereo equipment and boxes of books.

Well, fuck 'em, he thought, I like the stuff I'm working on now better. Besides, I'm not even sure they'd all work well together in an exhibition.

Of course, painting let him avoid the inevitable return to the Unemployment Office. He had only used their equipment and made a brief feint at looking for work. He liked this better than anything else he'd done since college. But could he make a run at painting now on his own?

It would have to be quite a success for a newcomer to the art world, especially since he had no one, not even a roommate, to share the burden of rent, car payment, insurance, and, that last bastion of the starving artist, food. And if he did not make it, what magic could he possibly use to massage his résumé into something useable in the wonderful world of insurance?

So with all of this on his mind, and even painting itself providing only a temporary refuge, it wasn't really all that much of a jolt to receive a call from James, however remote Flambet Insurance might feel. Paul quickly emerged from the contemplative state he'd entered while he painted, although James's voice over the telephone still took on the flat, remote quality of a radio announcer's.

"I'm in Detroit right now on another project," James said. "But I didn't want you to think I'd forgotten about you."

"No worries, James," said Paul, comfortable at last with using his first name. "I figured it was pretty busy for you with Graham gone."

"Actually, Paul, he may be more gone than we think. He hasn't been back to work since the polygraph, and he only called in sick that first day."

Paul paused, his paintbrush hovering in the air. "You're kidding."

"Nope, serious as a heart attack. I think, when he saw you, he took a *shitter* and that was that."

There was a sudden crackle of static, and Paul took a moment to absorb the word shitter. "I don't even know what to say," he finally managed. "Have you gotten the police involved yet?"

"Not yet. I've got Freddie Wilson on it, and we may actually take action as soon as I get back. Graham can't have gotten too far yet, I don't think, but I have to file the formal complaint if I'm going to press charges. I have to think about the media, you know, and at this point, I'm still waiting on the computer forensics."

He can't have gotten too far? Hell, he could be in Argentina by now. Paul allowed himself a sympathetic, "Jesus."

"Graham's polygraph results were inconclusive," James continued, "but that may have been enough by itself. That, and seeing you there."

"Sorry you have to go through all this."

James waved it off. "No need. If he's guilty, we'll get him."

Paul could not help feel his confidence unwarranted. Graham was a clever son of a bitch, and if anyone could get away scot-free with something this big, it was him. "Well, good luck with it. If there's anything else I can do, you can usually reach me here at home."

"Okay, Paul, thanks. We'll be in touch."

Afterward, Paul sat for a moment with the paintbrush in one hand and the other still on the phone. Was Graham really gone? It was impossible to imagine Flambet Insurance without him, but even more impossible to imagine doing anything about it now. He returned to the painting, thinking about Graham and James and even Suzanne, but more than ever determined to just get in some more work while the light was good.

CHAPTER 73

MAC FLAMBET COMPLETED the move into his new condo without fanfare, without so much as the help of a single soul he knew personally. On his salary there was certainly no need for the "get-friends-to-help-move-for-pizza-and-beer" party, and in any event he wasn't exactly rolling in friends. Marathon workdays at the law firm took the inevitable toll on his social life, and besides, he told himself, he'd rather pay movers to do the work. If they fuck it up, they have to pay you.

He brooded as the movers carried boxes of antique books and lamps up the drive to the wide tiled stairwell. It was hard to believe it had come to this—forced to give up the only residence that had ever held any sentimental value for him, but also to pay a much higher mortgage for a comparable place, thanks to property appreciation and higher interest rates. Fortunately, the real estate market had stagnated in the last couple of years, or his monthly payment would have been triple what he'd paid for the old place.

Still, there were advantages. A newer condo meant newer utilities: a state-of-the-art water heater with built-in water softener, the latest in energy-efficient central air, and a space age washer-dryer combination that looked like something he'd seen as a kid on *The Jetsons*.

The movers placed the last of the boxes in the master bedroom and gathered wearily in the foyer. They waited, wiping sweat from their brows, while Mac sat on the great leather sofa laconically writing them a check, contemplating whether or not to include a tip. He decided against it.

"Thank you, sir," said the man who took the check, apparently the manager or foreman. He looked at the check and then back at Mac, not hiding his disgust. "Have a great day."

Mac barely acknowledged him, flipping through some papers on the coffee table before him with utter apathy. "No problem. You boys can leave that door unlocked on your way out. I'm going out myself in a few minutes."

The door slammed, and Mac chuckled. Poor bastards. Oh well, that was plenty of money for a simple condo job.

He padded around the new place in his stocking feet, trying to think what he'd planned on doing before he went out. Then he remembered: he'd been wanting to call Andrea Heatherstone again. He hadn't called her in quite a while, but so what? She might still be interested.

Her husband had some kind of bourgeois marketing job, so even if his financial situation had somehow magically improved, he was still hardly able to offer the kind of stylish night on the town that Mac could provide at the drop of a Benjamin. And the body on that girl was fanfuckingtastic. He scrolled through the numbers on his cell phone until he found hers.

"Hello?"

"Hey Andrea, it's Mac Flambet."

"Hi Michelle," she said in a high, artificial register. "What's happening?"

"Ah, so the old schlub is there, is he? I've missed you. Been really busy with a case."

"Your grandmother? Oh, I'm so sorry to hear that." She paused, then continued before he could interrupt. "Maybe I can go to the hospital with you the next time you visit."

Mac chuckled. "Nice, very clever. How's Saturday night looking for you?"

"Saturday? Let me check with Bill." She held the phone down and said, "Bill, are we doing anything Saturday night?"

Mac heard the low Neanderthal voice. "Not that I know of."

"Michelle's grandmother is in the hospital again with her *sciatica*," she added.

There was a grunt. "She had to be hospitalized for sciatica?"

"I think she's really old." Andrea came back on the line. "Saturday sounds good. I can meet you there around 7:30 if that's all right."

"Well played. I'll meet you at Malio's around eight, how's that?"

"That would be perfect," said Andrea. "Tell her I hope she's feeling better."

Mac chuckled again. "Oh, you bet I will."

He sat back on the leather sofa, cell phone still in hand. What a trip. And she was obviously still interested, or she wouldn't have agreed to meet.

Andrea Heatherstone. With a last name like Flambet he couldn't exactly make fun of hers, but he couldn't help wondering what it reminded him of…a romance novel heroine? A porn star?

He considered it for a moment as he sat unmoving on the sofa, thinking mainly of the sex. It had been a while. He'd have to play it by ear, but any chance of getting her in bed again was worth whatever risk it might entail, what with the pesky marketing man husband always lurking in the background. Well, fuck him if he can't control his own wife.

He got up and slipped his shoes back on, then jangled his keys as he punched in the code for the alarm. After locking the place, he tossed the keys in the air playfully, catching them as they came down. It really was turning out to be a pretty good year after all.

CHAPTER 74

THE WEATHER FINALLY drove Paul out of his self-imposed exile, and he decided to take a day away from painting and just hit the beach. It was perfect, highs in the eighties and not a cloud in the sky. But heading west down the Courtney Campbell Causeway, away from the apartment and the paintings, his mind began to drift back to Flambet Insurance and the problem of Graham Woodcock.

When he got to Clearwater and lay on his beach towel beneath the Florida sun, the problem was still there, goading him. He had determined, for the time being, that the best thing was to stay away completely unless James Flambet himself asked for some kind of assistance. But the thoughts crept back in like uninvited guests. Troubled, he stood and shook out the towel, put his sunglasses back on, and walked slowly along the shoreline, looking at the sky and the water.

It all seemed so long ago and so unreal, Flambet Insurance. He managed to push it out of his consciousness again by focusing on the light and the colors of the beach, the steady swimmers, the pale, sweaty tourists. As he relaxed into the sights and sounds and smells of the beach, he noticed a woman of Middle Eastern or Eastern descent, up along the stretch of sand where he strolled. She sat cross-legged by the waterline, facing the Gulf and singing, her daughter behind her tracing figures in the sand. Paul passed behind them, eyes on the horizon, but as he glanced back at the girl, he saw that she was looking down, embarrassed by her mother's singing, so foreign, alien, while this American stranger strolled by.

But the singing was beautiful, and as he walked closer to the sandpipers and seagulls along the shore, the song drifted to him in a steady stream. Its mystery moved him. He felt as if he were in a play, a great drama, and he stood outside, watching himself. Suddenly, he couldn't wait to see what happened next. He looked back down along the shoreline at the woman and her daughter and he smiled.

Back at the apartment, Paul stood for a long time before the painting he'd been working on, not touching it, not even thinking about it. It was no longer a problem to solve, nor even a dream he'd once had. It was just color and space, paint on canvas. He looked through it, looked to another problem on the other side—not the problem of Graham, but the problem of Suzanne.

He picked up his cell phone, then thought better of it. This was no longer the time for text messages or phone conversations and all they implied and denied—words open to misinterpretation, the static, dropped calls, distance—not to mention the lack of touch, of facial expressions or eye contact. He needed more from her this time, and somehow he understood that she needed more from him, too, though he could not say how or why. He just knew it in his bones.

But showing up at her apartment and knocking on the door would be singularly creepy, so he needed to come up with some kind of contrivance allowing him to bump into her at the store or office, in the neighborhood somewhere, like in their last truly accidental encounter. He remembered how she'd practically run away from him, looking somehow both stunned and apathetic. He would have to do better this time. The only questions were when and where. He remembered the first time he'd met Pamela Mae Swenson, at the donut shop where she and Suzanne had their weekend chats. That sounded a little too contrived, showing up at the shop like that, too much a coincidence. Yet the idea had a subtle charm. At best, Pamela would be there as a neutral third party; at worst, Suzanne would see through him and think him a wimp for not going somewhere he would find her alone.

When he walked into the donut shop the following Saturday, it was still early, before the late breakfast college crowd's arrival. Already a few senior citizens shuffled in for an early lunch, salmon and dill salads on whole wheat, bagels and lox. Paul ordered coffee and sat at a large wooden table with a newspaper before him, slowly stirring cream into the swirling brown liquid, his spoon occasionally clinking against the side of the porcelain mug.

Absorbed in a news article about the real estate market—though it was more or less irrelevant to a renter like him—it wasn't until the two women passed Paul's table that he lifted his head and looked around.

"Let's sit over here," Suzanne said quietly.

Paul heard the voice, searched for its owner, and met the eyes not of Suzanne, but of Pamela Mae, who promptly said, "Hey, I remember you. How's it going?"

Instantly, he saw it was too late for Suzanne to do anything other than allow the situation to play itself out. She merely smiled grimly as Pamela Mae continued, "Look who's here, Suzanne. What brings you to this neck of the woods? It's Paul, right?"

Paul smiled up into Suzanne's eyes, then tore his gaze away and looked back at Pamela, to avoid being rude. "Yes, and you're Pamela, right?"

She smiled. "Right. Mind if we join you here?"

"Please, help yourselves." He cleared the newspaper out of the way, and they sat and began to eat their breakfast, while Paul stirred his coffee again.

Pamela turned to him. "I hope you don't mind if we eat in front of you."

"No, not at all. I actually caught an early breakfast. Had some errands to run and dropped in here to read the paper with some coffee." He glanced at Suzanne, who eyed him with suspicion.

"I've done that a few times," said Pamela. "Matter of fact, last time I ran into you two together I was on my way here. Remember, Suzanne?"

"I remember," she said.

Pamela's eyes widened at Suzanne's tone, and she looked from one to the other before saying, "I'm sorry, you guys. I totally forgot."

"Nothing to be sorry about," said Suzanne. "We're all friends here."

"That we are," said Paul, though he looked at her with the question in his eyes, *Are we?*

"God, I feel really stupid now." Pamela shook her head. "Are you sure it's all right?"

"Not a problem," said Suzanne, and Paul nodded in agreement.

"Listen, I'm gonna let you two talk. I've got to run to the store anyway, and I'll just take this with me."

"No, seriously, Pamela," began Suzanne, then stopped as they exchanged a glance. "Well, all right, girl, I'll see you in a bit."

They pecked each other on the cheek—an odd affectation that Paul had not noticed in the past—and then she was gone.

He broke the inevitable awkward silence. "I guess you were pretty surprised to find me all the way over on this side of town."

"You might say that."

"I've got to get some art supplies, and it's actually cheaper at this place over on Swann."

"How is the painting, by the way?"

He smiled. "Good, good. How are things for you?"

"Same as ever. You know Graham's gone, right?"

"I figured he might have bolted. Now, you remember you're not supposed to know all this other stuff, right?"

"I remember. My lips are sealed." She smiled and took a sip of tea. "Nobody's told us anything yet. We just noticed he was gone one day, and he hasn't come back since."

He stirred his coffee again. "You think I'm a pussy, don't you?"

"Excuse me?"

"I'm supposed to be a tough guy because I'm Latino, right? But I never even confronted Graham directly about the 401(k). All I did was tell James about it."

She laughed. "I don't think that makes you a pussy, Paul."

"I should have confronted him directly. Even if James said not to."

She began tearing her napkin into small pieces. "Come on, you know better than that."

"You know I saw him? I went in there and took a lie detector test."

Her eyebrows went up. "For real?" Suddenly, she looked relaxed, and somehow more interested.

"Yeah. Graham saw me in the conference room."

"I knew you came by, but I didn't know what for."

Now it was his turn to arch an eyebrow. "*Really.*"

"Yeah, Margie saw you when you came in. Wearing a suit, like a big shot, eh?"

He laughed. "Probably thought I was there for an interview."

Suzanne laughed again too. "Yeah, trying to get your old job back."

"No thanks. Whoever has it now can keep it."

"They didn't even replace you. Just piled all your old shit on the others."

"Jesus." He continued to stir the coffee.

"But seriously, Paul, I never questioned your courage. I think the way you handled it was the right way. And once you'd been fired, you really didn't have to tell James a thing."

He pondered it, staring into the coffee as he stirred. "I still thought I could have done better somehow. I just couldn't figure out how."

"And now you have?"

He looked up and saw the laughter in her eyes, the challenge. "No, I still haven't."

"So you think *not* being able to figure everything out somehow makes you a coward?"

"I guess not. I just wanted to figure it out, and I couldn't."

She tore the small fragments of napkin into smaller fragments. "Exactly," she said.

"So what *does* that make me, then? An idiot?" He laughed again, and she laughed with him.

"I'd say yes just to break your balls, but you know I couldn't figure it all out, either, Paul. I saw what you did with *Morningstar*, and that didn't give us the answer. Did you ever make any connections between all our stuff and that McDillon thing, or do you know if they were even separate issues?"

He shook his head, still stirring the coffee. "Nope, I never figured that out either. There were all these blank data fields in the spreadsheets, but I didn't have enough information to figure out why, or whether there was any connection."

She shook her head. "Too bad."

"I was really the Einstein of Flambet Insurance, huh? Good thing I'm painting now."

She laughed. "That's right, artists should be paid to create, not to think about data fields." Tiny shreds of napkin littered the table, and she scooped them up into a pile. "God, I'm really making a mess here."

"A little bit."

She glanced up from the pile. "You're not exactly chilled out either, Mr. Data Fields. You realize you haven't stopped stirring your coffee since Pamela left?"

His hand stopped in mid-stir, and he looked up from the coffee, laughing. "I guess you're right." He dinged the spoon twice against the mug and set it down on the table.

She relaxed a little, sipping her tea again. "You know why I walked away from you in the store that day?"

"No, I really don't. You were still angry with me, I assumed."

She shook her head. "I wasn't angry. I was hurt."

"I'm sorry. I never wanted to hurt you."

"And I never want to be hurt like that again."

He studied her, unsure whether she was rubbing salt in his own wound or just stating a fact. She looked away.

"I understand," he said.

"Let's not talk about it anymore," she said, meeting his eyes.

"Okay. Let's get back to the data fields, then, I guess."

She chuckled and glanced away again. "You always did know how to make me laugh."

"Current boyfriend not doing that for you?"

She looked back at him, eyes round. "Don't go there."

He laughed again, not without discomfort. "Okay, fair enough. Well, can we at least get together sometime? Just as friends, of course."

"Of course."

"You mean, of course we can get together, or of course just as friends?"

She smiled and shrugged. "Take it any way you want it."

CHAPTER 75

GRAHAM HAD THE taxi stop in downtown Winter Park, not knowing exactly where he was going to spend the night. He didn't want to leave a trail, and so he would not have the cabbie drop him at a particular location.

When Graham directed him to pull over, the cabbie looked at him strangely. "Here?"

"Yes, right by that pharmacy."

"All right, sir. That'll be one hundred thirty-nine dollars."

Graham let him keep the entire one fifty and stepped into the street. He walked past the pharmacy until the cabbie was out of sight. Feeling sufficiently paranoid, he wanted to avoid even a possible connection to the cab company.

Nothing in the area resembled a hotel, so he doubled back, ducking into a convenience store and out of the blazing heat to see whether he could find a recommendation for lodgings for the night. He approached the cashier at the counter.

"I beg your pardon, could you tell me where the nearest hotel is?"

The woman looked at him as if he'd asked to sniff her panties. "I don't know no motels around here except the Winter Inn, down the street."

"Is it decent?"

The expression remained on her face. "I never stayed there."

"Well, thank you," said Graham, returning the look of disdain.

Back outside, things looked even bleaker. He walked too quickly for the heavy humidity, trying to find the Winter Inn before the sweat soaked through his shirt. But it was nearly a mile away, and he hadn't a chance. By the time he stepped under the hotel's large grey awning, his face was bright red from the exertion, his shirt blotchy with perspiration.

He checked in as Jay Mercer and paid cash in advance for one night. No, he told the clerk, he would not be requiring room service or a wakeup call. He staggered into a dark, musty room, then flicked on lights, recoiled at the dingy bathtub, and wondered what kind of insects lurked within the mattress.

Impossible to stay in such a place for more than a few hours of sleep, and so he headed straight back into the heat, ready to catch a ride wherever someone could take him. He'd grabbed a handful of tourist pamphlets on the way out the door, and he flipped through them on his way to the donut shop across the street. He looked at the information, mostly Disney and other theme parks in nearby Orlando.

Thumbing through a pamphlet on something called simply *The Scenic Boat Tour*, Graham sighed. It appeared the way an oasis must look to a man in the desert—cool and green, peaceful and quiet, the kind of haven he had sought since the moment he'd left the condo at Redington Beach. And the kind of haven he would no doubt seek again.

He hailed another taxi and, within fifteen minutes, found himself on the tour.

The man's voice droned softly as he guided Graham and his fellow passengers smoothly through the heavy foliage in the small pontoon boat. By the time they cruised across Lake Osceola through Fern Canal and onto Lake Virginia, the stresses of laptops and pawnshops had fallen away, replaced by a dream of greenery that wrapped around Graham and held him in its soft grasp. He'd almost dozed off when the guide pointed out Rollins College and Knowles Memorial Chapel, and he realized it didn't matter where they were now. At least they were far from civilization, the real civilization, and there was no one on his trail. For the moment, he was safe.

Slowly, they doubled back through Fern Canal to Lake Osceola, then took the Venetian canal to Lake Maitland. It seemed quaint that someone had bothered to name these narrow canals, Fern, Venetian. A great canopy of greenery hung over them, reminding him once more of the Belize bungalow with its fronds of palm leaves and flowering bougainvillea. He sighed.

The humidity began to oppress him just as the sight of distant mansions on the green banks of Lake Maitland filtered, unwelcome, into his consciousness. The guide pointed them out to the group, identifying which had been owned by a captain of industry, which by the dean of a local university. To Graham, each mansion looked like the kind of place he'd always dreamed he would have himself. Each was worth far more than the sum total of funds he currently had, an amount that would have to last him the remainder of his days.

It was too expensive to buy booze at a hotel, he knew, so once he was back at the Winter Inn he took a short walk to a convenience store for a large bottle of malt liquor. It was cheap swill, the kind of thing he would have snubbed in the past, but he was well aware that cab fare and hotel expenses ate into his savings rather quickly, so it was a reasonable area to economize. He passed out after finishing the bottle, and slept badly, tossing back and forth on the lumpy, too-soft mattress.

CHAPTER 76

AFTER A NIGHT in a slightly less seedy hotel, Graham returned to Tampa on Monday morning, using a different taxi company to get to Oldsmar. He called Tim the passport contact from his cell phone on the way to make sure he was there. He was, and told Graham unceremoniously, "Just come over whenever," before hanging up.

The house was in a shabby older neighborhood not far from where Hillsborough Avenue intersected with Racetrack Road. Once Graham had wondered if there was a racetrack in the area, or if the name just occurred to some city planner years before. He'd been surprised to learn there was an actual greyhound track close by, where far-gone gamblers spent their last dollars watching the skinny, starving dogs chase a rabbit around the track.

A savage thing, he thought with repulsion. He'd always been more of a cat person, but he still hated to see cruelty, even against as lowly a creature as the greyhound. He remembered with disgust the posters he'd seen of dead dogs piled up for extinction, too old to race, and he shuddered.

Tim the passport man was tall and barrel-chested with a shaven head and all manner of arm and chest tattoos visible beneath the sweaty camouflage muscle shirt. He looked to Graham like he had done some hard time, armed robbery, maybe, or assault. Beneath a single bare light bulb in the makeshift office, various automatic weapons lay on the worn wooden table. Whether a testimony to an obsession, or simply a message to Graham, the sight made him shift nervously from one foot to the other as Tim glanced through the stamps on his passport.

"You got any more of these?" asked Tim.

"Passports? No, that's the only one I've got."

"Well, I can make you a brand new one, or alter this one. You need more than one?"

Graham paused. "No. I was thinking, actually, of changing the name and so on."

"From what to what?"

"From Graham Woodcock to Jay Mercer."

Tim arched an eyebrow. "Woodcock?"

Under normal circumstances, Graham would have had a much sharper answer. But considering the automatic weapons on the table, he only laughed sheepishly. "Glad to be rid of it for now, actually."

Tim laughed. "No doubt," he said coolly.

Graham stood back and watched as Tim slit the passport picture from its plastic moorings. "This is the bitch of it," he said, more to himself than to Graham, it seemed. "You see how you've got these red stars going down the side, right next to your face? How some of them are even touching your hair in the photo?"

"Mm, yes."

"Well, we've got to fake that. Plus, this stupid *Passport USA* crap at the top of the photo. You use that name anywhere else, Jay Mercer?"

"Just at a couple hotels. I didn't want to —"

"I don't want know," he snapped. "Don't make me an accessory to anything, man."

"Sorry."

"I don't really care, be honest with you. I only asked because I wanted to know if you've signed your name that way before. You should make a few practice signatures before you sign the new passport, that's all."

"Oh, right, of course."

He handed Graham a pen.

Within the hour, someone else's old passport became Jay Mercer's, complete with stamps for Columbia, Belize, and Guatemala. Tim passed it over to Graham, scowling with pride at his handiwork.

"Whose was this before?" asked Graham.

"None of your fucking business, dude. Mine, either, if you know what I mean." He began cleaning a snub-nosed pistol from the table. "Put it this way: look at the date stamps and countries, and you'll get the idea."

Graham flipped through it anxiously. For all he knew, it might have been anyone from a former CIA agent to a drug runner. "Just memorize the date stamps and countries on there, and old Jay Mercer will fool just about anyone."

Watching the pistol gleam beneath the bare light bulb, Graham decided the time for questions had come and gone: it was time to leave. He paid and headed for the door.

"Hey, Woodcock."

Graham turned back. "Yes?"

Tim paused, pistol in hand. "I wouldn't turn around if you hear that name again."

He laughed nervously. "Of course. Thanks."

"So long, Mercer. Where you going next, by the way?"

Graham thought about it. Then with some decision, he said, "Daytona Beach."

CHAPTER 77

MAC WALKED INTO Malio's tiled brown lounge before the appointed time, and when his hostess seated him in a booth by the window, he slumped back against the black leather and thought about when he'd been in the restaurant's original location. The eighties, that was the time for a place like this. He remembered being eighteen and his older friends getting him in with nothing more enterprising than a fake ID. Those were good days, he thought. Now that past was ever more distant, and the future looked blank.

Andrea Heatherstone arrived fifteen minutes late, so that, by the time she glided across the room in her conservative pale yellow cardigan, high heels clopping like hooves on cobblestones, he had already had a drink and checked his watch three times. She smiled invitingly as she approached the table, while he gave her a smile that was at best formal, at worst a sneer.

"Sorry I'm late. How's it going?"

"Fine. Tough time breaking away from the brute?"

Andrea settled herself across from him. "Don't be mean." She picked up a drink menu and flipped through it. "Anything look good?"

"I've already ordered."

She looked at his empty glass. "I see." He did not answer, and as a sort of preemptive strike she said, "Jesus, Mac, I'm only fifteen minutes late. I said I was sorry. I'm a little closer to the hospital where I'm supposed to be right now then I am to Malio's, remember?"

He grinned and shook his head. "I didn't say a word."

"Tough time breaking away from the brute?"

"Okay, so that's seven words. I lied."

"Yeah, like I lied to get here. Visiting your sick grandmother with you…Michelle, or whatever the hell your name is."

He laughed. "That was classic."

She closed the drink menu and picked up the dinner menu beside it. "So seriously, how are you? You look tired."

"Oh, I don't know. Got a new place. Did I mention that?"

Her face lit up. "No, you didn't. Congratulations."

"Well, the ex threw me out of the old one, actually. She had clear title."

"What?"

"Long story short, I had to bail out or pay her rent. I said fuck that and got a different place. Same size, bigger mortgage."

"Mac, I'm sorry."

"That's all right. Got some cool new shit, anyway. Nice washer and dryer."

She pursed her lips into a little girl frown, still sympathetic. "Poor Mackie."

"If the real estate market weren't so shitty now, it would be much, much worse." The server returned to take Andrea's drink order, and Mac eyed her while the two spoke. Her clothes were appropriate for a hospital visit, though he could still see the small firm breasts beneath the yellow cardigan. "Would you mind taking off that sweater, or is it too cold in here for that?"

She laughed, looking embarrassed. "You're really bad. Listen, I wanted to talk to you about…what happened before."

"What do you mean?"

"The last time we got together. You know."

"You mean the sex?"

She looked away as she folded her napkin in her lap. "I felt bad afterward."

"Why?"

"When you kissed me…you know, down there…and you kissed my wedding ring…."

"You mean I should have skipped the ring and just gone right for the good parts?" He shook with silent laughter, but she did not smile.

"It just made me realize how wrong what we were doing really was."

Her eyes met his again, and he looked into them with a kind of reptilian strength, the way a salesman would before the close. "Was it really so wrong?"

"I love my husband, Mac."

He hesitated, then decided to just launch at her full force. "Come on, Mr. Marketing Man with his bullshit sales job? Don't forget, I've heard him on the phone, more than once." He imitated the grunt. "Are you going to sit here with a straight face and tell me he's not a goddamn Neanderthal?"

He made a mental note that she did not say anything, glancing away again instead. The server returned and placed a large margarita glass in front of her.

"Are you folks ready to order?"

At the same time Mac said, "Yes," Andrea said, "I need a few more minutes."

The server laughed sympathetically. "Okay, I'll be right back, ya'll."

Andrea's silence infuriated him, but he decided that rather than get angry, he'd be better served just getting what he wanted. It was time to seal the deal.

"So, if you're really feeling remorseful, why are you here, Andrea? Don't you think maybe we should give it a chance to work?" He gazed into her eyes with infinite gravity.

"I wanted to talk to you about it," she began, "not do it again. I had to —"

Mac's cell phone rang, jolting him from the chair. He pulled it from his jacket pocket and examined it. "I have to take this," he said.

She sagged visibly as he stood to walk away from the table.

"This is Mac."

CHAPTER 78

PAUL'S PAINTING LED only to more painting, month after month. There were no gallery showings, no introductions to local museum curators. No sales. He merely stayed at home and painted, dropping into the Unemployment Office for the obligatory search of Bay area jobs, a pointless exercise. No one ever advertised for a painter of abstracts with a Master of Fine Arts and two years' worth of insurance processing experience.

He slowed his spending and milked the Flambet severance package as long as he could. No more eating out, no unnecessary driving. The bills were paid and the long humid autumn stretched out before him like a child's summer vacation, empty of responsibilities. The only thing missing was Suzanne, or even the promise of Suzanne, and after their breakfast with Pamela Mae Swenson, he was still unsure how soon to call her.

One dark afternoon, when the thunderheads piled up in the sky like giant tankers, he took a break from his largest abstract yet and drove down to the Artists Unlimited Gallery, just to test the waters. If nothing else, he would look at the work of the other current artists and get an idea of what was out there. He padded softly around the studio, his feet nearly sinking into the heavy green carpet, heart clenched in his chest like a fist. The works were all locals, which surprised him a bit. He glanced at the names and prices on the cards. Jan Brewster. Gail Hollings. Alexis Flambet.

He paused, too surprised to move on. The name confused him. She almost had to be a relative of James Flambet: the name simply wasn't common enough. Or was it?

He stepped back, looking at the painting. Crude, almost childish in its simplicity, but not a bad abstract. It was good enough to get into a gallery, apparently, but who was she? Not the daughter, of course; he remembered her name was Eugenie. At any rate, the piece was too disturbing for a child to have painted, something for a psychiatrist to analyze. Then again, he realized, to a casual observer his work probably fell into the same category.

There were others from Alexis, and the sight gave him confidence. He could not help thinking that his work was better. *I could get in here.* But he knew he could never approach a gallery with such an attitude. He had to be diplomatic.

"Excuse me," he asked the man behind the desk. "Are you the owner?"

"No, she's gone today. Were you interested in one of our pieces?"

Paul nearly blushed. "Actually, I'm a fellow painter. I was wondering about one of the artists, Alexis Flambet?"

"Oh yes. Lovely woman. What about her?"

"I may know the family. Do you know whether she has any relatives named James? Or Mac?"

The man did not give it more than a moment's thought. "No, I'm afraid I don't. In any case, we don't give out much information on our artists other than pricing, unless someone is interested in viewing other works for a possible purchase."

"I understand. Anyway, thanks a lot."

"No problem," the man said, returning to his work.

"Can I ask one other thing?"

The man looked up again. "Yes?"

"I was wondering what it takes to get into this gallery. Is there a way to contact the owner, or should I just call another day?"

"She'll be back tomorrow if you want to call her. Morning is best."

"Great. Thanks again."

He drove slower than usual on the way home, cruising just over the speed limit in the right hand lane, wondering about Alexis Flambet. He realized he should probably just call James and ask him, but he wasn't sure if he should wait until he heard more about what was going on with Graham. Maybe it had better wait.

CHAPTER 79

JAMES FLAMBET PICKED up the office phone to call Freddie Wilson but then paused and listened to the dial tone for a moment, pondering. He placed the phone gingerly back in its cradle, nodding as if in answer to a question. This call needed to be paid in person.

Freddie had not called him back yet, and it was nearly ten o'clock on Tuesday morning. Perhaps he was still waiting outside Graham's condo. Since James had returned from Detroit and Freddie did not know it, it only made sense to drive over and meet him in person, find out whether Graham had shown at all. Already James began to rethink his strategy.

Sure enough, there Freddie sat in his old Eldorado in front of Graham's condo complex, drinking coffee and looking blearily through the windshield as James pulled past and eased the gleaming Mercedes into the space beyond Freddie's car.

Freddie saluted with coffee cup. "Top of the morning."

"Hey, Freddie."

"Just get back?"

James nodded. "Yeah. Nothing, huh?"

"Nope. Hasn't been here at all, unless there's a back entrance I don't know about."

James shook his head. "No, the other side faces the beach. Listen, go ahead and see if you can get in there without causing a disturbance or getting caught. I'd like to know for sure he's gone before we make another move."

Freddie pursed his lips and nodded. "You want to come with me?"

James grimaced. "No, no. I want to be as far away as possible when you do it. Can you get in and out without it looking like anyone's been there?"

"Most likely. Want me to do it this morning or wait until dark?"

"Which is easier?"

Freddie reflected. "Depends. Sometimes it's easier to get into a place like this at night, when it's dark throughout the complex. Then again, there may be less people around during working hours. It doesn't really make a difference to me."

"Go ahead and scope it out, and just use your best judgment. But call me on my cell when you're inside. I'll have it on all day. You have a cell?"

"Yep. It's the only phone I got since the divorce."

"Thanks." He stuck out his hand and Freddie shook it awkwardly.

"You're welcome, Mr. Flambet. I'll talk to you soon."

James drove back down Gulf Boulevard from Redington Beach to the Tom Stuart Causeway, heading north on 275 across Old Tampa Bay, then up to Rocky Point. He looked out the window at the blue expanse of the gulf as he drove, thinking of the days when he and the whole family could go boating there. There'd be Sunday brunch at Landry's or the Grand Hyatt, Armagnac and Hennessy with the old man on the deck of a thirty-footer. Back then, they had the world by the tail, or at the very least, held it around the midsection. Now that past was all like a dream, or the recollection of some fifties movie he'd seen once: bluebloods on beaches, laughing, getting tanner and blonder.

He sighed, imagining Celia with Eugenie at the mall picking through discount bins.

An hour later, when Freddie called him back, James was in the middle of a meeting with a supply vendor. He pulled out his phone and saw Freddie Wilson's number. James looked apologetically at the vendor's rep. "I'm sorry, I have to take this."

He walked toward one of the building's large tinted windows as he answered. "Freddie?"

"Hey, James."

"You're back already?"

"It didn't take long. The whole place is emptied out, even his telephone. Nothing there but the largest furniture, couches and shit."

James breathed out slowly. "Well, that answers that question."

"I can bow out gracefully now if you want to get the police involved again, and you can just pay me for my time. I'd need Graham's cell number if we're going to try to track him by that, but I'll be honest: the police really have the muscle to do that, not me."

"Let me think about it, Freddie. Appreciate what you've done so far. Can I catch you at home later on?"

"Sure," he said. "Right now, I've got to catch forty winks, though."

"I'll call you in the morning."

"Sounds like a plan."

CHAPTER 80

PAUL MOSEYED OUT to the shore again to think about his painting and ponder the mystery of Alexis Flambet. He was ready for a break after nearly completing another large canvas that morning. He'd been inside so long it seemed as though he'd missed the entire spring, and now summer was almost over, which felt strange.

Rather than the noises of hip-hop and trip-hop and the Latino stations on the boom boxes of Clearwater Beach, he opted for Ballast Point, a quiet retreat on Tampa Bay that was less a beach than a public park. With a few benches and some green expanses of grass, picnickers could spread blankets and baskets and enjoy the day.

He walked slowly beside the shoreline, looking at smokestacks in the distance, a pelican preening himself, and four stingrays like big diagonal leaves moving slowly beneath the surface of the water. Smooth and slow, the water barely rippled. It was a windless day, and long lines, like fabric flowing east to west, cut across the slight north-south undulations, turning the whole pattern into a moving, rippling net. A jellyfish moved slowly along beneath it all like some exotic translucent mushroom, a blob of protoplasm from another era.

He slowed his pace further and looked into the water, thinking of James Flambet and Flambet Insurance, and wondering whether he would get a call, or even whether he wanted to respond to such a call. Of course, he would. Hell, he had to make the call himself.

He needed to get involved again, that much he knew. More than involved, really; he had to somehow become an integral part of the whole investigation. The company itself was the only thing that truly tied him to Suzanne now, and he couldn't just show up at a donut shop and expect her to regain any kind of interest in him. He had to be there. If he couldn't be a hero, he had to at least become a part of a team and quietly accept any role and whatever credit, if any, for discovering Philip Banks and Dolores Buenas. That was the bottom line. He had to make the call.

Still, dialing James Flambet's cell phone number was a little like addressing him as James for the first time, or asking a girl on a first date in junior high. It made him feel somehow less than, and he didn't like it. But he knew he had to do more than just launch himself back full force into the investigation. He had to talk about something else at first, and the best icebreaker he had in his pocket was the one other thing he wanted to ask James about anyway, the mystery of Alexis Flambet. Was she a relative, or if not, had he heard of her?

So when he returned to the apartment and looked at the painting, he realized he would have to abandon it, just as he eventually had to abandon every project, determining it "finished." With nothing left to do for the day, he decided to call James. He was too emotionally spent from the effort of painting to do anything else.

He dialed, expecting voicemail.

"Hey, Paul." The voice came across clear and strong, surprising him.

"Hey, James."

"How are you?"

"Good, good. Doing a lot of painting lately."

"Really," said James, sounding genuinely interested. "I didn't know you were a painter."

"That's what I went to school for, actually."

"Neat. What kind of painting?"

"Mostly abstract. I got my Masters in Fine Arts."

"I did not know that, but I'm not surprised you're the artistic type."

"Well, lately I've been trying to check out local galleries, and I thought of you when I was visiting one recently."

"Of me?"

Paul cleared his throat. "Yeah, I went to the Artists Unlimited Gallery. I was looking through the paintings and there was an Alexis Flambet."

"That's my mom."

Now it was Paul's turn to say, "Really."

"Yup." James chuckled. "She started painting a few years ago, and then when she shopped them around, she actually found that gallery owner interested in displaying her work. Nice guy. His name is Charles Swenson."

"So he just told her he liked her work and she brought the paintings to him?"

"Pretty much. She's sold a couple, too, which made her proud as a peacock. Not that she really needs the money," he added, chuckling again.

"Wow, that's great," said Paul. Must be nice not to need money, he thought.

"Tell you what," James continued. "Let me give Charles a call and get you an appointment with him. Maybe he'll want to bring you in too, assuming he likes your work, of course. I can't make any promises, but hey, at least with an introduction, it'd be better than going in there cold."

"That would be fantastic. Thank you."

"Not a problem. Listen, I've got to run, but since you called I wanted to let you know that Graham's definitely bolted. Condo emptied out, car gone…everything."

"Holy shit."

"It's kind of what I expected, but now that it's confirmed, well, that takes things to a whole other level."

"No doubt. Jesus."

"Anyway, I'm sure we'll be pursuing it further, but it's not with the police just yet, so keep that under your hat, all right?"

"Sure."

"We'll chat again soon, okay?"

"Great."

Paul sat back on the sofa and looked out the window, not even thinking of the gallery introduction, thinking only that Graham was truly gone. Gone, he said to himself. He did it.

CHAPTER 81

GRAHAM WALKED SLOWLY down Daytona Beach, grimacing at the long line of vehicles that crawled along the narrow strip of beach fronted by pink and grey condo complexes and hotels. The irony of having just sold the Lexus for barely more than half its worth weighed heavily on him as he gazed balefully at the cheesy pickup trucks and SUVs moving like fire ants across the sand. It was obscene, these redneck children with their oversized toys filling the salty air with exhaust, defiling a place that had no doubt been beautiful once.

He returned to the hotel and slumped onto the bed, pulling from a bottle of malt liquor much like the one he'd had in Winter Park. He flipped through the cable stations and found nothing, then decided at last on one of the hotel's thin selection of adult features. It felt like an extravagance, especially when he considered the cheap malt liquor, and the fact that he even had to think about the economics of paying for porn made him sick at heart.

Afterward, he settled the empty bottle on the nightstand and fell asleep at the edge of the bed. He thought he remembered getting up and going to the bathroom, fully clothed, but in reality he was dreaming. In the dream, he stepped back into the night, closing the hotel room door behind him. He began to walk down the street, looking at shadows in the shop fronts. Another shadow flickered behind his, just out of his range of vision, but he felt it somehow, and when he glanced back fearfully over his shoulder it receded, never quite reaching his line of vision.

He heard footsteps and moved faster, but then the footsteps grew faster too, and before long he was running, panting, the sounds of the two sets of footsteps echoing off the façades of storefronts as they whizzed by like dark lights. The sharp report of each breath grew louder as his chest heaved, until the pain told him he was going to die, but he could not run faster, could not breathe more, would inevitably trip and fall or else his heart would simply seize up and he would die on the streets of Daytona Beach.

He lurched up in bed, panting hard, sweat coursing down his back in an icy line, head pounding, the malt liquor nearly coming up in a bitter taste of bile that he had to swallow lest he vomit it out. He made it to the bathroom without vomiting, still panting, flipped on the light, and looked at himself in the mirror. The dark circles under his eyes testified to the nights he had suffered through all week. He washed his face and hands in the stained porcelain sink, dried them off, then went back out to get dressed. The eastern sky was already growing light, and when he looked at the clock he realized that he'd slept nearly until noon.

When he walked outside, the air was almost palpable, the heaviness of the tropics. He looked toward the horizon. Storm clouds piled up like mountains in the sky. The air's weight settled into his chest, and he breathed deeply and purposefully, as if he would smother. He thanked God the air conditioning worked back in the hotel room.

The dream of being pursued, hunted, made him feel as if the earth beneath him would open up and swallow him whole. Clearly, the world was his enemy, everyone was suspect. But the idea that the wolf pack was closing in, and all the frail defenses he'd erected might fall aside, trampled beneath their onslaught, made him walk faster, breathe harder. Surrender was out of the question. Telling his story was not an issue. That was a job for an attorney, if it should come to that.

He slowed his pace, scanning the horizon. In the distance, children splashed in the surf, and three seagulls wheeled overhead. Something about being on the beach felt ironic. How many other people had come to despair on a beach? It all seemed a great joke, some vicious version of cosmic tomfoolery, that he should feel like this in such a place. The sky pressed down on him. Even the slight breeze from the Atlantic blew rank and warm.

The poignant beauty of the shoreline filled him only with a sense of what might have been, just as the high-banked and man-sioned shores of Lake Maitland had the day before. He looked out across the waves and back again to the expanse of sand ahead and then above, where a pelican, like a great pterodactyl, cast a long fleeting shadow over him as it soared into the updraft. Beside him stood two great blue herons like some elderly couple waiting for a bus.

How close he had been and how quickly it all faded away. Just like this, too, would fade away—these birds, those women in bathing suits down the waterline—all would crumble into dust. He felt the weight of all time and all passion pressing down on him as he saw through the whole show. The world was nothing but a big act, everything was just surface, nothing more than what he could see: no underlying meaning, no design, no plan. No God. And it would all decay and blow away in the wind.

If he could find one thing that was almost good, he would say this: that the sharp pang of despair the knowledge brought made him feel more keenly alive than he had in thirty years. Maybe more. And it made a tear rise in his eye, sudden, unexpected. He resented the feeling, just sadness, soft sadness, and he flushed with shame. He wiped the tear away, quickening his pace, while all around him children ran laughing and splashing along the waterline and tiny sandpipers scooted across the wet sand, bobbing their beaks into it again and again, mindlessly, without a sound.

He had to get out of Daytona, even if it meant going farther north where it would most assuredly be colder. He would have to buy some warmer clothes and other necessities and find a little odd job to beat back the tide. He thought again of Belize, and grew confused as the laughter of the children and the long shadows of pelicans and the reiteration that it was all a sham made him more muddled and overwhelmed than he'd thought imaginable…as if he had reverted to infancy in sadness and had only been able to leap ahead to adolescence where his brains were jumbled up with bikinis and music and all the somnolent pain of the wide world. To hell with it, he thought. I'll think on it later.

He returned to the thought of his wallet and the job problem and how to manage the possibility of getting some ready cash without giving out his name and social security number. It would not do. He'd have to knock someone in the head, break into a house, or get a new gun at a pawnshop and hold someone up, some West Indian in a Circle K or gas station. Some old lady in a Howard Johnson's. He laughed aloud, and it sounded in his own ears like the laughter of the damned.

He could still see himself as an adolescent or, rather, see again the scene: standing by the Thames with his thumbs hooked into his suspenders, looking out at the water like a nineteen-year-old Churchill, whistling the tunes he'd heard on the Jazz Hour, old Billie Holiday and Sarah Vaughan and Ella Fitzgerald. And when he dreamed of America, he saw in his mind only a jazz club where smoke hung heavy over the piano player and the sounds of glasses clinking and men and women murmuring mixed with the voices of the drums, saxophone, piano, bass. When he dreamed of America, he thought of the daunting task of getting there and doing great things, never imagining he would be stuck in the insurance industry not just for a year or two but for five and ten and twenty, never imagining anything beyond the jazz joints and the grandiose vision of the house on the lake and the servants and country club and a great car, a classic Fairmont or Chevelle. He would sit behind the wheel on the right hand side of his parents' own car, dreaming on the visions that passed like ghosts through his mind, not knowing then that it would be another four years before he would arrive in America, hungry and lean and broke and twenty three, an age for martyrdom and grandiosity and the Boston Marathon. And when he ran it for the first time and saw those cheering crowds at the end, his heart pounding, he knew he would be king, he would be a ruler, he would rule the world, if need be.

He turned slowly, hands in his pockets, and walked back to the hotel.

CHAPTER 82

WITH FREDDIE ON Graham's trail, the first question he had to answer—without knowing Graham personally, or what his personal habits were—was where to start.

Of course, there were chop shops where the Lexus might have been sold, and even private dealers in stolen goods or goods that, for other reasons, needed to "disappear." Several pawn shops in Tampa Bay would take any computer or stereo system off someone's hands without so much as a question as to origin. Freddie knew them well, but it was, at best, a tedious task to go through them one by one and, at worst, a series of dead ends. Time was not on their side.

When Freddie got the call from Computer Recovery Services, he was hoping for something solid.

"It's a maybe," said John, the technician.

Freddie scowled. "What do you mean?"

"Well, those names you were looking for, Dolores Buenas and Philip Banks, they're on the hard drive all right, but there aren't any whole documents with them."

"Which means you'll have to do more research?"

John cleared his throat. "Depends what your client wants, my friend. It's up to you."

"I know he needs more than just the names being on there, John. We've got to have as much document reconstruction as possible. How do I explain it to him in layman's terms?"

"You know much about data recovery?"

"A bit, but I'm not used to trying to explain it like you are," Freddie said.

"Well, you know when you delete a file from a computer, it's not really gone, right?"

"Sure."

"The thing is, the hard drive was pretty full, and every time this Graham guy created a new file, Windows took up some of that unused space. There are still plenty of parts of these files, but he also made it worse for us by running the system defrag regularly to clean up the drive."

"So we have *only* parts of files."

"Exactly. Plus, any reconstruction of those files is only based on our assumption that we can fill in the missing blanks intuitively."

"Mind if I ask something?"

"Not at all."

"Why did it take two weeks just to get to this point?"

"Well, even though it only takes a little time to make a copy of the hard drive, we still had to go through the saved data, meta data, and deleted data."

"Did you say meta?"

"Yeah, that's information about the saved data: when it was updated, saved, and whatnot. We didn't look too hard through that yet, because we figured he'd delete the files in question. And that was the case."

"So now what?"

"Well, if we want to get farther into the deleted data, we can do an advance scan with this program we use called Data Recovery Wizard."

"What does that do?"

"It's a more complete scan, but I think it gives us a better chance to recover lost data. Basically scans all the clusters on the logical drive, then scans unused clusters for known types of files."

Freddie chuckled. "Which, in English, means…."

John chuckled too. "Sorry. It provides a lot more to work with than normal software. It lets us do a forensic byte-by-byte analysis of the data. It's a pretty good tool; it just takes more time. I mean, I could explain how we use a Cyclical Redundancy Checksum algorithm, but I don't think you really want to know all that."

"You got that right. What kind of timeline we talking?"

"Couple more weeks by the time we sort through all the data and try to reconstruct the documents."

Freddie nodded, thinking. "Well, that's about what I told him anyway, time-wise. Let's go ahead and do that. Is there an extra cost involved, or is this whole thing just by the job?"

"It's a little extra."

"I'm sure it's fine," Freddie said. "Let me know when you guys are done."

"Yes, sir."

Freddie hung up and sighed. It was time to call James again.

"James, Freddie Wilson."

"Hey, Freddie."

He explained the problem, adding, "The thing is, James, I have to know your first priority. I can try to track down Graham's laptop and see if we can get something more tangible while we wait for the forensic analysis. Or I can look for him, probably by trying to track the Lexus. He may be driving it, or he may have sold it. I can try to do both, but you've gotta realize that each process will be slowed down by the other."

"What's the deal with the forensic analysis? I'm not sure I understand all this business about sectors and clusters and whatnot."

"Well, the guy has to find the proper clusters to piece through the documents that Graham deleted. It could take as long as a couple more weeks, but after looking through it, he may find that even though a percentage of the document has been overwritten, most of the document probably will *not* have been overwritten."

"And the reason that analysis hasn't been done already is the amount of time it takes?"

"Right. Preliminary analysis showed that there are no longer any documents pertaining to Philip Banks or Dolores Buenas. However, examination of these sector boundaries or whatever they are showed that those names are on the hard drive. It's a long process to piece together parts of documents that have been deleted."

"Gotcha," said James. "That makes sense."

"And that's why it may or may not be worthwhile to track down that laptop. There may still be a similar document on there, maybe even a complete one."

"Or," James added, "there may not."

"That's the chance you take."

"And if we just look for Graham for now, focus mainly on him?"

"Another chance. We might not find him, and in the meantime, the laptop might get sold from a pawnshop."

"What do you recommend? I mean, we definitely need to find him, right, or what's the point?"

Freddie cleared his throat. "Yeah, I'd suggest looking for him first. Having a computer doesn't mean shit if we never see him again."

"Let's do it, then. Are you going to try to find him by his cell phone or his car?"

"Both," said Freddie. "I need his cell number from you first because, unlike the cops, I can't subpoena the phone company. I have to have a friend of mine tap into their records online."

"I'm assuming that's not legal, either."

"Not even close. Still sure you don't want the cops involved?"

"Positive. The more I think about it, the more I realize how fucked I would be by the bad publicity. Nobody wants to invest in a company that's had someone stealing from it. I've got enough problems right now as it is."

"Okay, what's the cell number?"

James gave it to him.

"And can you give me any details on the Lexus, the license plate and all that, from your employee records?"

"Damn," said James, "I'm out of the office now. I'll have my secretary call you, all right?"

"Sure. I'll start with the cell records, see who he's called, and I'll call you if I find anything worthwhile."

"Sounds good, Freddie. I'll talk to you soon."

"Oh," said Freddie. "One more thing." He held the phone away from him for a moment. "Shit. Hello? James?"

"I'm losing —"

"James, you're breaking up."

James' voice came back in fits and starts: "—Got—Fred—let me—" Then he was gone, and the line was dead.

"Shit." He called back.

"The cellular customer you are trying to reach is currently out of the calling area. If you'd like to leave a message —"

Freddie hung up. The question would have to wait.

CHAPTER 83

FRANK BRENKUS DID not return to the El Toro Sports Pub right away after that fateful night he'd hooked up with Mercedes Eden, but the two still spent the occasional weekend together in Frank's rooms at the top of Crump Tower, drinking margaritas and devouring each other like cheap pretzels. It seemed to be enough for her, and the sex was better than he could possibly have anticipated, so it wasn't likely to end soon unless Frank found himself a better option.

Nonetheless, the promise of a better option could usually be found grinding away to the sounds of hip hop or techno in the dark corners of The Red Zone or Empire. Frank wasn't ready to forego the possibility, though he was far too old now to move comfortably through those kinds of clubs. Somehow, he inevitably found himself trying to escape from Mercedes by going to one of the few places he might actually bump into her: the notoriously eclectic El Toro, where college students jostled with their elders for a spot at the bar.

Of course, Frank could always insulate himself somewhat from the general public if he met up with his fellow newscasters, since they typically had the VIP room to themselves. But if he went alone, and they turned out not to be there, it was no surprise to run into someone he knew from the younger crowd. This particular Friday evening, Frank was surprised by an unexpected glimpse of the incomparable Pamela Mae Swenson, the mere sight of whom made him forget Mercedes Eden immediately.

Pamela had stationed herself at a table with two people Frank didn't recognize. They had just arrived themselves and were still working on their first drinks of the evening when Frank approached their table.

"Pardon me, folks," he began in his most Rico Suave voice, indicating Pamela with one hand. "I believe I've met this young lady here before."

Pamela blanched, but recovered quickly. "Suzanne, Paul, this is Frank Brenkus. Frank, Paul Panepinto, Suzanne Beidertyme."

Paul stood to shake hands. "From WRYY, right? The weather?"

Frank grinned, giving the proffered hand a perfunctory shake. *"We've got our Y on you,"* he said with a chuckle, and everyone laughed except Pamela. "Mind if I join you?" Without giving Pamela a chance to speak, Frank moved beside her, as glib and comfortable with Paul and Suzanne as if they were great friends, or at least faithful viewers.

Paul shook his head, looking both amazed and amused. "So how do you guys know each other?"

Pamela opened her mouth to speak, but as he seated himself beside her, Frank jumped in. "We've got a few mutual acquaintances. You may know some of them from here, as a matter of fact: there's Arlen and Lakeisha…."

Paul looked at Suzanne, eyebrows raised.

"I know," Suzanne said to him. "Everybody knows Lakeisha except you, right?"

He shook his head, laughing silently.

Frank ducked his head around toward Paul. "Oh yeah? And then there's, let's see, Jill, Cora…."

Suzanne nearly choked on her wine. "Cora? Gable?"

Frank and Paul chuckled together, instant co-conspirators, while Pamela continued to look like she'd rather be just about any-where else.

"Oh yeah," said Paul, "we all know Cora. I used to work with her. Suzanne still does, as a matter of fact."

"Hey, speak of the devil," said Pamela. "Look who just walked in."

Sure enough, Cora Gable and Arlen Jameson were just enter-ing the crowded bar.

"Holy shit," said Frank, and again he and Paul laughed. "There's no escaping that one, is there?"

"How well *do* you know Cora?" Paul asked.

"Not very well, actually." He paused, concerned that Paul or Suzanne might actually be close enough to Cora that he'd better watch what he said. But their grins said otherwise.

"By the way," said Pamela, "how's Mercedes?"

Frank snapped his head so hard toward her that he felt a twinge of pain in his neck. "Mercedes? Ah, nice girl. We're just good friends, though."

"Friends with benefits?" Pamela's eyes sparkled. "Good for you, Frank. She *is* a nice girl, too."

Now Frank squirmed, and Paul and Suzanne exchanged a look of confusion. But before the conversation could continue, Cora and Arlen reached a point in the surging crowd where they could see Pamela's table, and Cora waved animatedly.

"Hey, guys," she called.

"Yep, here she comes," said Frank. "This one is a real piece of work."

Even Pamela snickered at that, and they all smirked as the two girls inched forward through the crowd. They were still a good thirty feet away, but even from that distance, it was clear that Cora had taken a few too many drinks somewhere else before El Toro, and Arlen's haggard look confirmed that she was drunksitting.

"Hey, Frank, hey, Paul," the girls said as they reached the table. "What's up, girls?" they asked the other two.

"We were just sitting here trying to decide whether to run or not when we saw you," said Pamela.

Cora belched. "That's mean," she said, but Arlen laughed.

"I think she's breaking your balls, Cora," said Arlen.

Frank knew the manager of some of the local talent in the fight game, and he started talking to Paul about boxing. He gave him a thorough breakdown of who was matched up, when, and the odds on some of the fights.

Arlen began to talk to Pamela and Suzanne about a girl they both knew, who Cora evidently did not, and Cora started to look around the room abstractedly, first glancing at the bar, then at the girls, until at last her gaze rested squarely on Paul and Frank.

"Hey, what are you guys talking about over there? Is it private?"

"No, Cora," said Frank, all teeth and squinty eyes. "Just some guy talk."

"Oh, well, guy talk," she said, rolling her eyes. "I know what that means."

"I'm sure you do," said Frank with a chuckle, and turned back toward Paul.

Cora stood a moment, swaying, then seemed to think better of it and sat back down. "Oh, I figured you were talking about the embezzlement at Flambet."

Paul looked up. "What?"

"Yeah," she went on, "Frank, you probably hear stories like this all the time in the news world, but just imagine how weird it is to find out your boss's boss is stealing from the company, and then he disappears."

"Cora," said Paul, "what are you talking about?"

She gave him a withering look. "Graham Woodcock stealing from Flambet Insurance."

Paul's hand began to tremble before him on the table. "How do you know that?" he asked.

"Oh, my father told me. I know you called him, Paul. See, when you don't actually *retain* an attorney for his services, there's no attorney-client privilege. Besides, he had to keep my best interests in mind. I have money in the 401(k) there just like everyone else."

Paul turned to Suzanne. "Are you hearing this?"

She nodded her head, clearly too stunned to speak.

"Cora, who else knows about this?"

"Hell, everybody knows." She gestured toward Frank. "Even he probably knew all about it by now."

"Actually, I did hear something about it from Mercedes, but I'm not familiar with the company, so it didn't mean anything to me. I just remembered the name Graham Woodcock." He chuckled.

Paul looked at each of them in turn. "Mercedes?" He shook his head, still not believing what he was hearing.

"Yeah," Cora went on, "I'm not surprised she heard about it. Probably from somebody at Flambet. The real question is, what the hell happened to old Graham?"

Indeed, thought Paul, that's the real question. He dropped out of the conversation, barely registering their comments. It was unfathomable. All along, this whole thing had been his baby, at least the Dolores Buenas and Philip Banks part, and now everyone knew? All of it? He sure hoped not.

Had James said anything to any of the employees? He continued to ponder it, until he became dimly aware that Cora was on her feet and swaying. She held a drink in one hand and pointed an accusatory finger at Frank with the other.

"Sure," she said, "if it weren't for all you baby boomers, maybe we wouldn't be in such lousy shape." She gestured with the finger, and part of her drink sloshed out. "I mean, the world your generation inherited wasn't exactly in great shape to begin with, but what the hell did *you* guys do? Said, 'Oh, I'd love to change the world, peace-love-dope-and-Hare-fucking-Krishna.' But so what? You just realized getting stoned and yelling stupid slogans wasn't getting you anywhere, so you stopped doing it, then spent the next thirty fucking years telling everybody how great it was. But what got done? Nothing. The sixties are so over, these people should just get over it."

Frank shook his head. "I'm only thirty-eight, Cora. Besides, you probably weren't even born then."

"You're goddamn right I wasn't, and good thing, too. I don't give a rat's ass about the sixties. It's ancient history, and all it did was create another nostalgia-fest, just like every stupid decade." She began to sing, mincing around the table: 'Looooove, loooove, loooooooove.'" She stopped in mid-prance. "Give me a frickin' break."

Frank stood up. "I think we're done here. Party's over." He faced her, then shepherded her toward the exit, one hand on her elbow.

"Oh no, you don't," she said, squirming away from him. "I'm not going anywhere, big boy."

Arlen came to the rescue. "Let's go, Cora," she said, standing and joining Frank. "It's pretty late."

"I don't wanna go anywhere else," Cora said, and then the tears began to stream down her face. "I wanna stay here and finish my drink."

Arlen steered her away from the table, saying, "I'll be right back, you guys," but they all knew she wouldn't be back again any time soon.

CHAPTER 84

THERE WAS CERTAINLY nothing unusual about James going in on a Saturday. Things were quiet at home, the news having sunken in, finally, that the business was in deep trouble. The divorce was inevitable; it was just a matter of time. Work provided the closest thing to an escape.

He sat at his desk, very still, looking down at a stack of paperwork but not really seeing the words. His brain churned with the myriad details of what would have to be done. Not until he began to focus his vision on the letters of the words themselves did he see a figure out of the corner of his eye.

It was Graham.

He stood in the doorway, leaning against the door jamb. His shoulders sagged. Defeated. James looked up and blinked, unsure what to say. It occurred to him that Graham might be armed, might, in fact, be there to do him harm. He made a feint toward his desk drawer as if to withdraw a weapon, but of course it held nothing more lethal than an old letter opener. He slumped back in the chair.

"Don't worry." Graham reached behind him and pulled the pistol from the waistband of his slacks.

James felt the blood drain from his face.

Graham lay the gun on the desk, adding, "It's empty."

"What were you going to do?"

"I dunno, James. Rob a Circle K?"

"What stopped you?"

"It's not that I couldn't have done it. I mean, it's not like I don't have the cojones."

"What, then?"

"It's just so fucking degrading, man. I mean, seriously? A Circle K?"

James picked up the gun cautiously. "You'll do time. They'll put you in prison."

Graham sighed, almost cheerily. "I know, but I can still retain an attorney. For something like this, I'll probably get less than five years, out on good behavior in a year or two. I Googled it. Hell, I'm a Brit: if there's one thing I know how to do, it's behave."

James laughed in spite of himself. "Mind telling me why? I mean, we didn't exactly underpay you."

"You know, it's not you, old boy. It's not really personal. But in a way, I suppose it was. All those years here, and I never forgot my boss was a trust funder who didn't actually have to work if he didn't want to."

James reddened.

"I worked hard for everything I've ever had, since before I came to the States. And for what? I wanted more, but there wasn't anymore to be gotten here. Not the legal way, at any rate. I'd already priced myself out of the market everywhere else. There was nowhere else to go. It wasn't for lack of trying."

"I suppose that's true, at least."

"So, here I am."

There was silence, and there did not seem to be anything else to do. "I'm going to call the police now," James said.

Graham did not even blink. "Do it." Even in defeat, his tone was imperious—as if still employed and giving his own CEO a direct order. "Make the call."

James pulled the cell from his pocket. He thought about calling Freddie first, but that could wait. His reputation was going to be shot anyway; the company was going down. Might as well call the police and let them take it from there.

"And what about McDillon? What was the deal on that?"

Graham looked sideways at him. "I really don't know about that mess," he said almost triumphantly. "Never did find anything there."

CHAPTER 85

"WHORE-HEY." EULA pouted. "Whore-hey, come in here."

Jorge Arce rolled his eyes, pulling the tray of tortillas from the refrigerator and walking across the kitchenette into the adjacent living room. "I'm on my way."

She glared up at him with an expression half exasperation and half…jealousy, it looked like. It didn't seem to make any sense at all, really, until he realized she was holding his phone.

"What are you doing?"

The exasperation seemed to subside, replaced with a cold, sudden fury. "Why is that girl texting you?"

"What girl?"

"You know what girl."

He sighed. "Lemme guess —"

But she was not about to let him say the dreaded name alone, and together they said, "Pamela Mae Swenson."

Again he sighed. "What does it say?"

"She's asking you about the Flambets again."

"Well, that ain't exactly a love note, is it?"

Eula threw the phone down on the table, where it clattered to a halt. "Why she always gotta be texting you? Why?"

"Because I still work there. I'm not out of a job yet, but you know, I probably will be in a week."

"Come on, you don't really believe that, do you?"

He sat beside her, guarded, not touching her. "Yeah, I do. Celia is gonna divorce him. After that shit with Graham hit the news, she hit the road. I found out yesterday. Freaking company is gonna go out of business, I bet. It's all about the money. Money, money, money."

She glanced away, and it was hard to tell what she was feeling. "I wish we had some."

"What? Money?"

"Yeah."

Now it was his turn to sulk. "Hey, I've gotten every penny I can outta them. She ain't exactly the type to give out a Christmas bonus. Cooking for them is like working in a sweat shop. Surprised she hasn't asked me to walk the damn dog."

Eula looked at him without expression. "Remember how we used to talk about opening our own restaurant? So you wouldn't have to just be a cook? How it would a combination Chinese and—"

"And down home Southern style cooking," he said with her. "Sure, I remember. What about it?"

Now she held his gaze. "Doesn't look like that's happening, is it?"

"Well, I can't start a business with no money, babe. I mean, neither one of us makes that much. How are we gonna do it? Are you gonna do it?"

Eula stood and walked away from him a few paces, then turned. "This just isn't working, Jorge."

"What do you mean?" He looked up at her, searching for a clue.

"It's not working," she said. "It's not working anymore." And that was all.

CHAPTER 86

THE TABLE WAS all women—Suzanne Beidertyme, Pamela Mae Swenson and Lakeisha Bennefield—until Paul Panepinto walked into the shop. Pamela saw him first and had no problem getting him to their table, announcing, "There he is," as if she knew him well.

"Hey, ladies." He sat down comfortably in the one unoccupied chair, three days' growth on his face and a look of satisfaction after a job well done. He reached out his hand to Lakeisha. "I'm Paul."

"She knows you, Paul," Suzanne said.

"So *you're* Lakeisha." He chuckled. "Everyone seems to know you except me. We went to school together somewhere?"

Lakeisha giggled. "High school French class with Mr. Mathers."

"Aha, okay." He snorted. "Long time ago. Forgot I even took that one. C'est la vie?"

The women laughed, though with some apparent disapproval.

"And so," Suzanne said, "what's this I hear about a gallery opening? You're not going to come back to work with us wage slaves at Flambet Insurance?"

"Oh, thank you, thank you. Well, I might have to get a day job again soon, but for now it's okay. What's happening with all that insurance stuff now, anyhow?"

Pamela Mae's eyes widened. "Didn't you hear?"

"No."

"Celia left James. I think Jorge was let go last week, and I'm sort of the last man, or woman, standing. It's a messed-up situation. I'm still there, but James is so distracted with work and the press and all that, he doesn't seem to know I have a life outside of taking care of his daughter. I would have thought Celia would take her, but apparently not."

Suzanne frowned. "Her own daughter, not a priority."

Lakeisha shook her head, frowning too. "Mm mm."

After coffee, when Lakeisha and Pamela Mae discreetly found reasons to disappear, and Paul and Suzanne found themselves alone, it felt oddly calm, not at all awkward the way he would have thought. He went back to her place later that morning, and they sat on the same old sofa, as if they'd never left. There was something reassuring about it all, not just the familiarity but also the excitement of starting anew, of salvaging something that was much more than just a fling, something that needed to be kept alive and was probably inevitable after all. The road ahead seemed as uncertain as ever. And yet, it looked like an invitation.

"What are you doing?"

He laughed, playing with her hair and kissing the side of her neck, so that she squealed with laughter from the tickling sensation. "Doing? Oh, nothing much."

"Stop." She laughed and tried to squirm away.

He began to unbutton the long tails of his shirt and pulled her closer, wrapping the shirt around her like a cloak. She laughed, hands on his chest, and they embraced, sparkles of wonder swirling around them like snowflakes in the warm morning air.

ACKNOWLEDGEMENTS

COUNTLESS INFLUENCES SHAPE an author's life and work, and space does not permit thank yous for all of them. But on some level or other I am gratefully indebted to the following people whether their help was inspirational, editorial, instructional, emotional, spiritual or all of the above: the lovely and wonderful Sunny Sotgaew Sahno, Bob Sahno, Evelyn Sahno, Cory Andrew, Lou Berkman, Don Booth, Geodie Baxter-Bowen, Xena Brown, Paul Bouyea, Martha Calligan, Michele Carrell, Bruce Cockburn, Janet Davidsen, Linda Rurka Dooley, Christie Bracciano, Jim Ellis, Tara Engstrom, Cha Gray, John Guzzardi, William Hanna, Lori Jewell, Gemma & Larry Kay, Tom Kelly, Mark & Elizabeth Leib, David J. Lipani, Virgil Mandanici, Joni Mitchell, Lyle & Caroline Mosier, Donna Murphy, Jennifer Nolen, Lorin Oberweger, Phil Ochs, Craig O'Neil, Angela Perkins, Fred Rezler, Liz Rosenberg, Ron Scott, Paul Stober, Sr. Marguerite Tarleton, Scott & Lauri Toler, Nick Vukasinovic, Ed Whittle, Dot Wilson, Brenda Windberg, Lisa Zackowski, Frank Zappa, Mike S., Rob D., Dick & Judy P., Brenda D., Kenny & Pat H., Ron B., Paul G., Kathi W., Eddie H. and Nancy A., the late Stan Geda and Jeremy Crowe, and above all, Mr. G.